PREY

By

Tim A. Majka

THANK YOU FOR
THIS OPPORTUNITY
TO INTERVIEW.
ENJOY!!
ALL THE
BEST

DEVIL DOG
PRESS
SWANVILLE, MAINE

Edited by Rob M. Miller

Cover art by Dane@ebooklaunch

DEDICATION

For my hero, best friend, and biggest fan.
Dad, thank you … I'll keep trying.

ACKNOWLEDGMENTS

Gratitude is owed to many:

First and foremost, to my bride Bridget, and sons Jacob and Alex, and all of my family. Thank you for not conspiring to send me to the funny farm because I wanted to write a book.

To Melissa Leffel, for encouraging … *no*, pushing me to keep writing after you read the first draft of part one.

To Mark Brazill, Wendy Corsi-Staub, Sean Patrick McGraw, Christina Calph, and Bob Rusch for inspiring a hometown boy to chase a dream.

To LeeAnne Krusmark, EJ Hayes, Mike Kirst, Mary Mistretta, and Renee Gravelle, for being my trusted readers.

To Sidney Mosher, legal eagle.

To Tracy Tufo and Devil Dog Press for offering me this opportunity and partnering me with such a great editor.

That leaves one very special thank you to be extended. To my editor, Rob Miller, whose patience, generosity, knowledge, and ability to teach made this such a rewarding endeavor. You showed me what it means to be a writer. I am eternally grateful. Let's do this again sometime

PART I
THIS WASN'T MEANT TO LAST

PROLOGUE

HOURS AGO, THE delivery room medical staff was elated to see the second healthy baby squirm free of its surrogate mother's womb. Janice Pontillo, however, was vexed. There had to be something she'd missed in the scrolls about needing twins to fulfill the prophecy. Regardless, she was not going to let these two end up like the last pair of infants. These boys would be strong and fearless.

Gods among men.

Having learned from her mistakes, she now had a much better handle on the steps needed to ensure their success. She wouldn't fail these children and they damn sure wouldn't fail her.

The pediatric nurse lifted the infants, one at a time, from the hospital baby cart, walked them over to the chair where their real mother sat, and nervously placed them into her welcoming arms. Janice couldn't help but notice the look of horror that washed over the nurse's face, could almost feel the deep chill stitching down the nurse's spine. As each infant came in physical contact with their true mother, for an instant their eyes turned completely black, just long enough for the hospital caregiver to notice. The disbelieving look on her face, the way she fumbled for the crucifix hanging around her neck, brought a smile to Janice Pontillo. After all, she knew what it meant. Her boys had the gift. One that would set them apart and guide them on their road to greatness, one that she would have the pleasure of honing to a razor.

The surrogate, having done her job, would now have to be eliminated. The vessel for the newborns was simply a loose end. The father, however, was a different story. His sacrificial blood would release his soul, or his *élan vital*, which, in turn, would strengthen the boys. As stated in the prophecy, it had to be done before the children reached their first birthday.

Janice chuckled and closed her eyes.

Conditioning the newborns and getting rid of two adults would be an easy enough task. After all, she'd had plenty of practice. It would just be time consuming and boring. But as she gazed at the infants, her smile morphed from something sinister to another warm and loving, as she thought: *All part of the price of doing what's right for my boys.*

CHAPTER ONE

DARKNESS.

Silence.

Then light … screaming—blinding PAIN.

And breathing. The filling of giant, newly-fleshed lungs.

It worked. I'm alive.

ALIVE!

The beast's thoughts were jumbled, a mess of recollections and … and feelings—the pleasure of … of success. The old ones, the Elder Gods, the gatekeepers, seekers, the wardens of the threshold … all the snobbish hoarders protecting their own, ignoring him, denying him (*I'm a him!*) his rightful place in the other realms.

The last of his kind and he'd beaten them all.

But now what?

He couldn't remember. Not yet. But he would.

He'd be the god-king of this realm, this land of flesh and blood and breath. The body, this new form of … of the physical, of the *touch-able*, would serve. Clawed hands flexed. Rows of teeth clacked against each other. And a belly hungered for blood. But there was something else … a thing that made him sick, that threatened everything.

Fear.

He had to destroy this nagging, tormenting *feeeling*.

His plans were not yet final. His position not yet firm. He couldn't quite remember *who* or *what* needed to be dealt with, but they were out there, their mere existence a threat.

Nostrils flared, a scent was caught.

A homing instinct that would lead him to what needed to be done turned on. His hungry stomach concurred. Wherever this invisible trail led, the destination would take care of everything.

He'd destroy what would dare make him afraid.

And whatever that turned out to be, it would also satiate his hunger.

CHAPTER
TWO

ЄDWARD ARCHER LIKED to think of himself as an alpha-male, and perhaps he was—most of the time. But never with his wife, though he did try to fake it. With Ellie, instead, he'd always been wrapped around her finger, superglued there since the day they'd first met. And now they were here, old but still together, sipping coffee out on their wrap-around deck, this their ritual, an early hour that typically afforded some relief from the Western New York mid-August heat.

But not today.

Today threatened to be what he liked to call *from the depths of Hell*. Where the westerly breeze did not offer any surcease, but mimicked the quick opening of a blazing oven, the wind nothing more than a *whoosh, whoosh, whoosh* of furnaced air, instantly bringing sweat to skin.

No, today there would be no heroes on the farm.

No heat stroke victims, either.

Then again, who was he to complain, what with him and his bride sitting out and not-so-wisely tipping back mugs of joe, the both of them, victims to the power of habit and ritual.

He squeezed his wife's hand and felt the pang of

arthritis cut through his gnarled fingers. He quickly flashed and almost regretted it. They'd agreed to not be so frivolous about such things, but there were times to cheat. His wife cheated, too. Her hips were bad, but she still always managed to do that one sexy—

He brought his mind back into focus and decided it was time to take the plunge—again. "You know, Ellie, we're pushing our luck."

"Why's that? Because we're gonna work in this heat? We've done it before."

"Naw, not the heat. The years. Thirty of 'em, count 'em. Gawd! Thirty damn years, and not so much as a shiver up the spine with regards to that thing, until today. Mark my words, we're playin' with all our lives. I can feel it in my bones."

"What do you want to do about it, Ed? Go off and tell Eric 'bout everything? You know that boy's nature. He wouldn't let it rest. Has too much of your piss to let anything lie." Elena Archer put her hand on her husband's knee. "I haven't often put my foot down in all the years we've been together, but I'm telling you, you are, in no uncertain terms, *not* going to inform our son about any of those events. It's ancient history. Let the story stay buried right along with that thing."

"You're right, dear, as usual."

"I love you, Ed, heart and soul. But let's not burden our child. Not and if'n we don't have to."

"Children."

Elena stared into her husband's sullen eyes. "We … we jus' can't think about that. Eric is our one and only. That's just how it has to be. Don't you go makin' me think of such things. Do you mean to make on old lady cry?"

"Maybe I'd hear you more if you'd call me Eddie, like everyone else?"

"Eddie's a boy's name. And you're a man—*my* man, *my* Ed, *my* Edward." Elena took to her feet and beckoned for him to stand. "And you need to stop cheating."

"What?"

"You heard me. If we're going to be sweating like pigs, anyway,"—she motioned towards the house with a tilt of her head and a wink—"then we might as well do something fun to earn it."

Ed the MAN laughed along with his wife. "Right again. Save the power for when we *really* need it." He made his way into the house and over to a bookshelf in the sitting room. He ran a wrinkled finger along the spines of several of his favorite novels before pausing at a copy of Dante's *Divine Comedy*.

He pulled it off the shelf and flipped through the book until it revealed its secret. Of course, the book was warded, but only against strangers, not anyone Ed trusted. About 50-pages in, the hollowed out copy held a small leather-bound journal. *I don't care what Ellie says, Eric needs to see this. I'll give it to Andy. If the need ever arises, he'll put it in Eric's hands.*

The old farmer entered the kitchen, and quickly snatched the keys hanging on the wall. In doing so, he snagged his finger on the brass hook and it started to bleed. "Damn, hooked like a trout." He licked the blood off his finger and yelled back to his wife, "Ellie, I need to run into town for a few things. I shouldn't be long." He exited the house without waiting for an answer.

LATER THAT EVENING, Ed stood looking out the screen door of his back porch, confident he had done the right thing by tasking his best friend with the journal. Andy wouldn't fail to get the truth to Eric about who he was.

About *what* he was.

He watched as his dog took off like a bullet into the darkness. "REGGIE." After spending an hour earlier in the day giving the finger to the BLUE PILL, this was not what he'd had in mind for the evening.

Man's best friend, my ass. The beast knew better than to run away. He was only supposed to go out and do his business, not scurry off. *Somethin' must've gotten a hold o' his nose and tugged—hard.* He looked over his shoulder, thought a moment, then walked back to his wife in the next room. "ELLIE, I've got to get Reggie. Damn dog took off again."

"Hurry back."

"I will." Ed suddenly felt sick, and a wash of fear hit stronger and far deeper than just his mere bones. Whatever it was, it made him feel they were all threatened this very night. A wiser more Alpha Ed might've strode out, and with every ace held, but right now, he was Eddie, and if there was a danger to be dealt with, he wanted to make sure his wife was as safe as possible. "And, honey?"

"Yes?"

"Catch my kiss." Eddie then—and not Ed, but Eddie, a young and in-love Eddie with his beautiful wife—blew a kiss. One that he'd flashed as strong as he could. An instinctual transfer of power that he'd be sure to answer for later. An imparting of virtue unlike anything he'd ever done before. But now was not the time to ponder the flood of *whys* that would come if he allowed for the distraction.

Watching his smiling wife catch his kiss, but then questioning him with fearful eyes, Ed moved quickly back into the kitchen and pulled on his barn boots. *Ornery mutt's going to be the death of me yet.*

Stepping onto the porch, he could hear the dog barking fiercely, and then … silence.

Somethin's wrong.

Immediately, he was out and heading in the direction where he'd last heard his dog, completely unaware that he'd instinctively grabbed the 12-gauge problem solver kept leaning against the wall by the kitchen door until he'd racked the slide.

CHAPTER THREE

AS HE DROVE the patrol car up the familiar dirt driveway, Andy Pontillo, towards the end of his sixth term as sheriff, felt every one of his 62-years, every ache and pain, and *pang* and *pop*, and *creek* and *crack*. Gravity and years behind a never-ending pile of admin had rolled into bubble gum a once commanding physique. Still, when he walked into a room, everyone snapped to a smart *May I have another?*—just the way it should be.

Perseverance, commitment, and sheer will trumped youth every time.

At least in his case.

His moment of ultimate vindication was finally at hand. In the meantime, he'd enjoy every arthritic step he took. Sear it into memory. Wouldn't be too much longer when his body and every other mundane thing he could think of wouldn't matter a lick.

For the moment, though, it was time to be somber-faced. His idiot of a deputy would be expecting it.

"Who would do something like this, boss?"

The poor man's voice was shaking. Andy could almost feel bad for his trusted second. True, he'd just thought of the man as a dullard, but that was only in the way that just about everybody stood a fool, spiritually blind and completely undiscerning. "It's alright, Tom, just take a moment, then you can fill me in."

Andy let the man have a few seconds. To pull this off, things needed to unfold organically, and that meant grief had to be factored into the equation, the genuine kind from everyone else, as well as his own particular brand. With Tom Deering, there was no façade. The man was true blue, all the way, and when it came to such temporal matters as upholding the law, Andy couldn't have been any luckier. Tom was the quintessential deputy, a man who did his job to the best of his ability and never complained. Serving and protecting the town he'd grown up in was a source of pride. The kind of man that if his bestie died from a heart attack, he'd do the bastard a solid and clear his Internet browser.

Then again, the man had little in the way of *real* imagination or wonder or thirst for true knowledge. Didn't have a clue that such things even existed. Such was the fate of the bulk of the human race. Andy looked at his friend, giving him his most understanding eye-to-eye contact, just two men on the job, both doing their best to handle an ugly night's work.

Andy, not for the first time, wondered if maybe he shouldn't have gone into acting.

"The Archers were the nicest of people." The deputy motioned towards the prairie barn at the end of the driveway, and started walking that way, Andy pacing alongside and giving the younger man a pat on the back. "You're not going to believe this. I can hardly believe it. Like some damned animal ripped through

14

here."

More right than you know, thought Pontillo as the two of them moved closer to the activity in and around the Archers' barn. "Just take me through everything, one step at a time. The Archers need us now, Tom, need all of us—to do our jobs. Bring some sense to this mess."

Their shoes crunched in unison on the crushed stone driveway as they approached the flurry of deputies and investigators scurrying about. It looked like chaos, but Andy Pontillo knew that none of the crime scene investigators would leave any clue or evidence undetected, especially with the Archers involved. Everyone knew them, and to know them was to love them.

Andy had known Edward and Elena Archer for the better part of 30-years. The both of them, model citizens. Community minded, kindhearted, the type of people always willing to lend a hand. Years back, he'd helped them purchase a run down, foreclosed upon farm in the village of Pine Creek. They'd held no outside jobs, just the farm. And they had made it work. Soon after arriving, the only child they raised, Eric, was born.

No one knew anything about the Archers' life before Pine Creek, no one but Andrew Pontillo, and of a truth, the one thing he could say for sure was that the two of them were no kind of idiot.

As Tom and Andy were walking up, Deputy Jessica Benitez emerged from the door of the barn. "Sheriff, no one can make heads or tails of this. It's the most horrendous scene any of us have encountered."

Pontillo knew Benitez to be a good deputy, a little

green, but with excellent instincts. He was glad she was one who'd answered the call. She would play an important part in what was coming. She would be exactly what Eric needed to get through all of this.

"What do we have, Benitez?" The sheriff's eyes scanned the barn in all directions; it was a mess, with the floors, walls, boxes, crates all torn apart. "It looks like a tornado went through here."

"Exactly, sir. This was an exhaustive, motivated search for something specific. It's the same inside the house."

The sheriff's mind kept coming back to one name, one name that would bring death to all the others, but a new life for him.

Feigning concern, Pontillo sputtered, "Where are the Archers?"

Deputy Deering answered, "Mr. Archer, or what we assume is Mr. Archer, is in the back of the barn. Mrs. Archer is already being transported to Forbes Memorial, but the EMTs aren't holding out much hope."

"She survived?" Pontillo's eyebrows raised about as high as the pitch of his voice. He had to give Elena Archer credit; the bitch was tough. "Who's the crew running her?"

"Wolfman and Lurch."

Shit. "Well, at least the woman's got them … couldn't ask for better. Hell, maybe she'll make it." *Fuck me, if she does.*

As the sheriff approached, crime scene investigators were taking notes, pictures, and measurements, everyone going through the motions of their job. He saw the head of the county CSI unit,

Ricky Mack, striding towards him. Pontillo thought he looked a little queasy. "Ricky, you're turning all shades, buddy. You've been to countless scenes like this. What gives?"

"Hey, Andy. This is *not* your run of the mill gore-fest, man, that's for sure. Have your work cut for you on this one." He got his comments out right before he vomited at the base of a tree.

The sheriff retched at the sight of Ricky losing his lunch. As he turned away, he noticed Deputy Benitez had positioned herself closer to Edward Archer's body, so he moved in that direction. There was Edward Archer hanging on the back wall of the barn. It was a gruesome sight, like something out of a horror movie. His arms and legs impaled by railroad spikes through the forearms and shins; heavy tow chains splayed his limbs in a macabre jumping jack pose, frozen, like the anguish on his face. Every inch of his body burned or carved. The incisions were not random, not with the skin charred between the cuts to make them stand out.

Pontillo could tell that Deputy Benitez was trying to hold her feelings in check.

The words stumbled out of her mouth. "He … he was beaten. Markings carved into his skin seem religious or ritual in nature. Have you ever seen anything similar to this, sheriff?"

"Can't say that I have, deputy." Pontillo knew immediately that the carvings were religious and ritual. Edward Archer's body had been dealt with in the same way the ancient Greeks had used tortoise shells, as an oracle to receive messages from the gods. Except the perpetrator of this heinous act wasn't calling upon a god, he was one. This was a feeding. A quest for information. Pontillo now knew that his years of preparation had not been in vain. The ancient god had answered his call and he was in Hurley County.

Pontillo tried hard to keep up the façade of surprise regarding the gruesome scene that had unfolded at the Archers' farm. There were a lot of questions to be answered, some he could already. Others, however, he would need help with, and that is where Eric would come in. Pontillo was about to introduce Eric to a world he didn't know existed. He was about to be force-fed the truth about his parents. The sheriff relished the part he had played in the Archers' past finally catching up. All he had to do now was wait for Eric to arrive and the next piece of the puzzle would fall into place.

CHAPTER FOUR

IF COMMON SENSE wasn't enough to let Eric Archer know that a knock in the middle of the night, or coming home to a ringing phone was never a good sign, then his decade in law enforcement had certainly cemented the concept. He'd sure put in enough time on the other end of things, making both long distance notifications and the always awful face-to-face delivery of always awful news. So as soon as he stepped off the elevator and heard his phone ringing, it was with a sinking stomach that he rushed to the door, fumbled for the right key—the phone stopped and instantly started again—and pushed open the door, keys still in the lock, dropped his duffel bag, and sprinted to the phone. "Detective Archer?"

The voice on the other end was familiar, but that didn't make the call any more comforting.

There was hardly a memory of Eric's life that didn't involve Hurley County Sheriff Andy Pontillo. The sheriff and Eric's dad were the best of friends, inseparable for as long as Eric could remember, and it was Andy Pontillo who'd been an integral part of his pursuit of landing a position on the job. Andy had given Eric his first shot as a deputy, and eventually pushed him to spread out from the rural Western New York area he had spent most of his life, and into Pittsburgh homicide for the last three years.

And now it was Andy calling him in the dead of night. And something, indeed, was wrong. Eric knew it, heard it in Andy's voice, heard it in Andy's *professional* voice. Eric felt his adrenaline dump and his nausea start to build. Professionalism now would be his shield. "Sheriff?"

"Listen, son, you need to come home, there has been a … a, well, an incident at your parents' place."

Eric glanced at a picture of his parents. "What kind of incident?"

"It's better if you just come home."

"Why won't you tell me anything?" Only silence on the other end. "Sheriff? Andy?"

An eternity before Eric heard Andy's voice again.

"Eric, just come home. We need you home. Head right to Forbes Memorial. Your mom will be there."

Discipline once again in the driver's seat, Eric answered, "I'm leaving now … should be there in about three hours."

"Be careful. You need to make it here safely." Andy's voice took on an even graver tone. "It's of the utmost importance."

Eric grunted and hung up. He'd wanted to push the issue, but if Andy, the man he'd looked up to since a kid, and his dad's best friend, was going to be tight-lipped, then that was that. What was worse was Eric knowing why—*Suspecting why, you dumbass … suspecting why.* After all, like good ol' Uncle Andy, Eric was also a cop, and not just any cop, but a detective, a homicide detective. He knew the script.

Hell, everybody on the job for any length of time ended up knowing it.

He looked again at the framed picture of his parents sitting on his roll-top desk, back when they were still young. *Young-minded and young-backed*, as his dad liked to say. It was their 20-year-anniversary, with him about 10. The pic taken at one of their favorite local haunts, Rusch's Restaurant. And somehow his mother had gotten Dad to wear his monkey suit, which he hated to don, and one could tell, with his dad in the picture looking simultaneously smitten by the woman on his arm, while uncomfortable with the fancy occasion. What his mom called: *Dressed to the 9.5s.*

She looked gorgeous, too, hair done up fancy, fingers and toes taken care of at some spa, and with all the get-up, her dorky necklace, that she rarely took off. Her half to his, a silver heart pendant with the words HE WHO HOLDS THE KEY CAN UNLOCK MY HEART above and below the outline of the other fitting part.

He still had his half, the key, bound up in a black paracord survival bracelet, always on him, save for when he had to suit up for the job—a key that his mother had made him swear, and swear again every one of his birthdays, to fit with hers, in case of—

"They're fine," Eric said aloud in his living room. "And if they're not, they're going to be." He took a breath. "Until I know different, their hearts are beating, and they are A-friggin'-okay."

But they weren't okay.

He knew it. Could feel it. All he could hope for was that he'd misinterpreted Andy's intent, but there was fat-chance for that. There was a reason why Andy had been a cop on the phone, had spoken the vague words that he had. The same kind of words that had fallen from his own lips on too many an occasion.

... an incident at your parents' place....

He had to get moving. Put on his mother-effin' bracelet and pray there'd be no promises to keep. Get some of the strongest, blackest coffee in his system and go pedal to the metal.

... an incident at your parents', Eric. Did you hear that?

A goddamned incident.

INTERLUDE I

IT HAD ONLY been six months since the babies were born, and the father and surrogate mother had already been taken care of, the loose ends tied up faster than even Janice Pontillo had anticipated. She'd staged their demise to appear to be victims of an apparent lover's quarrel that had ended in a murder/suicide. Janice was very convincing in her grief. Everyone bought the story, including the authorities.

She was now free to raise the boys as she saw fit.

Sympathy for her, the babies, and her situation poured out of everyone she knew. Friends, in disbelief, consoled her. She heard all of the clichés. How she would be better off without him. They had both gotten what they'd deserved. They would help her and the babies however they could. Janice graciously accepted all the well-wishes, knowing full well she would never need the help of these people.

They were so ignorant.

They had no idea of the amount of power her babies had the potential of wielding.

She shook the thoughts out of her head and turned her attention back to the infants next to her. Little Andy coughed and rolled over in his crib. He was recovering faster than his brother. The boys were only six months old, but she had already introduced four different diseases to their developing immune systems. They needed to be strong. She was taking every precaution to protect them in the future. The boys had been very good since coming home from the hospital. The only person they knew or trusted was their mother. That was just the way she wanted it. She doted on them, treated them like the princes she knew they would one day become. Once she was finished with the boys, they wouldn't care about anything but fulfilling their destiny.

And they would praise their mother for all she had done.

CHAPTER FIVE

THERE WERE FEW things in life the wolfman enjoyed more than screaming down the highway in the Monster M.A.S.H. with his bestie Lurch, heel to steel, hauling ass to save a person's life.

In fact, it'd been a lifelong dream.

He'd grown up with his partner Nick *Lurch* Stephens. More than 26-years before, their mothers had shared a room in the maternity wing of Forbes Memorial, both giving birth within an hour of each other, and starting the relationship of their boys as hospital brothers.

When he'd started sprouting hair everywhere in the fifth grade, it'd been his bruthah-from-anutha-mutha who'd dubbed him The Wolfman. In kind, when Nick had shot up to six-foot-two in the seventh grade, before topping out with an additional five inches by the age of 19, there'd been only one moniker fit for his friend for life.

From elementary to middle to high school, from buddy-enlisting to graduating as medics from Fort Sam Houston, to two tours in Iraq, everything had led them to this, EMTs with their own business—Monster M.A.S.H.—and in their own customized rig of the same name, a converted Humvee, tricked out to the max. It sat on jet black 17-inch Allied Beadlock rims which held 40-inch Pit Bull tires. Coupled with a six-inch lift kit meant no amount of snow or debris would hold back their beast. The body was fire engine red with yellow and black flames painted on the front fenders. A custom carbon-fiber body and grill guard caged in a 572 Hemi 650 hp big-block engine that could top out at 130 MPH. The roof was outlined with a roll-bar of the same material and included an enclosure for the combined light bar and siren. Their 4x4 home away from home was fitted to meet anything a first responder could demand.

A fuckin' fortune—and *that!* without all the medical shit.

With both of their sets of parents investing into their business, plus everything they'd put in, along with other investors, they were both ass-deep in debt—but they'd also been saving lives. After only two years, they'd already become the *go-to* response team for those living out in the sticks, and for the most gravely injured. They were also able to make some cash on the side showing off their baby at car shows in the tri-state area. It made them the rock stars of Emergency Medical Services.

All the better for staying up to their pits in adrenaline.

God bless America.

Derek Matthews glanced at the speedometer, took in the steady 80 MPH, and kissed two fingers before tipping them to the side of his head and saluting them to his heavenly Father, all in gratitude for being the only ride on the empty road.

26

Only 30-minutes out ... but this gal's not going to make it. Not the way she's been ripped open.

Then, over the speaker from the back: "Wolfie, if only you could see this!"

"Say again ... what's happening?"

"This bitch ain't going down. And it's more than her being a fighter ... this is some ... this is some *X Files* shit."

"Spill it, Lurch. What's going on?"

A pause.

Some rattling from the back.

Finally, "She's healing right in front of me. Hell, I've had to remove some of the clamps ... her body, it's ... it's zipping itself up—going slow, maybe too slow, but I'm fucked sideways if that ain't what I'm seeing!"

For a moment, Derek didn't feel like The Wolfman. Instead, he felt scared. What in the hell was going on? His mind, however, through force of habit, quickly ran down the possibilities. *No, Lurch isn't joking. Yes, he could goof around, but never for reals ... not when they were on-mission. No, Lurch isn't crazy, either. So what's that leave?*

Only one thing.

Lurch was telling the truth. And that truth was something never encountered before.

Keeping his eyes focused on the road, he called back, "She still doing the mutant-thing?"

"Hell, yes, and I'm dyin' if I'm lyin'. You gotta see this?"

"I wish ... but we still gotta get her to Forbes. Do whatever you can to help her out."

"I am ... I'm already on a third unit of blood, and

I've been stitching her up like crazy."

"Lurch, I—" Something moved in front of the vehicle and The Wolfman's hands jerked out of instinct.

The vehicle tipped,

"What the hell …"

threatened to roll—*fuckfuckfuckfuck*—and by the grace of God, only, his hands somehow managed not to overcompensate.

"… is going on?"

"We're okay, we're okay, we're—"

They were *not* okay.

Something pounded on the roof of the cab, and something happened that hadn't occurred since The Wolfman's first firefight.

He pissed himself.

A hand punched through the roof of the cab, once, twice—*Is that a fuckin' claw?*—and then a third time, impacting the Wolf's shoulder.

No, not impacting.

Penetrating.

Oh, God. Nononononono!

Derek screamed: "I'm dead, Lurch, I'm dead." And he was, or would be within seconds. His right subclavian hadn't just been hit; it had been ripped out by some … by some …

"WOLFMAN."

… demon, some demon from—

Dead hands no longer controlling the high-speed vehicle, Monster M.A.S.H., this time, started its devastating roll.

THE BEAST MOVED to the back of the now at-rest vehicle—which had, surprisingly, rolled and rolled, only to land on its tires—his eyes taking in—and enjoying—the destruction he'd wrought, his feet uncaring and immune to the bits of metal and glass and polymers littering the ground. Other than the massive cosmetic and mechanical damage suffered, the ambulance was still remarkably intact; nonetheless, it was a dead contraption—never to move again.

What did hold some interest, however, was what might still be alive inside.

The beast grabbed the dangling door from off the back of Monster M.A.S.H. and tore it free. His eyes, unhampered by the darkness within the belly of the camper, took in the scene, a tallish man no longer looking so tall, his mouth bubbling forth blood, his body sporting multiple compound fractures, his life-force quickly draining … and, the target of the moment, his *real* quarry, the old woman, her body safely strapped to a gurney locked to the floor of the vehicle, still badly injured, but not even close to the damage expected.

He'd previously thought her dead.

Now, this time, he'd be sure of it.

Stooping his shoulders, he moved as far in as he could, and grabbed the foot of the broken, dying man, and pulled.

"Fu … fu—"

The beast brought the man's face to his, curious to

hear his final words. A talon brushed away another wash of coughed up blood, bile, torn flesh and shattered teeth, and then its three fingers held aright the head, even as it canted its own with an inquiring ear.

The man blinked, his eyes going dreamy, but then a flash of intelligence lighted, and he smiled. "Fuck … fuck your canoe."

And he fell forever silent.

The beast let the head go and watched the body crumble, his previous hunger already satisfied by the killing of the other man, the letting loose of his blood, the absorbing of the man's soul.

But now, there was this woman, she who would dare to even tempt him with thoughts of failure. How laughable now it seemed that he'd brought anything akin to fear with him into this realm. This, indeed, had been his only folly. The temptation that something, some-*one*, as feeble and spindly and weak as this, a woman on the cusp of death, could ever hope to threaten something as powerful as himself.

Reaching forward and grabbing the secured gurney, the beast pulled with a commanding jerk, ripping free the bed even as he backed out of the ambulance.

The other one, the old man, had somehow managed to keep his silence. But even with that, he'd gained what he'd needed. Knowledge. There was something in his blood, something ancient—and powerful, but something that in the end still couldn't save him. This same blood, he could smell, resided in this woman, and he'd learn even more, even as he permanently ended her life.

He moved to the head of the gurney, and gripped

the skull of the now-moaning, but still unconscious woman, and prepared to—

A flash of LIGHT.

He staggered back in pain, and forced his squinting eyes to focus.

There was a figure standing beside the gurney. A silhouette.

"She is not yours to take. Not she who holds the sacred ...

The beast tried to move, to attack, but stood frozen.

"... bloodline. Take heed, Difatos, you have no claim to her power."

Angry, the beast watched through slitted vision as both the old woman and the apparition disappeared, the two, he presumed, or at least the one, thinking him defeated.

But they were wrong.

The side wall of the ambulance buckled from the force of the beast's blow. "Brother, I will end you." *I have a brother? Yes, many brothers.*

He was stronger than before. More knowledgeable than before, and with that knowledge, his power continued to grow.

For now, he knew something critical, and with it, memories were flooding in. Now he knew who he was!

He was Difatos.

The god-king Difatos.

CHAPTER SIX

ƒPEEDING UP INTERSTATE 79, Eric's mind raced along with his car. At least he'd had enough presence of mind to report in. There was no way he was making it into work tomorrow. He hadn't even given his boss, Captain Howard, a date-of-return. Screw it. He couldn't care less. Fortunately, the man hadn't pressed him for any details, which was good, 'cause he didn't have any deets to give.

He could hear Andy's words running through his mind—again and again, even if perverted by his tortured imagination.

There's been an incident, Eric. Did you catch that? An incident.

What the hell kind of incident could've possibly happened that Andy couldn't have told him over the phone?

You know what kind, Eric.

Did you catch that?

Just talkin', cop-to-cop, you know what kind.

He ran a hand through his light brown close-cropped hair and imagined how much better it would feel to be … to be wringing Andy's neck. God knew he loved the man, but it bordered on sadistic, his mentor keeping such a sensitive matter secret.

Then again, as much as his mind could mess with him, he could also imagine Andy giving him reproof. *Whatever's going on, boy, I need you to get here, and that means getting here in one piece. Control your thinking. Be professional.*

Yeah, right.

Be pro-fessional.

As if....

He needed to know what had happened. Mom off to the hospital and no mention of Dad. WTF. What was he supposed to make of that!

There's been an incident, Eric.

His parents had to be okay. They were his world. Always had been. Everything he was, everything he *would* be … it was all them. He owed it all to them.

Dad's okay Dad's okay Dad is breathing and he's o-friggin'-kay.

The man had to be. Eric just couldn't picture him any other way. The man was too smart, too strong— and too … well, too magical.

Sounded stupid to the ear, even the mind's ear, but it was true. His father probably wouldn't believe Eric remembered, but he did.

He remembered everything.

"Dad?"

The man stared at him from across the fire. "Yes?"

"Seems like you've got me studying everything?"

"'S'at so." The man grinned. "Sure it feels that way, but it's far from the truth."

Eric scooted to his dad's side of the blaze. "One thing I've noticed, though, that's missing. There's nothing about God."

"God, huh?" He put a hand on his son's knee.

"I'm doing the three R's, social sciences, world history, geography … you even got me doing boxing, karate, and wrestling. Then there's the farming, our hikes, killing chickens and prepping them for dinner. I'm getting homeschooled in everything but relig—"

"Check out that sky? Look at all those stars."

Eric did.

"What would you have me say about all that? Could say something, sure. But what? Did God make all that?" He looked up at the night sky. "All this?" He glanced around their campsite and beyond. "Or was it gods? Or a bunch of goddesses?"

"I don't know."

"Religion's man's attempt at explaining what he doesn't know." A long pause. "Maybe way back, he knew a little bit, some mysteries here and there, but they've been lost a long time. And maybe there's a few out there still that know some stuff, but those people, those shamans, you're not going to find in town on Sunday, standing behind a pulpit."

"I've just been wondering if there's … you know, anything more."

"There's always magic."

"Yeah, right."

The man turned and straddled his log. "Face me."

Eric did.

"Let me give you something to ponder."

Laughter. "Won't be the first time."

"Won't be the last, either. But this'll be fun—and hopefully, a bit scary."

Eric's smile vanished. "What does that mean?"

Another long pause. "Magic is real. It's in the

heart, in the imagination, and sometimes, might be something that gets stumbled upon, and even then, might not get noticed. Or worse, it might get dismissed. But it's there. Magic. And it's a wonderful, amazing, exhilarating ... and sometimes terrifying thing." Edward Archer started rolling up his shirt sleeves, all the way to the elbow. "Got any change?"

Eric reached into his pocket and pulled out a quarter.

His dad held up his arms, palms out, then palms in, demonstrating there was nothing there but skin. "Lemme have it."

Eric handed over the coin.

"Which way does George Washington face on the coin?"

Eric thought a moment. "Towards the left."

Edward held up the coin and showed that Honest George, indeed, faced to the left. "But if there's such a thing as magic? Then perhaps he could face the other direction."

"No way."

Eric's dad passed a hand in front of the coin, and when it came back into view a moment later, George, miraculously—*magically*—was facing towards the right."

"NO WAY."

Edward chuckled. "People would do far, far better if they'd just farm, just enjoy nature, and see how things grow. And they'd do far, far better if they'd just stay curious, and full of wonder, and never presume to think that they've got the answer to all this"—his eyes quickly flashed to the stars—"when they don't."

"How did you—"

"Wait now." The man's hand closed on the quarter. "Which way is George facing now?"

"You made him face to the right."

"Did I?" He opened up his hand and held up the coin, its face illuminated by dancing flames. "Is he still facing to the right?"

"No." Eric studied the coin for a moment of time … and then it hit: "OH, you trickster! He's bald!"

"Is he now?" He handed over the coin. "Just a bit of magic. Put it in your pocket. Let your mom see it when we get home."

And he did.

Somehow, he'd managed to keep it in his pocket and not look at it, despite wanting to, even needing to. He kept it put away, and when he and his dad returned home, while sitting down to eat lunch, he pulled out bald-headed George on a twenty-five-cent piece and handed it over, before sitting down to eat lunch.

"So, your old man's a magician now, is he?"

Eric pointed at the coin. "Look at it, Mom! Dad's the real thing."

Elena Archer looked at the coin, then held it high in the light coming through her kitchen's bay windows, and canted her head. "Um, no. George has a full head of hair—and! he's facing to the left." She tossed the coin back to her son.

Eric looked at the coin and verified his mother's observation. "Darn. He's back to normal. No one's going to believe me."

"Maybe what your dad was showing you for just for you and nobody else's business."

Eric, sitting in front of his half-eaten sandwich, continued looking at the coin. "And I told you. Last night, Dad made the president face back the right way."

Elena walked over to her son, and pointed at the coin. "He also told you about the dangers of not noticing things, about dismissing them."

Eric broke into a wide grin. No, he hadn't noticed it. All he'd perceived was George's bald head now back to sporting his traditional weird wig.

But the coin was different.

This time magicked by his mother.

At the back of George's neck, instead of saying: IN GOD WE TRUST, it read IN MAGIC WE TRUST. "You and Dad are magicians! *Real* magicians."

His mother kissed his forehead. "Maybe we are and maybe we're not. Not too hard, is it, to buy some trick coins and do some sleight of hand? But if, just *if* we did have *real* magic, just imagine what might've come from us, and landed in the likes of you?"

Later, of course, the coin had returned to normal. He could never get his parents to confess to switching it out from his keepsake drawer, and he always wondered if maybe they hadn't. He still had the coin, its rim painted red so he'd never confuse it with any other. A lesson from his youth about the secrets of the universe, about wonderment, about magic.

He remembered everything.

But were they right? Was there magic? And if there was, couldn't it have prevented any kind of incident? Couldn't it be helping his parents even now? And what about his mother's words? Did he have anything special inside of him?

Maybe not magic. He'd certainly never seen any of that. But he'd tried hard to make his parents proud, and they showed every sign of loving him, and loving him with such burning pride that it was almost painful.

They were always there for him. When he'd tested out his high school graduation, and later, when he'd graduated from Chadwick Bay University with degrees in History and Anthropology. They'd been there crying and clapping and hugging when he'd become honor grad at the Sheriff's Academy, and had cheered him on when he'd landed the job he'd wanted with the Pittsburgh P.D.

Thirty years, it'd been. His life.

And always there, his parents. As much a part of him as anything, and way more than most, and most people.

They had to be okay. Had to be.

He'd find out. He'd get his answers.

Magic or no, he was going to make some shit happen.

CHAPTER SEVEN

THAT FUCKING CAR.

Andy Pontillo heard Eric's restored classic black and white 1974 Chevy Laguna S3 before he saw it pulling into the hospital parking lot.

Last of the muscle cars, Eric had once said. The hours spent scouring the country for parts and pieces, all to make a faithful restoration. The patience and bloodhound attitude Eric had showed during the rebuild, had not only sold Pontillo on Eric's skills, but his commitment and passion.

Pontillo remembered the look of joy on Eric's face the day he proudly drove the multi-year project up his uncle's driveway. The news he was about to deliver to the young man today, though—the man he had known since birth—would bring an entirely different kind of feeling. But that's what life was about, wasn't it? The moments spent between times of pleasure and pain?

Pain-pain-pain, good ol' pain. But none for me, thanks ... I've more than filled my quota. Now if only Eric plays his part, like the good little boy that he is.

And he will!

After all, I'm the good guy—I'm Uncle Andy!

He could almost taste the sweetness of the words he was about to speak to Eric. They would sound downright melodic—a recessional hymn cascading into the air as the sheep filed out of their misbegotten house of worship. The end of the journey started so long ago by him and his brother.

Pontillo smiled. The parents had been a pair of side-sticking thorns, sure. But they'd been taken care of. Now there was only Eric left to carry out his last bit of business. He was so looking forward to never thinking about them again.

It had never been about them, anyway.

It has been about me ... always about me—me and power.

Andy put on his game-face. He even had his booby-trap ready in the trunk. Wait till Eric got his hands on that.

But now it was time to get serious, at least enough to pinch one out. *Besides everything else, fuck Chevy.*

THE LAGUNA'S TIRES squealed to a stop on the parking lot blacktop of Forbes Memorial Hospital. Eric was immediately out the door, moving towards the ER, and looking for signs of life—his life, *his* world.

But no, there was no mommy and daddy.

Andy had said his mom was going to be here ... which meant that if his father was okay, then the man, if he couldn't be with his wife, would be outside waiting for him, along with Andy, or perhaps the pair just inside the ER, but all he saw was empty cars, some people walking around, and a couple of parked ambulances.

He'd been expecting—*hoping*—to see his dad, *needing to*, yet from the time he'd left his house, he knew that was a stretch. He'd been driving for hours—nearly four, instead of the three promised, 'cause making it alive and coffeed-up was more important than being stupid and causing any further damage on top of what had probably already happened. Nearly four torturous hours, with his phone, fully-charged, but still plugged in, sitting on the passenger seat, cursed and silent, yet reminding him with every passing mile that if there had been any good news coming, he'd have heard something from someone.

When his eyes finally locked onto Andy, standing just inside the ER's sliding doors, the look on Pontillo's baggy-eyed, somber face told him everything he needed to know.

His dad was gone.

Eric's shoulders slumped.

Walking up to Andy, he took the man's hand in his, and with the other, brought him in for an embrace, their traditional *shug*—but then he held it a bit too long. Maybe for just a few extra seconds at the most, but it was enough, Eric was sure, to let Andy know that for a moment in time, he was a little boy again, a lad who didn't want to be a man, who didn't want to deal with such verboten issues, who didn't want to man-up and be the grown-ass murder dick that he was, who didn't want to follow the sacred script, mouthing the obligatory questions he already knew the answers to.

Finally, stepping back, barely able to form the words emanating from his mouth, Eric asked, "Dad?"

Andy stared for a moment, then, as a tear bubbled from an eye and started to trek down his face, he gave the slightest shake of the head, almost imperceptible—except to Eric.

Silence.

Eric felt a coldness wash over him, and he was thankful, a numbness working as a shield. His cop armor was back in place. After so much time worrying, at least now he knew. "So, for the moment, Dad's a non-issue."

A slight nod.

"Mom?"

"I don't … I don't really kno—"

"Where's my mother, Andy?"

An awkward pause. "Monster M.A.S.H. was bringing your mom from the house. But … but they never arrived. We have patrol cars out now looking for 'em."

"What? Wolfman and Lurch? They didn't make it here? How the hell does that happen?" Eric was incredulous. "It's been almost four hours since we talked?"

Andy just stared.

The silence was broken when Deputy Tom Deering's voice squawked through the radio in Andy's patrol car. "Sheriff, we found the ambulance. It looks like it was in a nasty accident. I don't know how this could have happened, but the top is ripped off. It's opened up like a friggin' tin can."

"What about my mother?"

With Eric riding his hip, Pontillo moved to the car and picked up the handset, while Eric walked around Andy's cruiser, looking in through the windows.

"Okay, Tom, calm down. How is Mrs. Archer? Where are the EMTs?"

"Wolfman and Lurch are dead, sir, and there is no trace of Mrs. Archer."

"What is your location? I have Eric with me, we'll come to you."

"Old logging road off Route 62, between Dredge and Leon Road," the deputy explained. "And, sheriff, please hurry."

"We're on our way." The sheriff started to settle into the driver's seat, but Eric waved him back out of the car from where he stood by the trunk.

Andy Pontillo walked to the back of the car. "What's up?"

"My parents, they were attacked?"

"Yes."

"At their home?"

"Yes."

"Then their home's a crime scene."

Andy gave him a funny look. "So?"

"C'mon, sheriff, I'm not some cherry on his first rode—"

"I'm not getting y—"

Eric slapped the trunk. "You were there. And *if* you were there, you *took* pictures. Your duty-bag's not in the car. So it's in the trunk. Get it out."

Andy looked down and shook his head. "Eric, I did take some pics, but they're not anything you want to see. Not Ed and Ellie."

"What, not the way I should remember them?" Eric glanced at the trunk, then back at his friend and mentor. "You're really going to tell me that, a homicide detective, and a guy who's read the same manuals you have? Gonna hit me with that line?"

Pontillo held his stance. "It is a good line! And for this situation, it's the right one. Was right enough to make the manual. There's reasons for—"

"Open the trunk."

Andy sighed, took the ring of keys that were already in hand, and inserted one of them into the trunk.

Seeing the sheriff's bag, he quickly fished out the digital camera that he knew would be inside and then looked at Andy. "Let's get to the Monster M.A.S.H. and find my mom."

A moment later, they were speeding off to meet the deputies at what was looking like another crime scene. Eric couldn't hardly believe what a nightmare this was turning into, but the worst blow had already landed. His father was dead. And it wasn't looking too good for his mother, not with two of the best paramedics one could have out for the count.

Eric, sitting beside Pontillo—who was all-business speeding them towards their destination—powered up the camera. He started to cycle through the photo-gallery stored on the device's hard drive.

Click.

Click.

Click click click. Fuck me. Click click....

The first several pictures were of the outside of his parents' house, the driveway, the back door and porch, and finally the barn.

As he moved through the stills, he got a tour of the house and barn, two structures that should have been intimately familiar, but now, due to the incredible amount of damage, felt completely foreign. It could make a person cry—though not him, not now, and maybe not for some time—with the way their place looked, and after all the pride they'd had in their property. *Oh, God, am I already planting my mother before I even really know?* To see these pictures now, of what had happened, was a perversion.

Click.

Click.

Click.

Continuing on, he grew increasingly angry—and he welcomed it. Welcomed the pain. Liked how it was feeding his adrenaline, keeping him going, despite a lack of sleep and a ton of worry. He enjoyed the personal Hell this was putting him through, because it fueled his desire for vengeance, and a righteous kind of payback, because there would, indeed, be a reckoning.

Click.

And there he was—his dad.

The man had been pegboarded to the wall of the barn with spikes, railroad spikes—*It's not my dad, not this, not anymore ... just a body, and a crime scene that needs to be worked—so work it, you sonuvabitch*—and with the rest of the ... of the *deceased's* body looking like it had been carved, like scrimshaw, meticulously flayed, opened up, gutted, burned, shit moved around, and with glyphs and other crap scalpeled into the skin.

Eric looked over. "What's this Lovecraft shit carved into the body."

"The fuck? Body? This is your dad we're talking about—not some goddamned body!"

"Get a grip, it's a body now. The manual, remember?"

45

"Yeah, well … well, touché for you. He was my best friend."

"Don't I know it, but the question still stands; what's this writing about?"

Andy Pontillo grabbed a water bottle from its holder, the liquid warm, and God knew how old. "You're asking me? Satanic killings in this country, though they do happen, are so damn rare, they hardly register." A long pause. "That leaves us two choices; we either have some stone-cold Devil worshippers we're dealing with, or it's some whack-jobs fucking with us on purpose."

Silence.

Finally, Eric gave Andy's knee a squeeze. "Look, I love you, you know that. And I thank you for try—"

"Trying to"—Andy grabbed the camera on Eric's lap—"protect you!"

Eric watched in shock, as next he knew, Andy's window was down, and the camera went flying at 75 MPH. "Christ, man, what you do?"

"Fucking vented, that's what. Shoulda let good enough alone. I wanted to save you from seeing that bullshit."

"I needed to se—"

Andy glanced over for a flash. "Maybe you did … maybe you need to know everything. But what about me? Have you thought that maybe, just maybe I didn't need you to see this shit? If I might've had a shot to pretend before, I sure as hell can't now. Known you since before you were knee-high to my ass, and I didn't need you seeing that nasty, evil, vile business."

"What about the pictures?"

"They're fine. Crime scene guys downloaded all of

'em on-site. The only thing lost is the damn camera. A statement of charges will be damn well worth it. I needed to fuck something up."

"I'm so … so sorry. Been thinking about things from my perspective, and all the while making sure I keep my shit together for this … so I can work it, be of some benefit. Didn't stop to really think about what a loss this has to be for—"

"Don't worry about me. I just wanted to spare you some pain. There's only so much a man can take; think of it like a quota. The barrel can only get so full—I know. Those images you saw … they're never going to leave you."

"My mother was on that camera. I've handled my dad, I should've seen her, too."

"No." Andy let out a long sigh. "No, my boy. Not her, not after what she went through. God, son, didn't you see your dad?"

"Yes, so?"

"Your mother was worse, boy. Way, way worse."

"How's that possible?"

"Because she was still alive."

Eric kept silent, and just let the man drive, his mind working feverishly to process everything, and doing so while taking Andy into account. He had been roughshod with the man, and that hadn't been fair. But then some things started to come together. "You said *some*, you said *whack-jobs*, *whack-jobs*, with an *s*."

"You saw the pictures. Enough of 'em, anyway. Think one guy did all that damage? Hell, I don't even know how structurally sound the barn and house are anymore. No single guy did all that destruction."

Eric thought a moment, then said, "My parents live

out in the sticks—"

"Yeah, you're a smart one, alright. The question is how did we even know to go out. Could've taken some days. But while I was off-duty, at home, trying to enjoy my evening, probably just the same as you, some *anonymous* tipper called it in."

"That changes everything."

"It does—how?"

"This wasn't just some home invasion on steroids. That's private business. Those folks don't want po-po showing up."

"Right, go on?"

"We may not be dealing with some weird cult, but we're certainly not dealing with a group of whack-jobs. This was planned. If it had simply been a ritual—again, that'd be private business, but some-bodies wanted their work found, and soon."

Apparently, it was Andy Pontillo's turn to give Eric's knee a squeeze. "Knew you'd be good for something."

"You know what this was?"

Andy gave a tired, but enthusiastic smile. "Tell me."

"This was a message. This whole bloodbath of a mess. Some kind of effed-up message."

ʃHAKEN BY THE night's events, Deputy Deering started rambling as soon as Pontillo and Eric exited the patrol car. He wanted to get the words out and away from his thoughts. He didn't want to have to think about them again.

He hoped as the words escaped his mouth, they would take the pictures of the horrors he had witnessed this past night and morning along with them. "Well, Benitez and I drove back out to the farm to retrace where the ambulance left from. When we all left the farm, we went south on Cross, and took Kent Switch Road back to the station. I figured the ambulance took off north, then up to Dredge, so we drove out there, and when we got to the bridge over the creek, it was gone. It looked torn away or washed away, or something.

"I radioed the highway department and they didn't know anything about it. Figuring they couldn't have gone that way, we headed to Route 62. South on 62, just after the corner, there were two massive pines in the middle of the road. They looked as though they were snapped off at the base. So they were cut off there, too.

"As we went north, there were tire tracks that burned off onto this old logging road. We followed them and found all of this." Deering swept his arms out in both directions. "The EMTs are here, but there is no sign of Mrs. Archer."

The sheriff put his hand on Deering's shoulder. "Where's Benitez now?"

"Taking pictures of the surrounding area. Be back any moment."

CRIC WALKED AROUND the scene—stunned.

The destruction was unbelievable. He and Pontillo

surveyed the area. They inspected the mangled corpses of Wolfman and Lurch. "Damn, all the good these two did in their life. They deserved a better end than this. And those wounds aren't … uh, human. No person can do that to a body."

"I'd be inclined to agree with you, son. Look at their ride, Monster M.A.S.H., that thing was built to withstand the apocalypse. It is mostly intact, hell the damn thing must have flipped three or four times, the roll bar hardly looks dented. The cab, though, is popped open like a tin can, and Wolfman got ripped up through it. The back door here wasn't jimmied by a crowbar, it was torn off. Poor Lurch looks like he was wrapped backwards around a tree. This certainly has the feel of something inhuman."

"Who could do something like this, Andy, why these guys and why my parents? It doesn't make any sense."

Pontillo met Eric at the rescue vehicle. "I wouldn't say *who* as much as *what* did this to your parents."

Eric shot Andy a look of disbelief. "You're saying this isn't the act of a person or group of people? Enlighten me, then. Do we have a sleuth of really pissed, super intelligent black bears running around here since I've been gone? I was half joking when I said the wounds weren't human."

"I don't have all the answers yet. That's why I wanted you back here so bad. I won't be able to get the answers I need without you."

"It's not like you to be this cryptic, Andy. I'm not sure I like it."

The two climbed into the back of what was left of the rescue vehicle where Tom Deering was already situated. "Sheriff, Eric. None of this adds up. There are no signs of a struggle. No footprints. And look at the jagged nature of the hole in the ambulance. It wasn't cut apart; it seems ripped, just like the bodies of the EMTs. Their wounds are similar to claw marks, large, deep, vicious claw marks."

"We were just commenting on that very same thing, deputy."

The site of the empty gurney caused Eric to shudder. All that was left on it were clothes and a necklace, his mother's clothes and the necklace holding the heart-shaped pendant, matching his key, that she had worn nearly every day of her life. He picked up the jewelry, lamenting how out of place it was, being in his hand, instead of around his mother's neck, so terribly out of place, like everything else in his life right now.

"Look at this." Eric pointed to a black mark that looked like a powder burn on the sheets of the gurney. "What the hell is that?"

"Not sure, better let CSI try and figure it out."

Deputy Jessica Benitez appeared and approached the trio. "Sheriff, in our preliminary searches, we found no evidence that another vehicle came down this road. Nothing in the underbrush is trampled. It's like no one else was here." She handed a digital camera to Pontillo. "These are of the bridge and the trees that Tom mentioned. Near as we can tell, all the damage was caused by something slashing through the … uh, the uh, items."

Pontillo, with his classic sheriff's hat in-hand, tipped the bill in the deputy's direction. "This is Deputy Jessica Benitez, she replaced you on the force."

51

Eric stepped out of the rescue vehicle, slowly extended his arm and opened his hand. "Here's another item for you to catalogue."

As Benitez reached out to take it, there was a moment in time where they both were holding onto the necklace—

—and they couldn't break contact with each other; their eyes were locked, and something happened in that instant that neither could explain … a confluence of time and space

weaving and coalescing, tangling

then stret*ttttccchhh*hing   untanglinggggg.

Immutable laws of physics, biology, mind-boggling Stephen Hawking shit, the essence of life itself—all fell by the wayside.

Time

Stopped

Pontillo and Deering were in the periphery

But were no longer animate.

thecrashscenewastherebutwasnolongertangible

The pair existed in a plane just a sliver off of

REALITY.

ERIC'S SHIRT, SOCKS, pants, everything, became soaked from the cold sweat that broke out—everywhere. Chills moved down his spine as if administered by a staple gun, every joint in his body stiffened, then ached, a pulsation of painANDpleasure. It was the worst of flu symptoms all at once, but with the hint—*possibly?*—of something better to come.

—

Then a wash of adrenaline flooded throughout his body. He was concurrently agonized, energized, vulnerable and invincible—ALIVE.

And it felt … it felt right … no, *nonono*, it felt natural, the most natural thing that could ever be, and in that moment, Eric knew he could overcome anything.

JESSICA SAW THE auras—*she had never before in her life used that word*—of Tom, Andy, and Eric, the three of them standing in front of her, and traces of Kirlian residue ... *kir-lee-un what?*—radiating from the empty gurney.

There was the … the signature of two others, but not people, not animals, not birds, nothing mechanical—but something else, something beyond her mind, something even beyond whatever had been piping these new words into her.

Everything was washed in a bright white light. Images flashed through her field of vision:

an island

a struggle between two figures

three young adults with babies

ruins in a jungle

millions enslaved

a shadowy avatar beckoning her to come closer.

Something didn't want to just scorch a gurney. Shit no. Something had plans to scorch the world.

Squeezing her eyes shut, she stopped the visions and was able to pull away from Eric.

WHEN THE PAIR broke contact, Eric stood frozen, eyes unblinking, vacant, then suddenly aware, and his body started shaking, shuddering, reeling from the shock of coming back to his senses.

Tom Deering—"Are you okay, buddy?"—moved to catch Eric as Jessica found herself dropping to her knees.

Eric shook his head. "I must be coming down with something."

Jessica came to her feet, brushing off her pants, looking stymied. "How long were we out of it?"

"Out of what? Eric just handed you the necklace to enter into evidence. You dropped it and Eric tripped."

"But, I … um, saw images. Well, it's hard to explain."

Pontillo moved to her side. "What exactly?"

"I can't quite remember anymore, they're gone, just a foggy recollection of a dream, it's faded."

"I guess you just stood up too fast." Eric nudged Pontillo in the shoulder as he walked by. "So, my idea about super intelligent bears isn't sounding so bad right now, is it?"

ANNOYED BY THE sarcastic remark, Jessica Benitez scrunched her nose and mumbled something under her breath. She had a tendency to be too expressive and had a low tolerance for bullshit in the field. It was something her father had cautioned her against as she was growing up. It was also a topic she and the sheriff had broached on several occasions during her time as one of his deputies.

"Jess, don't mind Detective Archer." Pontillo nodded towards Eric. "He's had the longest day of all of us. And his attempts at humor tend to make him feel better."

The penitent deputy replied, "I'm so sorry, Detective Archer, I didn't mean any disrespect. I've heard a lot about you in my time here. I'm very sorry for your loss."

"No harm, no foul, deputy. As for hearing a lot about me, I hope you have taken the source of your information into consideration. I only say that because you can't believe half of what comes out of Deering's mouth, and *nothing* that Ricky Mack spews." Eric gave a nervous-looking grin. "Andy is right, though, I do tend to make lame jokes at the most inappropriate times. Now let's have a look at those pictures."

As Jessica handed the camera over, the look on Eric's face was too much to ignore. His stare was brief, but intense, soulful even.

"What was that earlier?" Deputy Benitez slightly cocked her head.

"What was what? Did I do something?"

"I guess it's nothing." *But there was something.* Not only the look on the detective's face, but when their hands touched. Why was he ignoring what happened? Or maybe nothing happened to him? How could that be? Maybe she had imagined it. *Hell, no I didn't imagine it. C'MON. Keep your cool and be professional, pro-fessional.*

Eric turned to Pontillo. "SITREP, we have my father ritualistically cut, burned, and murdered, it looks like my mother spontaneously combusted, Wolfman and Lurch deceased, their vehicle ripped apart, a destroyed bridge, and two downed pine trees. All with cuts of similar depth and matching slash marks."

Pontillo nodded. "And very little in the way of leads."

Eric shook his head. "To think I left this area for more excitement in the big city."

Jessica guessed that sarcasm must be a staple response to difficult situations for Eric, and it was in very full and very lame effect.

Tom Deering tugged Jessica's arm to move out of earshot of the sheriff and detective. "So, what do you think of Eric. He's handling this pretty well, considering. I'd be sitting in a corner sucking my thumb like a baby if it was me."

"He's unprofessional. There's nothing special about him. I don't have any feelings for him at all."

"What the hell are you talking about? I didn't ask you if you wanted to date him."

"Let's just drop it, Tom. We've got a job to do here."

ERIC'S FINAL WORDS were trailing out of his mouth as Hurley County CSI coordinator Ricky Mack joined the group. "This is bonkers, man. Crazy. Far out. Whatever you want to call it. I can barely keep up with all of this shit. Oh, and hey, Arch, sorry about your folks, man. Tough break there."

"Good thing your patients are already dead, Ricky, your bedside manner would kill them."

Ricky Mack furrowed his brow and sneered. "Like I said before, Andy, not your run of the mill scene. Without a formal autopsy, I can't be 100-percent sure, but the wounds on Mr. Archer, Derek Matthews, and Nick Stevens are all consistent with those of surgical instruments, very *large* surgical instruments."

"How large are you talking?"

"Mighty Joe Young large. In Mr. Archer's case, the cuts were actually more precise than those of any scalpel. They are more in line with the incisions made using obsidian blades. They are rare, but have a cutting edge many times sharper than high-quality steel. Even the sharpest metal knife has a jagged, irregular blade, but when viewed under a microscope an obsidian blade by comparison, is still smooth and even. That's my working theory, anyway."

"I'm assuming you think that is what we will find with these two newest victims?"

Ricky Mack popped the Dum-Dum grape sucker he always seemed to have, out of his mouth and pointed it in the sheriff's direction. "Bingo, boss man."

Eric rolled his eyes; he had forgotten how much Ricky liked to show off his knowledge of *everything*.

"I saw that. Very un-cool, Arch, but you know it would be irresponsible of me to not share my gifts with the world." A toothy grin filled Ricky Mack's face as he walked off.

Jessica pulled out the pendant, looked at Eric, and mouthed *What the hell?*

Later, Eric mouthed back.

Pontillo placed a hand on Eric's shoulder. "Why don't we let Ricky and his boys finish up here and find someplace for you to get some sleep? We can get a fresh crack at this in the morning. It will be a while yet before everyone is done at the farm. Why don't you come to our place? Your aunt would love to see you and some good ol' home cooking is good for the soul."

"I do want to see her and I will, but I'm going to hang around here a bit longer. Besides, I miss Aunt Julia's cooking. Your offer is more of a case of misery loving company. I'll get one of the deputies to give me a lift back to my car at the hospital."

"I'll be here a while longer, sheriff. I can make sure Detective Archer makes it wherever he needs to go."

Pontillo removed his hat and genuflected in the deputy's direction. "Well then, I'll leave you in the capable hands of Deputy Benitez, but the offer stands. If I don't see you at the house, make sure you stop by the station after you get some rest."

"Thanks, I'll see you later." Eric waved as Pontillo backed the patrol car down the driveway.

Pontillo's car pulled onto Route 62 just as another pulled in. The driver got out clutching a folder and ran over to Ricky Mack. Jessica nudged Eric in the arm as she saw Ricky's eyes light up as he rifled through whatever the folder contained. Jessica and Eric strode in his direction. He motioned for him to hurry over. "You are going to want to see this, Arch!"

Ricky handed the folder over to Eric. "These are the results of some tests we ran based on samples we found in your parents' barn and by the bridge and the downed trees. Remember how I said the wounds were similar to obsidian blades?"

Eric nodded.

Ricky continued, "Well, we actually found fragments of obsidian at each of the sites. Near as we can tell, we have a few more tests to run, but it looks like it all came from the same source. Cool, huh?"

"Not all that surprising, we kind of thought the incidents might be related. It would mean to me that the same person or people are responsible for all of the events of the last day. Any DNA pulled from the scenes?"

"Not surprising? Jeez ... you're hard to impress. Guess the big city has jaded you." Looking frustrated, Ricky threw his hands in the air. "We need a bit more time to see if we can extract any DNA or tell the origin and age it."

"So now we have the commonality of the same person or people at each scene," added Jessica. "Looking at the events from that perspective, whoever this was saw the ambulance leave your parents farm and somehow took the bridge and the trees out forcing the ambulance down into this desolate area."

"It had to be multiple people. There is no way a single person could make all of that happen in the amount of time needed to reroute the ambulance."

Jessica followed up Eric's thought. "I agree, but where are these people and how have they left no trace of themselves?"

"Let's wait and see if my guys pull any DNA from the scenes and go from there. I'll be in touch." Ricky Mack headed back toward the crime scene.

Eric rubbed his eyes with the heels of his palms. "Well, Deputy Benitez, I think I will take you up on that offer of a ride back to the hospital."

"GIVE ME A few minutes to wrap up some notes with Deputy Deering and we can be on our way." In reality, Jessica needed a minute to compose herself. She had such conflicting thoughts about Eric. What the hell was that look of his about? It was like he had seen a ghost. And the *event* she experienced. She wasn't an overly sensitive person. It perplexed her usually calculated thought process. She tried to put herself in his shoes. She had never known her mother, but she knew just how unfathomable the thought was of her father no longer being in her life. Eric had that multiplied times two.

The urgency to call her dad overcame all other thoughts. It had been a few weeks since they last talked. She made a mental note to do so first thing in the morning.

JESSICA WALKED OFF, leaving Eric to review the scene.

His head hurt from trying to wrap his brain around all that had happened. There were so many questions. He knew if he was going to be any good to anyone he had to distance himself from the fact it was his parents he was dealing with. He needed to approach it as a detective, not a grieving son. He wondered if he could do that and how long it would take him.

"Whenever you're ready, detective."

Eric felt a light tap on his shoulder and was jostled from the trance he was in. "We can leave right now, but should we talk about the elephant?"

"Elephant, detective?"

Eric gave a nervous grin. "No playing around, you know what I mean."

"Why don't you tell me, sir."

"You know … with the, uh, with my mother's necklace. About what happened."

Jessica Benitez opened up Eric's door, and then walked around to the driver's side. "Maybe we should just let things percolate for a bit, and give it some time to process."

The pair got into the patrol car and started down the road. Eric looked out the window only to see Ricky Mack's famous 1000-watt smile as they passed by. Eric gave a tired wave and Ricky just kept smiling. As annoying as Ricky Mack could be, Eric appreciated his efforts to put his mind at ease. He thought he heard Jessica mumble under her breath again. She was going to have to lighten up or she wouldn't last very long in the field.

After a few minutes of silence, Jessica struck up a conversation. "What do you think the next step should be? There has to be a witness somewhere. We also have to find some trace of where these people entered and exited the crime scenes or we will already have hit a wall in the investigation. Someone had to have seen *something*. Don't you agree, Detective Archer?"

Eric made a few barely audible sounds: "Hmm … uh—"

"Sorry, detective, didn't quite catch that." Jessica glanced over and saw that Eric had fallen asleep. "Okay, I guess I'll have to talk this through with you later." Back concentrating on the road, Jessica continued the drive to the hospital.

Deputy Benitez dropped Eric off at his car, still parked in the NO PARKING zone at the hospital.

"I better move this lest I get a ticket from a good ol' Chadwick Bay black-and-white. Thanks again for the lift."

"I'm sorry again for your loss, do try and get some sleep, detective. I'm sure I will see you in the morning."

"She needs to lighten up." Eric muttered to himself as he climbed into his car. Sitting behind the wheel he wondered where he should go. He didn't want to see the Pontillos; they would just remind him of his parents. He decided that what he needed was a drink. He checked his watch. There would still be time to have a few before last call. He eased onto Central Avenue and made his way north toward the lakefront.

A right turn onto Lake Shore Drive brought him to his destination. *Stelmach's Watering Hole*, called *Sheik's*, by everyone in honor of the owner's nickname, one of the best and oldest bars in the area. He had heard the story more than once growing up that it was a distribution hub for liquor during Prohibition, as well as a speakeasy, although at that time it fronted as a malt shop and candy store. It was a throwback to old-time neighborhood bars, and the best place to go if you wanted to drink and not be bothered, or drink and find a room full of friends.

Eric pulled into one of the angled parking spaces at

the side of the building, hoping tonight it was the former. As he stepped through the doorway, the dingy lighting from wall sconces converted from gas to electric a generation prior, worked to partially conceal him and all of the other patrons. For Eric, the smell of decades-old beer soaked into the hardwood floors and the crunching of peanut shells underfoot was like heaven, and already these familiar comforts were starting to soothe his overwrought soul. No one lifted his head or noticed him. Being in a place like this so late in the evening usually meant you had some demons to chase away, and everyone in the bar seemed to be doing their best to be invisible.

Good, just what I wanted.

At the bar, he ordered two of the establishment's specialty: a Na Zdrowie lager, complete with its time-honored Polish Falcon label. The proprietor had started brewing and bottling his own beer on-site only a few years after he'd taken over, and decades before the microbrew craze had taken off. People would come from all across the state just to savor the libation unique to this establishment. The owner/brew master didn't even sell it to go, though he probably could have made a fortune. Whenever anyone asked about it, he would respond, 'Dem guys come here looking to take my beer back dere wit dem. No way, I says. Da beer is made in dis here city, and it should be enjoyed in dis here city.'

Expansive with the heavenly relief of Sheik's beer, Eric left the change from his 10-spot on the bar. Sheik deserved the tip. You couldn't get anything this good in Pittsburgh, and the popular craft beers went for eight dollars a pop. But none of them could hold a torch to

Na Zdrowie.

He grabbed the *comfort in a bottle* and made his way to one of the high-backed dark cherry booths that lined the outside walls of the place. He chose one in the corner. No surprises that way. He could see the whole bar from there, the seat chosen from a habit that was either a benefit or a curse from his police training. He slammed the first beer on his way to the table, then slumped into the booth and started to compartmentalize all the shit going on in his head.

Halfway through his third bottle, which Sheik had hand-delivered to his table, he started to cry. The sleep depriving grief coursing through his body was starting to wane. It was replaced by loss, and agonizing, gut-knotting pain. He feared it was settling in for a very long stay. It was the thought of his parents: their *torture,* their *final thoughts,* their *final actions,* their *final sounds,* which ate away at his insides.

Would things have been different had he stayed closer to home?

It was a futile line of thought. If not in light of common sense, then from his training.

You cannot turn back time.

Now his feelings were turning from pain to anger. Realizing how hard he was squeezing the bottle in his hand, he stopped, and not because he was afraid it would shatter—it was too thick for that—but because it wouldn't, which meant he wouldn't have the satisfaction. He wanted to hurt, physically, and he wanted to hurt something physical.

At the edge of his vision someone approached. *God-damn-it.* The last thing he wanted was company. *Then again, maybe I d—*

"So look who it is, the mama's boy, Mr. Home School." Matt O'Donnell stood next to his brother Phil, both now a little too close to Eric's table.

"What's the matter, little Eric?" Phil piped up in a mocking tone. "Couldn't make it in the BIG city? We all knew a flake like you would flame out and come running back here. Did you come back to cry on mommy and daddy's shoulders?"

Eric reached back and unclipped his holster, stretched his arm over the table and placed it down, patting it as he did.

Phil and Matt turned to face each other and let out a *"Whooo!"* in the grand fashion of wrestling legend Ric Flair, and then proceeded to further cement their bond of brotherhood with a high five, fist bump, and chest bump. Same routine they had in high school. A couple of years older than Eric, they had terrorized him in his youth, catching him on the weekends, getting to him from behind, when he was alone, and always two-against-one.

Things don't tend to change too much in a small town.

"Nice to see you two still joined at the hip." Eric took a swig from his beer.

"This guy," Matt turned to his brother, jutting a thumb in Eric's direction, "always the wiseacre."

The brothers glanced at each other and then looked at Eric. He'd seen the look of disdain on people's faces before. His shot across the bow of the S.S. O'Donnell had gotten a rise, and now he was begging them to make a move, had decided on it as soon as he saw them. *I need to hit something.*

Phil O'Donnell was the first one to comply with

Eric's silent request, stepping in swinging his beer bottle at Eric's head.

With more dexterity than he should have had in this early morning hour, Eric took to his feet as he ducked and parried the swing, his right hand moving under the bottle, turning, and catching the back of the man's hand, while his left cupped the back of his head and bounced it off the thick wooden tabletop like a rubber ball—opening up the man's nose like a bloody flower, and sending him staggering back before falling unconscious.

Immediately, Matt attacked, connecting with a hook to the jaw, and driving him back into the booth, jamming him against the wall, and pummeling him with ham-fisted blows and not quite righteous brotherly rage.

Eric's body felt numb as he did his best to curl up, and shield himself with upraised arms and knees, but the swings kept coming, some connecting to his head, the rest landing on bone.

Then it happened.

"MUTHERFU—"

Peeking between forearms, Eric saw Matt shaking his busted hand—or busted something—and kicked out, right at the man's holy-of-holies.

And connected.

Matt crumpled, gasping for air. As Eric climbed from the booth, miraculously unharmed, a bloodied Phil attacked from his left. He swung at Eric, who easily blocked the punch with his forearm. At the same time, Eric landed a shot to Phil's solar plexus and then a quick uppercut to the jaw.

Bone crunched.

Phil took a few steps back and was standing next to his brother, who was just picking himself up off the floor. Eric ran at both of his dazed opponents with his arms ready to clothesline. He slammed the both of them into the wall between the restrooms. Phil slumped to the floor unconscious, while Matt required one more, well-placed fist.

Rubbing his jaw, Eric looked down. "Thanks, guys, for repaving memory lane."

Once the dust had settled, the owner crept over, sleeves rolled up on his shirt, white apron on and push broom in hand. Leonard 'Sheik' Stelmach was in his early 80s, but could still handle himself. He'd ran the bar since he was 16, when his father hit the dirt. A man as much a Chadwick Bay fixture as the waterfront itself. A living history of the city in his head, he knew all the names and the secrets that went along with them. Everyone confided in Sheik because over time he proved that he could keep those same secrets.

"I knows what happened wit yours folks, kiddo, dey was good people. I am very sorry for your loss. I can cover for yous and take care of dese here guys, but you better make yourself scarce, nonetheless."

"Thanks, Mr. Stelmach."

CHAPTER EIGHT

POUNDING ON HIS window roused Eric into consciousness. He narrowly opened one and saw one of Chadwick Bay's finest leaning down looking into the driver's side window of his car. Eric smiled and the officer motioned for him to roll down his window. Eric leaned over, grabbed the handle and cranked the window down.

"Good morning, officer, what can I do for you?" Eric looked around to see just where he was. It came back to him. After leaving the bar he had stopped at the local supermarket only to find it was no longer a 24-HOUR store. He must have passed out trying to decide where to spend the night.

"Detective Archer, I am well aware of everything you have gone through in the last day so I'm not going to give you a ticket for parking in a FIRE ZONE, or for loitering. But you do need to move the car. The store manager is beginning to complain."

"Thanks for the courtesy. I was just about to leave." The car's engine roared as Eric turned the key, hit the gas at the same time. He slid the shifter into gear, wink to the officer and gunned the car out onto Central Avenue. *I wonder what Mom and Dad are doing?*

His green eyes stared back at him from his rearview mirror. His mind snapped back to reality. Images of his dad's brutalized body cycled through his mind, snapshot after snapshot, *click click click.*

Realization shot a surge of adrenaline through him. He was suddenly wide awake and filled with purpose. He steered the car out of town towards Route 83 and pressed the pedal. The car responded in kind. He sped off to the sheriff's office to see if there were any new leads as to who murdered his parents.

CHAPTER
NINE

ERIC PULLED INTO the parking lot of the Hurley County Sheriff's Office a little after 10:00 in the morning. The August heat and humidity was already in mid-day form, so much so that on the drive over Eric could barely see the road from the heat coming off of it. It was going to be one of those Western New York scorchers where the slightest movement resulted a bucket of sweat. He saw Jessica Benitez in street clothes placing her helmet on the handle of her crotch rocket. He hurried to catch up to her as she made her way toward the granite steps at the front of the building.

"Hey, Deputy Benitez, wait up!" he called out to her, hand raised in the air as if he was hailing a cab.

"Well, good morning, detective." She looked him over. "So … is this the uniform of the Pittsburgh Police Department, or are you like Einstein and just have a closet full of the same clothes?"

Eric must have been a sight. He looked himself over, pulled at his wrinkled shirt and thought he did have the look of someone who had just spent days in the same clothes. "Ha … no I'm not that organized or intelligent. As sweet as my car is, it isn't the best place to sleep, and I haven't found a shower yet."

"Well, I'm sure the sheriff can help you with that."

All in due time. So, what brings you to the office on what I assume is your day off?"

They reached the front door, and Eric opened it, allowing Jessica to enter the building first. She nodded in thanks and walked in.

"It's this case, your parents, the EMTs, the damages, I can't get it out of my head. I was coming in to see if any leads had broken in the last few hours."

"I appreciate the dedication … and, um … thanks for the lift last night. Sorry I wasn't better company. The stress finally just took its toll."

"It's completely understandable. I'm used to talking to myself, anyway."

Jessica pulled her hair into a pony and tied it off as they walked. For the second time in less than 24 hours Eric had to pause at the sight of Jessica, thoughts of his mother flashed in his mind. Neither was paying attention as they turned the corner, and nearly ran over Ricky Mack, carrying manila folders and evidence bags.

"What's with you trying to scare the crap out of me, some new pastime you've taken up?"

Eric and Jessica looked at each other, smiling.

"Very funny, I assume you're heading to the Boss Man's office. I'll walk with you. We found out a little more since last night."

The three started down the hall and took a few more turns before arriving at Andy Pontillo's office. The walk was one that Eric had taken countless times in the past, it never felt as long as it did today.

The office was adorned with reminders of a long

and successful career in law enforcement. Plaques, certificates, framed photos hung on the wall. His desk was tidy, clean, and clear of clutter. There were two pictures on the desk, one of Andy's wife, Julia, and the other was a picture of Eric, Edward Archer, and Pontillo the day that Eric bagged his first deer. In many ways, Eric was like the son Andy never had. Married to the job is what Andy would always tell people. The reality of the situation is that he and Julia had worked with fertility doctors, but none of their efforts resulted in a pregnancy.

Andy walked into the office. "I remember that like it was yesterday," he said motioning to the picture Eric was holding. "By the way, things get squared away back in Pittsburgh?"

"I do, too, we had a lot of good times." Eric put the picture back in its place. "And, yes, I did. I'm now officially on leave."

"Kinda like the reminiscing you did with the O'Donnell boys last night, huh? Don't worry, they're all taken care of. No charges are being filed, they want it *hush-hush* that Mr. Homeschool cleaned up the floor with 'em. Man, are they beat to hell, though. You did three numbers on them. Phil's nourishment's gonna be delivered via a straw for the foreseeable future."

"It went south fast, they were in a heap quick. Details are fuzzy."

Ricky Mack cleared his throat as a reminder that he was standing there. Eric, Andy, and Jessica turned their attention to him.

The CSI chief smiled and adjusted his glasses. "A few things since we last spoke. We found no fingerprints or DNA at either of the crime scenes, save for those of the victims. There is no trace of how this person or people got *into or out of* both locations."

"So, what you're telling us, Ricky, is that we don't have jack. Ghosts, ghouls, goblins, or maybe," Eric's sarcasm in full effect, "I know … flying monkeys. Or do we need to go to a psychic at Lily Dale to clue us in?"

"Calm down, Arch, don't kill the messenger, man," Ricky continued. "We did find some interesting similarities at all of the locations, though. What we thought were pieces of obsidian, are in fact, just *that*. Small flakes were found embedded in the Archers' barn, the pine trees, the metal from the bridge, and the top of the ambulance. We are close to finding the place of origin. It's found in over a dozen places throughout the world. I won't bore you with the scientific mumbo jumbo, but this particular obsidian was odd in that it had an organic component to it. So, we're attempting to match it with known samples."

Eric interjected, "Organic? As in alive? Is there any scientific reasoning for that? Any animal that has been known to have obsidian or a substance like it for claws or teeth?"

For the first time in all the years Eric had known Ricky Mack he was speechless.

Finally, Ricky offered a terse, "I don't have an answer for that."

ANDY PONTILLO SOAKED in the information presented to the group. He knew exactly what the organic obsidian was and what it meant. He could answer the question for the Ricky in a heartbeat, but it would complicate things. Complicated was not what Pontillo had in mind; besides that, he didn't feel he owed any of the idiots he dealt with on a daily basis any kind of explanation. No one but Eric, that is; he needed to get Eric alone and explain to him what was going on. "Thanks for the update, Ricky, please keep me informed of any developments. Jessica, go enjoy your day off. We'll keep you in the loop. Eric and I need to attend to some family matters."

"Thank you, sir." Jessica closed the door.

"We have some things to talk about, Eric." Pontillo sat down, pulled his chair up to the desk and laid his elbows on the table, making a tent with his hands. Eric had taken a seat in one of the chairs on the other side. He leaned in toward the desk, head down, elbows resting on his knees.

"I know what killed your parents. I mean, I have knowledge of what your mom and dad confided in me many years ago. Things they showed and told me didn't seem possible. But I can see now all of their planning and preparation wasn't in vain."

Eric's head shot up, eyes wide open. "What the hell are you talking about, Andy? This isn't your first cryptic message. Come on, out with it. What aren't you telling me? And what do you mean *what* killed my parents, don't you mean who? Planning? Preparing? They were farmers, for Christ's sake! You aren't making any sense!"

Andy sat for a moment looking at Eric. Suddenly he got up went over to a picture of his brother John and him holding up a flag at the top of Mt. Marcy and swung it out of the way, revealing a wall safe. He spun the dial in the requisite directions and opened the door. Inside was a leather-bound journal and a mahogany case. He removed the journal, closed the door, and turned to Eric.

"This will begin to answer your questions. Its better you read it from the hand of your father than to have me explain it. When you get done, come back and find me and then we'll talk."

Pontillo saw the stunned look on Eric's face as he took the journal, turned it over in his hands and absently flipped through the pages.

"I don't get it. What is this? Where did it come from?"

Andy motioned toward the door. "Eric, I'm going to be cryptic with you one more time. Go to your parents' house. Sit down, read that book, and learn about your legacy."

"I've heard that word too much over the last 30-years. What are you boys prattling on about?" Julia Pontillo entered the office, keeping her daily ritual of providing the love of her life with his homemade lunch. "Eric, my dear sweet boy." Julia wrapped her arms around her nephew, stepped back, and with both hands, pinched his cheeks. "I'm devastated about your mom and dad, we all are. You're coming with me, right now for a proper meal."

"I … um, okay, Aunt Julia. I'd love it, haven't had a decent meal in some time. And I still hate it when you do that."

She pinched him again. "Good choice, son, it's never wise to say no to your aunt. But remember, get to that book before too long."

—

Eric held the door open for Julia. "Thanks, again. I'll be in touch when I'm done with it."

The latch clicked and Andy Pontillo plopped into the high-back leather chair. "Perfect—another wheel set in motion."

PART II
ENCOUNTER WITH DESTINY

CHAPTER TEN

ERIC ARCHER WAS on auto-pilot, the turns and bends of the roads taken by reflex. He drove, soaked in the late summer weather, his thoughts consumed by his parents and all that had transpired. Then, an intruder, Jessica Benitez, the deputy, flashed into his head. Who was she? Why did she get to share his private moment with his family? Walking past Eric earlier, she had given him a gentle squeeze as if to say *I'm with you.* Her touch elicited a warm sensation that washed over Eric's body. That sensation seared into his mind. Twice—in two meetings. It calmed him. Why?

As he approached the farm where he grew up, he saw his mom out in the garden by the house, his dad on his John Deere tractor out in the field, and their black lab Reggie II, who undoubtedly was a reincarnation of his first-ever pet the regal Reggie I, exuberantly bounding up and down the driveway announcing his arrival. He pulled into the dirt driveway. The mirage disappeared. The farm was desolate. Cold. Lifeless. A skeleton where there had once been the full body of a family. He brought the car to a stop along the side of the house. His usual spot. He shifted the car into park and turned off the ignition, He slumped forward, rested his forehead on the back of his hand that was choking the steering wheel. He began to cry. His shoulders heaved as the sobbing became uncontrollable. But he couldn't hold back any longer. Between the sobs, came low anguished screams of *Why?* coupled with his fist pounding on the steering wheel. He was alone. Truly alone. He didn't have the strength to keep up appearances, to put on a brave front.

The pain. It hurt so bad.

Wait, what was that feeling?

Doubt.

He hadn't doubted anything in years. Yet there it was. Front and center, getting smashed into him.

Are you really that weak? a foreign voice whispered in his ear. Eric raised his head, looked around and saw no one. *Are you finished now? Done feeling sorry for yourself? You have a job to do. Go do it.*

The feeling of being watched wouldn't go away. Someone—something had spoken to him.

He is near. The voice, louder now. *He grows more powerful. If you don't learn, you'll lose everything. Go learn. Defeat him.*

Eric clenched his teeth. "Who are you? Get out of my head."

It's who YOU are that is important. This is why you were chosen. Your destiny. To tell more is forbidden.

"Forbidden?" Eric pleaded. "What do you mean? Chosen?" He waited for a response. There was none. "That's just great. Now you're going crazy, Eric. Good job." A loud thud startled him. His eyes widened and his spine got stapled again.

INTERLUDE II

THE LEATHER BELT struck John's behind with the force of a hurricane. Between blows his mother lectured him. "How many times have I told you? The weak are weak because they're supposed to be. They are not to be coddled. Weak people fit into two categories." She paused. To John, it was these short recesses that were the worst part of *mother's conditioning*.

She turned her attention to John's brother, Andy sitting in the corner of the room, half-shielding his eyes from the beating his mother was putting on his brother. "Andy, don't you dare sit there and shy away from this. You watch what happens when one of you screws up, or you will get the same conditioning today."

Andy immediately sat up straight and put his full attention on his brother. The whole situation had happened because some older boys in the neighborhood were picking on a little girl who wore braces on her legs, and Andy had stepped in to help. Mother always conditioned the child who had done nothing, making the other watch. It would teach them to look out for each other and keep one another in line. Andy was again amazed at his brother. John never cried. Mother's shrill voice broke his thoughts, "Two categories. The weak either fall in line or get removed." Again came the leather, and continued, with a lash between each of the words of her last sentence. "We *ckhwak* do *ckhwak* not *ckwhak* HELP *ckwak* the *ckwak* weak."

She held out the belt and Andy ran to take it from her. She straightened herself up, smoothed out her dress, and brushed her hair away from her eyes. Within the blink of an approving eye, Mommy Dearest was gone, replaced again by June Cleaver. "Now both of you go get cleaned up for dinner. Tonight, I'm making your favorite."

The boys knew the drill.

They stood before her, hands at their sides. She poked each one playfully in the stomach and continued in a sugary sweet voice, "And if you boys finish all your dinner and are good helpers after, Mommy will take you for some ice cream. You would like that, wouldn't you?"

They looked at each other and then back at their mother with wide smiles and nodded.

CHAPTER ELEVEN

THE ANCIENT GOD had other adversaries to vanquish and the divine weapons were near. He had no doubt he would find the last of these enemies and the implements that could be used to destroy him.

He was growing stronger with each life extinguished, absorbing their *soul* or *ba* or *kundalini.* Humans had so many names for their life essence. The woman with ancient blood would have revealed much more to him, had his brother not interfered. A brother who thought he was better.

But still, with each passing moment he knew more. Remembered more.

He would be the one to reign over this realm of existence. Father, The Absolute, had held this prize at arm's length for long enough. He was done being lackey for his brothers, the *higher gods*.

His time was near.

He could feel it.

The ancient weapons were close. The hum of their enchantment ran through his head. He tore through the human dwelling. Items inside the barn flew like fallen leaves in a windstorm. Crates and drums shattered. Animal stalls ripped apart—all manner of destruction.

He was going about his mission at a furious pace, when suddenly he fell to one knee, sticking his clawed arm out to steady himself. He let out a small, anguished cry. He stood back up and straightened his leg, which resembled the hindquarter of a horse, the limb covered in oily slick black scales, just like the rest of his body.

He shuddered again.

A brief wave of weakness came over him. The last time he'd experienced such a feeling was in the presence of those who had defeated him so long ago. He stopped and listened, his elongated snout lifting into the air.

He caught the same human scent.

Could smell its ancient blood.

He winced as his clawed appendages wrapped around his midsection.

Pain.

He loved the pain. It made him alive. Struck by another wave of weakness, he buckled to the ground.

Who was this adversary?

He crawled like an animal to the back of the barn. There in the shadows he waited for what was outside.

CHAPTER TWELVE

ERIC STOPPED AND listened. He didn't hear anything else. *Maybe I imagined that, too. Why the hell did I let that happen? Damn, I never lose control like that. You were taught better than that, trained better than that. It's gotta be this fucking heat driving me crazy. No, bullshit, the fact that someone murdered your parents is driving you crazy.*

"And now I'm talking to myself, again. Good job, Mr. Detective." Eric chuckled nervously.

He reached back and fumbled around the rear of his car for something to wipe his face. He grabbed a balled-up T-shirt and wiped his face, hoping it would take his emotions with it. He could do without them right now. He sighed into the T-shirt pressed to his face. As his exhale faded away, a new sound took its place, a violent, animalistic noise exploding from the barn just a few feet away. There wasn't supposed to be any-*one* or any-*thing* here. Eric, eyes fixed on the barn, felt the seat beside him for the cold comfort of Austrian tech. He held the Glock Model 37 semi-auto in one hand and quietly opened the door with his other. He slid out and crouched behind the opened door. He focused on the noise still emanating from the barn. He stayed in a crouched position as he crept to the front of the car. The cop in his head was back in control. He held the Glock in a shooting position, ready to double-tap center mass whatever threatened to burst from the structure. Silent as the middle of the night, he moved forward. He got about 10-yards away and the crashing stopped. There was a shuffling sound, like someone had fallen and then stumbled as they got back up. Someone or some*thing* was in the barn.

A strange sensation originated in his gut.

It burned.

Trust your gut, son.

The twinge—similar to the feeling he got around Jessica—was intense enough to stop him in his tracks.

But different, something off—not soothing—instead, foreboding.

Evil.

Why evil*? Why is that the word popping into my head?*

He hunkered down, made himself a smaller target, trained his weapon on the door of the barn and waited….

CHAPTER THIRTEEN

JESSICA BENITEZ DECIDED to take the sheriff's advice and make good use of her day off. She needed to blow-out her head-space. Since meeting Eric Archer, she couldn't string together two coherent thoughts. Distance would give her a fresh perspective.

It always did.

She hopped on her Suzuki Boulevard S40 and made her way along some winding backroads. The feel of the bike was instantly exhilarating. There was nothing like the freedom of a motorcycle.

She'd been hooked since her first ride.

"Daddy, are you sure about this? I'm a princess. Princesses are supposed to arrive by horse and buggy."

"But you're no ordinary princess. You are the BEST kind. A warrior-princess. And this steel horse is what you ride. It's faster and more powerful than a team of those boring old regular horses."

"I like that, Daddy. Jessica Benitez: Warrior-princess." She hopped down off the motorcycle. "I'll be right back."

"Where are you running off to? We're going to be late to the costume party."

A few minutes later, Jessica emerged from the house. She had one of her dad's belts looped over one shoulder and under the opposite arm, so it hung diagonally across her body. She ran back to her dad. "If I'm going to be a warrior, I gotta have a weapon. You know, to defend my people from the bad things."

"What do you have there? Is that my belt, and a shoelace?"

Jessica turned around, and looked over her shoulder. "Well, I needed something to hold my sword. I had to improvise. Just like you are always teaching me when we're out camping and stuff."

"That is true. I'm impressed. But couldn't you have just grabbed a magic wand or something?"

"C'mon, Daddy, everybody knows there's no such thing as magic."

"You'd be surprised. But we'll leave that for another day."

Jessica wrapped one arm around her dad and pulled the plastic sword from its sheath with her free hand. She pointed it forward. "Onward, to the party, where I will vanquish my foes."

As the bike roared down the street, and within a *wink* of time was cruising down a backroad, Jessica the cop giggled with delight.

Magic, ha.

The stories of warriors of old fighting ancient evils came flooding back. She hadn't thought about them for some time, but the strangeness of the recent deaths had brought them back—in spades, and especially after having shared a touch with Eric.

Had Dad been trying to tell her something all those years ago? Was he preparing her for something? *Ugh, like I really need something else to think about.*

After reaching Route 20, and then the entrance

---

ramp for I-90, Jessica headed east to I-190. Getting into Canada on a Saturday, and especially at this time of day, could be a bear. She thought it would be best to avoid the Peace Bridge. The Rainbow Bridge wouldn't be as crowded. She was heading home to St. Catharines and her dad. Eric Archer pushed his way into her thoughts. A twinge of guilt came over her knowing what waited for him at his parents' house.

Her thoughts vacillated between Eric's life and her own. He had been on her mind since leaving the station that morning. There was an undeniable surge of *something* that had flowed through her when she'd touched Eric's arm. She didn't know what to make of it. She had no real attachment to the detective. She had never been an emotional person.

It vexed her.

Eric vexed her.

He was stoic and businesslike in the face of such a personal tragedy, yet affable and witty at the same time. Jessica certainly knew *of* him from her time in Hurley County, but didn't know a lot about him. They were the same age and he had already made detective, something she wanted badly. She hoped he was as good a cop as everyone made him out to be. He certainly had the respect of Sheriff Pontillo, respect that she still sought. There was definitely a glass ceiling in Hurley County. Her career had started the same year Eric had left for Pittsburgh. She had gotten a late start after serving in Mexico, spending three years of post-collegiate time in the Peace Corps. When it came time to apply for jobs after graduation, Hurley County was the first and only place on her list. She had never been there before she applied, yet the town carried with it, the sense of destiny. Dad had tried to dissuade her from taking the job. *Don't jump at the first thing offered to you*, was his advice.

He couldn't have been more wrong.

She wanted nothing more than to make investigator. Helping Eric bring the people responsible for the death of his parents and the two EMTs to justice might go a long way to making that happen.

There he was again.

Eric Archer.

Commandeering her thoughts.

One of Eric's exchanges with Ricky Mack entered her brain and she chuckled as she thought of the one certain thing she and Eric had in common; they both had a healthy aversion to the personality of the Hurley County CSI director. She wondered what else they would find in common as they spent more time together.

And again … her brain was like a broken record.

What *was* it with him?

Why did she feel so connected?

The bike roared as Jessica pulled off the Q.E.W. and onto Thorold Road. Backroads would take her the rest of the way home, allowing her time to enjoy the Southern Ontario countryside. She hoped her dad had caught some walleye out of their favorite spot on Twelve Mile Creek. Her stomach growled at the thought of a home-cooked meal. She pulled off Linwood Drive, taking a left onto Centennial. The bike easily slalomed through the winding street toward the end of the cul-de-sac, where she entered the familiar driveway leading to the white ranch style house she'd grown up in.

CHAPTER FOURTEEN

ROBERT BENITEZ HEARD the bike pull into the driveway. *Jessica!* He made his way to the front of the house, both excited to see his only child and intrigued to find out the reason for the unannounced visit. It wasn't like her. Not that he minded. It had been too long since they had spent time together. As he rounded the corner, Jessica was just taking off her helmet. She allowed her shoulder-length hair to fall down. She instinctively pushed a few wisps of the dirty-blonde highlights away from her green eyes. His *jade-eyed princess*, he liked to call her. People told Robert she should have been a model, praise he always acknowledged with some kind words and a *thank you*.

What he always thought, though, was that would be a cold day in Hell.

Not with her upbringing.

Not with the events that were to unfold at some point in her life.

For now, she needed the trappings of a normal woman—even if of a policewoman. There were things that Jessica needed to learn, and it didn't leave much time for dance lessons, pageants, or modeling. Raising

Jessica alone had not been easy, but he'd done the best he could, and from all accounts, he had been successful.

"Hey, Dad!"

They met halfway across the drive and Robert gave her one of his bear hugs, lifting her off the ground. Giving her that squeeze comforted him, because it meant she was *still* with him. He hoped it comforted her just as much.

"To what do I owe the honor?"

"I need a reason to visit the best dad in the world? It's been a while, and I just didn't think a phone call would do."

"I see you're still riding the worrier?" Robert motioned to the motorcycle. "I was hoping when you hit 30, you would have outgrown 'em."

"Ha ha, very funny. You're the one who taught me to ride, remember?"

"My gray hairs won't let me forget."

"Fair enough."

Robert took her hand. "You timed your ride perfectly, I was just about to start grilling."

"Music to my ears. I was hoping we could have a nice dinner and I could bounce some ideas about this case I'm working on."

Robert wasn't in law enforcement, but his daughter liked to tout him as the smartest man she knew. He made a very comfortable living running a small combatives school. He even spent time teaching advanced hand-to-hand combat to LEOs. Several times Jessica questioned why he didn't do more with his talents.

He never answered that question, but always hoped

he had done enough for Jessica.

"Come on, let's go out back, I'll fire up the grill." Robert started to walk toward the backyard. "I have some fresh walleye we can cook."

Jessica grinned.

It was good to be home.

CHAPTER FIFTEEN

AFTER A GREAT meal of grilled walleye, steamed brown rice, and a homegrown romaine salad doused in Robert's own raspberry vinaigrette, father and daughter made their way to the deck at back of the house. Robert took up residence on his favorite lounge chair and Jessica sat on the porch swing opposite.

Jessica, completely relaxed, was home.

"So, what is this case that has you all mixed up?"

"It's the craziest thing." Jessica crossed her legs, picked up her bottle of Labatt Blue Light and took a sip. "I know I haven't been a cop for that long, but I don't think I could've ever imagined encountering anything like this." She went on to explain the details of the case to her father, leaving out the names of the victims.

Robert lean forward and pinched his chin. "I can't help you with the fact there doesn't seem to be a trace of anyone coming to or leaving these scenes. Something that heinous, though, these people had to have wronged someone in a big way." A pause. "That level of violence isn't a random act, not at all."

"That's the thing, Dad. We can't find anyone that has a bad word to say about the two primary vics. I mean NO ONE. They were best friends with the sheriff. I got to know them quite well. Edward and Elena Archer were the salt of the Earth. Nicest damn people you could ever hope to know. I can't imagine how it's eating away at their son."

The rocks glass that contained Robert's nightly after dinner Canadian Club and Seven-Up shook in his hand, then slipped and spilled. Robert's jaw went slack, he felt the blood rushing from his face. The brutality and eccentric nature of the crime now made sense to him. A long-forgotten nightmare had suddenly rushed back into his head. "Edward and Elena … it can't be, can it? They wouldn't have stayed there…," he mumbled. He turned his attention to Jessica. "How old were they?"

"What can't be? What's wrong Dad? You act like you know them. Edward was a few years older than his wife. But I'm pretty sure Mrs. Archer was around 55, same as you."

"What about Eric? Is … is Eric with them?"

Jessica recoiled. "Eric? How do you know Eric Archer and his parents?"

Robert could see the look of disbelief on Jessica's face. He said very slowly and methodically, "Is he with them?"

"He's in Pine Creek now, yes. But he's been working as a detective in Pittsburgh the last few years. He drove in after the sheriff called him with the news not long after we discovered the scene. Dad, what's going on?"

Robert Benitez sat up, planted his feet on the deck, and leaned in toward his daughter. He locked in on her eyes and soulfully admitted, "Jessica, I have known

Edward for decades, and Elena for a lot longer. But we haven't been in contact more than a handful of times over the last 30-years." He paused once again, took Jessica's hands in his. "Even though I prepared you for this, I never really thought the day would come."

"What day? What do you mean? You're scaring me."

"You and I have a lot to talk about. And you have every right to be scared."

CHAPTER SIXTEEN

NO SOUND OR evidence of movement had come from inside the barn for a while.

Screw this.

Eric crept forward. When he reached the barn, he flattened his back against the side and inched toward the door. He peered around the corner. The door was closed. He couldn't see inside the barn. "Damn." He edged to the door. Reaching across, he slowly turned the handle with his left hand, keeping his gun raised in his right. In one swift movement, he swung the door open, dropped into a shoulder roll and came up in a kneeling firing position.

Alternating strips of light and dark covered the barn as sunlight from the second-floor windows filtered down through the spaces between the floorboards above. There was a flash of movement in the back corner of the barn. His eyes, adjusted to the lighting, scanned for the source of the noise. The barn was a mess. Crates were smashed, drawers opened. It was a frantic search for something. A pungent odor permeated.

Sweetness mixed with decay.

Smelled like death.

Someone or something had been in here.

Something, there you go again, Eric. Now you sound like Andy.

He felt a presence. He thought he heard a low hum coming from the direction of the stairs. He navigated through the barn, checking every area. When he reached the back, he froze; shuddering at the very spot his father had been slain and left hanging as a ceremonial sacrifice, tears welled in his eyes. He shook his head. *Get a grip or you're not going to be any good to anyone.* He walked toward the steps in the corner. He relaxed for a minute, shut his eyes, bent at the waist, put his hands on his knees, and let out a deep breath.

Whiskey, Tango, Foxtrot.

Eric was still bent over, struggling to compose himself when he saw them.

HUUUUGE damn hoof prints.

He opened and closed his eyes—again. Shook his head. *Yep, they're still there. Holy hell. What could have made those?*

He looked around. There was only one pair. Maybe it's the light. Maybe the other pair got wiped out. There was nothing bipedal that left behind hoof marks, giant hoofmarks.

A horse, back here, standing on its hind legs? Yeah, that seemed likely. If you believe that, I've got a bridge I can sell ya. Another one of the million sayings from Dad over the years.

The sweet decay smell was even stronger back here. He looked up the stairs. Then he slowly started to ascend.

CHAPTER
SEVENTEEN

THE WEAKNESS WAS still there. This human was strong with the blood of the ancients. Difatos stood in the back of the structure, cloaked by the staircase in front of him. He could see the entrances to the dwelling. He wanted to lay eyes on this adversary that had weakened him.

The door flew open and he saw the figure roll into the room and stop. He saw an object in its hands. Was it one of the tools of the divine?

Another shot of pain.

Difatos realized he was not prepared to confront whoever had entered the barn. Retreat was in order. He needed to recover and consult with his mortal contact to learn about the power this one held.

He chanted a few lines and was gone, transported out of the human's sphere of influence, and now standing in an open field, confused.

He looked around. He could still see the barn. He should have been miles away from the structure. Again, he chanted the incantation. And again, he'd only moved a few hundred feet. A strange feeling stitched up his spine.

Was this the fear that others felt in his presence?

How could a human, even a descendent of the ancients, make him feel this way?

He needed more knowledge.

He needed to kill.

Another soul to devour.

CHAPTER EIGHTEEN

AFTER FINDING THE loft empty, Eric left the barn and checked the immediate perimeter of the property. He turned his attention to the house, searching it from top to bottom, with the same result, nothing. He couldn't shake the sense someone or something had been there.

It was much more than a hunch.

He knew.

As he made his way through the house, it was still in shambles. It would take months to repair the damage, holes in walls, doors ripped from their hinges. He did his best to straighten up the living room. Grabbing the duffel bag he had previously retrieved from his car, Eric headed up to the bathroom. An affinity for the writing of Ian Fleming had led to a showering ritual described in every James Bond novel. He turned the water as hot as he could stand and then cold as he could stand. It really did work. He felt more alive, senses on high alert, ready for anything. He stepped from the shower to the sink. Wiping the steamed mirror, he looked at himself. He worked hard to keep his 210-pounds toned, all six-two of it. He was only 30-years-old, but vigilance now would keep the younger officers wanting to replace him in the department food-chain at a safe distance. He stared for a minute. Looking back from the mirror was his father. People constantly told him he was a dead ringer for his dad in the man's younger days. He had never really noticed it before. *Looking like my dad? I'm all right with that.* He threw on his favorite pair of Levi's, a well-worn Chadwick Bay University T-shirt, and Teva sandals. He clipped his holster to the small of his back, plucked his father's journal from the top of his duffel bag, and took the stairs two at a time down to the living room. His dad's favorite reading chair seemed like the appropriate place to examine what his father had written.

The journal was well worn. Eric flipped through it, and with a sudden pang of sorrow, recognized his father's handwriting. *Learn about your destiny*, Andy had said. "Okay, then, let's just see what's in store."

January 1, 2011

Writing this was my New Year's resolution to your mom. It has been a long time coming and it should have been done before now.

As you are reading this, you are no doubt aware that something terrible has happened to me and your mother. I'm sorry we never had the courage to tell you what you're going to read in here. We should have once you were old enough. Your mom wanted to and I kept talking her out of it. Somehow, thinking that if I didn't say these things out loud, we wouldn't have to worry about them, and you could have a normal childhood. Please don't take any of your anger out on Sheriff Pontillo. We swore him to secrecy, and he has been a great friend to our family over the years. I know you didn't always have the ideal childhood. I know it must have seemed like we were overly strict, but every skill and lesson you learned growing up will serve you well with what lies ahead. Your mother and I did the best we could to raise you. We are so very proud of the man you have become and all of the things you have and are yet to accomplish.

Once you have read all I have written, there will still be questions that only you can answer. I pray we have prepared you well enough and have gathered enough information to help you. Please know that everything you are about to read is absolutely true. Do not hesitate to believe even the wildest things you read.

Everything we told you about our family history, aside from where we each grew up was a fabrication. Least of all, we didn't have a small vineyard in California and decide to move east for a change. I know you will be upset when you read this, but please know we did what we did to protect you. I was born Edward Wolownik, and your mom Elena dos Vidas. Your mom has a twin brother named Roberto. So, yes, you have an uncle that you have never met. Again, it was all for your safety. We have only contacted each other a handful of times over the last 30-years, but we couldn't have you two get together.

I met your mom and uncle at the University of the Southwest in New Mexico. I was an archeology grad student. They were undergrads. We were part of a group of students picked to accompany Dr. William Dirk (an expert on Mayan culture, and if you ever meet him you will be impressed with his knowledge) on a dig out on the Yucatan Peninsula.

An excavation company building a small resort near the Mayan ruins in Campeche discovered what they thought was just another sink hole (which are common there). Jonathan Pontillo (Sheriff Pontillo's brother) was an advance man for the excavating company. In an area that rich in history and artifacts, companies will hire archeologists to make sure they are not destroying anything valuable (at least a company with a conscience will). When they entered it, they found several partial stone tablets covered in glyphs. The head of the company (who was a longtime friend and benefactor of Dr. Dirk) contacted him about what was found.

We set off on what was supposed to be a six month dig. Several locals became members of the team. There were no problems getting to the site. We were still in the process of setting up the dig and your mom wanted to be the first of our team to see the area where the tablets were found (in her younger days, your mom was not as patient as you know her to be). We were already involved in a serious relationship (one that Dr. Dirk would not have approved of, so we had to keep it quiet) so there was no way I was letting her get out of my sight in a foreign country, AND underground no less.

It wasn't long after we lowered ourselves into the sink hole that your mom was in serious pain. It started as a burning sensation in her stomach. The longer we stayed in the chamber the worse it got. I took her back to the tent site to rest and to get checked out by the team medic. Once she was comfortable, I joined everyone else in continuing to set up the dig. Part of the dig site collapsed and revealed a second passageway. It was at that time your uncle (impatient as your mother) careened down the hole. He moved deeper into the cavern and came upon what looked like a large door. He began to scream in agony. We pulled him out. He was explaining what had happened when one of our local contacts came running into the dig area. She was frantic, yelling that your mom was being possessed by the ancients. The level of hysteria in her voice alarmed all of us.

I beat everyone back to the tents. When I came upon your mom, she was writhing in pain and moaning.

She was sweating and burning up. I felt helpless. Your mom started gasping for air. She clutched my arm, and between heavy labored breaths, looked at me and said over and over again, 'Help me ... help me get rid of him ... it's the only way.'

Her brother was the next to arrive. As he approached the cot where your mother lay, her breathing became better. She calmed down. Both of their pain had subsided. I cracked a bad joke about twins feeling each other's pain. They didn't appreciate my humor. After an hour or so they both felt fine, and we went through the rest of the first night without incident.

Eric set the journal down and cupped his face. He squeezed his eyes shut then rubbed his temples.

I have an uncle I don't know, archeologist parents, and ancient Mayan artifacts to find. Yeah, this is a typical day. Eric's thoughts spun like a bald tire on a patch of ice. *Why didn't they tell me any of this before? Why couldn't they? What could be so awful that someone wanted them dead? Jesus ... this would be a lot easier if I could talk to them.*

He dreaded what the rest of the journal would reveal. He thought of not picking it up. *Some things are better left unknown.* That thought departed as quickly as it came. *I have to do this. I have to do this. Quit being a baby, Eric.* The journal now weighed a ton when he hoisted it off the table. He cautiously turned to the page he left off on and began again down this frightening path:

January 2, 2011

After the incident of the first night your mom and uncle didn't enter the chambers for a few days. They were held back and put in charge of cataloging the items brought back from the site.

Everything was proceeding normally until we found the box. We didn't know what it was at first. Hell, son, we are not even sure we know exactly what it is now. We had unearthed a limestone box with a lid. At first we thought it may have been a sarcophagus, but it only measured 2-feet x 2-feet x 1.5 feet. Etched into every free space around the outside surface were what turned out to be Mayan glyphs. We set to work immediately trying to decipher the symbols.

Even after our local contacts brought a VERY OLD man who claimed to be a Mayan shaman, we were only able to translate a small portion of the glyphs on the box and the partial tablets. We learned of a previously (and still) unknown lowland king called Lord Janab Pakal, a minor king of a city-state at the time of the "great Mayan collapse." Several times in what we decoded, the god Cizin (God of Death) was mentioned.

The deciphered glyphs made reference to the declining population. Sketchy information about people just disappearing, a 'dark road,' and something called the Island of the Dead, but there are no islands off the coast of the Campeche region, so we didn't quite get that reference until later on.

Once we had everything deciphered, your mom and uncle joined the team back down in the chamber. They both got a little queasy as we worked to open a large set of stone doors that had been unearthed. We thought maybe there was a natural gas vein that was hit and making them sick ... but no one else felt any affects. Pushing on, we were able to open the doors only after your mom and uncle had joined the rest of the team. They were able to find and figure out an elaborate trigger system that needed two people working in unison to open the doors. The doors turned out to be to the outer chamber of a much larger area. In the outer chamber several items were found. A jade and obsidian necklace, two knives, one jade (in our possession), one obsidian (your uncle has that one), and a Mayan manuscript with more glyphs that we could not decipher.

We spent the next few days examining the artifacts. Our local old shaman fellow told us the knives were weapons that were cursed or some-such thing ... we really didn't pay much attention to his ramblings. He couldn't decipher the glyphs or wouldn't ... we never found out which it was.

The first night after opening the outer chamber we lost two locals. They disappeared without a trace. Strangest thing is, the second night we lost two more. By the third night everyone was staying in the large mess tent. That night we all heard what we thought were high-pitched howls emanating from the area of the chamber. We listened through the night. No one got much sleep.

January 8, 2011

It's been a few days since I've been able to write. We had some troubles with a few of the cows. Good thing I'm not sending this to you piecemeal, or that last entry would have been quite the cliffhanger. Ha, ha....

Anyway, things really got interesting the following day. We decided to attempt to open the inside chamber doors and see what awaited us. Much to our surprise we came across tools and four sets of clothing. Clothing from the missing locals. No bodies or signs of foul play anywhere. There were four scorch marks on the ground near the clothes. The inner chamber door was open.

A few of the members of the team went back to camp and gathered the few rifles and firearms we had brought with us. Dr. Dirk and I were the first to enter the chamber. It was small and dank. There was no exit out of the room we could see. Your mom and uncle entered and a loud hum started. As they moved to the center of the area the noise grew louder. A wind started swirling throughout the chamber and a dazzling display of lights filled the room.

The next thing we all remember is waking up groggy on a rocky beach. Looking around, we realized we were off the coast of Campeche, not far from the shore. This was an odd occurrence because there are <u>no</u> islands off the coast of Campeche, and it was an ODD OCCURENCE because we'd been in inside of a chamber—and now we were on an island.

In the center of the island was an entrance to a cave. There was nothing else around. We heard the same howling noises we had the previous night. Something was moving inside the cave. John Pontillo, your mom, and Uncle Roberto were the first to approach. Pontillo took off toward the cave, yelling something as he went. It almost sounded as though he was chanting. We didn't know what the hell he was up to. A black blur is all we saw and John Pontillo was gone.

Screams came from the cave. We all backed away. The creature that emerged (the ancient god Difatos) standing at least eight-feet-tall, with shoulders about one and a half times wider than an average doorframe. It had a long snout, and beady black eyes set far back in its head. Its body was covered in black, shiny scales. Its legs were similar to the hind legs of a horse, hoofed feet. In place of fingers it had three-pronged razor sharp talons that moved independent of each other.

We drew closer together. Me, your uncle and mom were out front. Your uncle and I fired our rifles, aiming for where we thought the heart would be. The monster was injured but continued toward us. We tried to encircle it. As one of the locals with us moved to the right, it lashed out, cutting him down. We moved in closer and the beast whined and recoiled. Dr. Dirk and the others moved toward the cave as me, your mom, and Uncle Roberto closed in on the ancient god.

We emptied the clips from our rifles and it fell to one knee and howled again. And then it was gone, leaving behind a terrible smell of decay.

After the initial surprise wore off, we entered the cave where the others had retreated, and once again, the same wind and lights emerged. Next we knew, we found ourselves back at the dig site in the inner chamber ... we ran as fast we could and scrambled back to camp.

January 9, 2011

At camp we told the old shaman what had happened. He mentioned the name Difatos. This was apparently the name of the ancient god. He resided on the Island of the Dead (Dr. Dirk and I traveled to the coast to check it out, but there was no island visible) and stole the essence or souls of people to get stronger.

Generations on the peninsula had lived in fear of Difatos. Over the years, he became the Yucatan version of the bogeyman. His return was prophesized, but he couldn't tell us much more. We couldn't make heads or tails of why Difatos had appeared or disappeared. A few more lines of the glyphs had made mention of warriors and defeating Difatos. We thought that your mom and uncle may have some connection (their sickness at getting close to the chambers, transporting to the island, Difatos's recoiling as we moved in and eventually disappearing), but they thought it was me, because the English translation of the surname Wolownik is "Warrior."

We didn't know where to turn next. The shaman left us for a day to consult the gods. When he returned, he had the pelts of freshly killed jaguars and several wineskins filled with their blood. He told us we needed to banish Difatos back to his island prison. We were going to need the necklace and knives he found along with what he had brought back. He also cautioned that he didn't think our actions would be a permanent solution. The prophecy was unclear and he didn't know all of the information. It was bizarre. Local leaders had come to us to tell us that several people had disappeared in the last few days. So, we did what we thought was right. We made plans to trap what we now knew to be an ancient Mayan demon.

January 10, 2011

We went back to the inner chamber. Uncle Roberto, Dr. Dirk, and the shaman were with us. Not knowing what to expect or what our roles were to be, we split up the artifacts. Your mom wore the necklace, I had the jade knife, and Roberto had the obsidian one. The shaman chanted an incantation of protection over all of us and made all of us wear a jaguar pelt as a poncho.

Dr. Dirk, however, refused, saying that since he had the explosives he would be fine. The plan was to subdue Difatos and blow up the entrances. We were hoping that collapsing the chambers would stop anyone else from stumbling upon Difatos and what we had done. We did just that. We were transported to the island from the chamber. Difatos, though, must have felt our presence and materialized in the cave mouth where we were. Dr. Dirk blew the mouth shut. We'd trapped ourselves inside with the demon. He swung at us like a mad beast. We attacked. Mom and Dr. Dirk stayed back and fired their rifles. The shaman chanted. Roberto and I attacked with the knives from different sides.

The demon was weakened for some reason. We assume from all of us being in such close proximity. It stumbled to the ground and the shaman pounced, covering the demon's head with the jaguar pelt. The demon dug its claws into the back of the shaman which sliced open the wineskins, pouring the jaguar blood all over this ancient terror.

This seemed to stun him.

Roberto and I moved in and drove obsidian stakes through the demon's hands and legs. I was slashed on the shoulder in the fray (so no, son, that scar isn't from a football injury).

With the "ancient god" immobilized, we set charges to bring the cave down on it. We didn't see this happen because we had already transported back. We quickly helped Dr. Dirk set the charges. It wasn't a precise operation as none of us were demolition experts. Dirk was struck by falling debris as we exited. He saved your mom from being hit by it. The accident left him paralyzed from the waist down. We were able to concoct a story with the local authorities about an accident with explosives and an unstable cavern system to account for the deaths that had occurred. We told no one what really transpired.

We figured if we took the box and weapons back with us there was less of a chance of someone stumbling upon them and Difatos getting free from the island.

The group decided it was best to separate from each other, so that if Difatos returned we would be harder to find. Dr. Dirk took the tablet sections and the manuscript with him. He went off to take a teaching position at the University of

Anchorage. Roberto kept the obsidian knife. Your mom and I kept the other knife, necklace, and the box.

Our first stop after the events in Campeche was in Pine Creek. We returned Jonathan Pontillo's personal effects to Andy. We decided to stay in the area. Andy and I became fast friends and it wasn't long before he knew the whole story. He worked with us throughout your life to mentor and uncle you and keep you safe.

We found out not long after arriving that you were on the way. Your mom was three months pregnant. Your uncle stayed with us for a few months until you were born. He would be the one to contact us through Andy. We only spoke a handful of times over the years. He never told us where he was living, and he never knew that we had stayed in Pine Creek.

January 11, 2011

The rest of the story is what you know, son. The people who you thought were relatives that we visited on adventure vacations were experts in their respective fields that I located and arranged to train you in different disciplines. We didn't want to leave anything to chance, should you have to face Difatos in the future.

I constantly watched for any news reports from the Yucatan about any strange occurrences or people disappearing. It wasn't until December of last year that the first stories broke. I knew the demon had reappeared. I don't know how I knew, but it was such a strong feeling. He was coming for us. And now you have to be ready. Andy has some information and an item for you. You need to see Dr. William Dirk. He is actually now on staff at Chadwick Bay University. So he should be easy for you to find. I'm sure you will do the right thing. There will be more surprises in store for you. I know you can handle whatever is thrown. You were born to.

You were raised to. I don't know the extent of harm Difatos could cause, but I know you will do everything in your power to stop it. Above all else, Eric, remember this, you are the best son that parents could have ever dreamed of.

There is more, so much more, but I can't get into it now. There is more ... stuff that was necessary, but for your mother and I, it's to our shame. When the time's right, uncle Roberto will fill you in. I so wish we could've done things differently.

We will always love you and watch over you, and the both of us terribly wish for your forgiveness.

Dad

Eric slumped in the chair and the journal slipped to the floor. He was no less stunned or confused now than when he had started the read. The waterworks started immediately—

—with fat tears taking the path of least resistance, hugging the crevices in Eric's face until they dropped onto his shirt.

Who the hell are these people? My whole life's been a lie. God, why couldn't they have just told me? Maybe I could have saved them if they'd just let me know. We could have moved away ... I could've protected them.

There were still so many questions that needed answers.

He didn't know where this would finish, but he knew where it was going to start.

Andy Pontillo.

PART III
TRUTH AND CONSEQUENCES

CHAPTER NINETEEN

ANDY PONTILLO STOOD in his study, silk bathrobe hanging open, exposing a pair of matching boxers. He poured himself three fingers of Knob Creek, drank it in one gulp, slammed the glass down, and poured himself another. Then he repeated the process. On his third go around, he skipped the formality of the rocks glass and snatched the bottle by the neck. He couldn't get the image of Edward and Elena Archer's tortured bodies out of his head. The dream he had last night was so realistic; the dark figure held them out like marionettes as they pleaded with their oldest friend to make the pain stop.

Pontillo needed this to be over.

Once the pieces were put together for Eric, the final stage would be set and his plan could come to fruition. The memories, though, still assaulted. The bottle of distilled nectar he hoped would bring on a sudden case of amnesia was frozen halfway to his mouth.

The doorbell broke the trance.

The surprise of the sound made the libation slip from his hand. The bottle bounced off the table, spilling the whiskey. "Damn it!" He paused to mourn the wasted spirit, then made his way from the study to the foyer. He could see the distorted figure of Eric Archer on the other side of the leaded glass. He took a deep breath, composed himself, tied up the robe, and opened the door.

"Hey." Eric cocked his head to one side and waved his hand in Pontillo's direction. "Catch you at a bad time?"

"No-no-no … haven't been very motivated today. I couldn't sleep much last night, your parents' case and all that goes with it. It has me vexed. Care for a drink? I was just going to fix myself one."

"A person without a nose could have smelled the Knob Creek. So, maybe *another* one is what you mean? I'm good, thanks. After all, Andy, it is only 7:00 A.M."

Pontillo slowly turned and pointed a finger. "Now *you* are starting to sound like Julia, like the song says, 'It's 12 o'clock somewhere,' and it was a rough night." He turned and walked from the entrance of the house and back into the study.

Eric followed at a distance.

Waving the leather-bound book in the air like a bible-thumping evangelist, Eric pronounced, "So this journal tells a pretty amazing tale. In it, Dad says that you would have some more information for me."

Pontillo nodded in agreement. He picked the bottle up from the floor and poured himself another drink. Once again he offered it to Eric, shaking the bottle in his direction. Eric dismissed him with a wave of his hand. "Suit yourself."

Pontillo sat down in one of the leather club chairs in front of the floor-to-ceiling bookshelf that made up one wall of the room, and motioned for Eric to join him.

"My parents were lucky to have found such a good friend in you, Andy. They had to have been in a rough place coming out of the events of the dig. The way you helped me my whole life, I never realized, I owe you so much."

Pontillo smiled, amused that Eric might be hoping for a genie to pop out of the journal and grant him three wishes. "Your parents needed a sympathetic ear, and so did I, for that matter." Pontillo lifted his glass, took a swig, rinsed his mouth, and swallowed. "Listen, we will be more than even as soon as you pull all the pieces together and put an end to this."

"I was shocked and sorry to see that your brother was one of the people killed by this … this demon-god, whatever he/it is."

"It was a hard time for me and my family, Eric. Much like what you're going through. Johnny was a great brother. We planned on doing great things together in this world. Life has a way of coming up and biting you in the ass sometimes." Pontillo raised his glass.

"No argument from me." Eric, fixated on the journal in his hands, started thumbing through the pages. "Tell me what I need to know. How can we defeat this thing?"

"First of all, there is no *we* involved. It's all you, buddy. Somehow over the years, your mom and dad figured out that your bloodline is tied to this demon-god, this ancient deity called Difatos. Only the bloodline, the *blood of the ancients* has the power to vanquish him." Pontillo walked over to the antique oak and leather-topped executive's desk in the opposite corner of the room. He pulled a mahogany case out of the drawer, the same case that until yesterday was secured in the wall safe with the journal. He walked back to where Eric was seated. Eric took the case as Pontillo held it out. Placing the journal off to the side, Eric opened the box to find a .40 cal. Beretta M92, and three 10-round magazines.

"That gun was your father's, the rounds custom-made. If you find them, you may have some advantage over Difatos. Your father wasn't sure if the bullets would make a difference or not. The shell casing and bullet will be black and green." Andy retook his seat. "They're manufactured from the jade and obsidian removed from the dig site your dad wrote to you about. He figured if Difatos were to return, a modern weapon might be more useful."

Eric placed the gun back inside the case and then examined the clip. "Dad's journal mentioned a box and other weapons and items. Maybe the bullets are there. Do you have any idea where they are?"

"That's where you come in, son. The hope is that once you have all of the information, you'll be able to piece it together. I know your dad had some of the stuff at the farm. But he never let me in on where it was. He thought it would be better if fewer people knew. If I were you, the first thing I would do is call on Dr. William Dirk, and then try and find your uncle. I have been unsuccessful in contacting him for many years, or getting any information from him in the past. But for you it may be a different story. They just might hold the key."

"Apparently, Dr. Dirk moved into the area a few years ago and took a position with CBU. It's odd, though, he would pick this area of the country, of all places to relocate to."

"Not as odd as you think. I would take it as a sign that things are lining up."

"Hope you are right. I'm going to head home, change, and gather my thoughts before seeing Dr. Dirk. It may very well be that he thinks I'm crazy and sends me packing."

"I'm sure that won't happen."

Eric stood and stuck out his hand. Pontillo swigged another pull, and took the handshake with a strong grip. "Thanks, Andy, and again I don't think there is any way I could repay you for all you have done for my family."

They walked toward the front of the house and Pontillo held the door open for Eric. "Don't you worry about what I've done for your parents. They have done just as much for me. Just as you have, or I should say you *will* have, once you put all the pieces together."

Eric gave a nod and made his way to his Chevy Laguna and drove off.

Pontillo lingered on the porch. Difatos was out there somewhere. He could *feel* it. He turned and went back into the house.

Time to pour himself another drink.

CHAPTER TWENTY

AS THE DOOR closed, a dark figure emerged at the edge of the woods surrounding Andy Pontillo's property. Beady eyes glowed with a deep red hue. He turned his head, watching Eric's car pull away and Pontillo reentering the house. Difatos sneered as a feeling of satisfaction came over him. He felt his confidence grow that he would soon triumph over the last of his adversaries.

A hollow voice rang out from behind. "I wouldn't get too comfortable with your situation, Difatos."

Difatos spun and saw a cloaked figure. "My big brother, the King of Lie—"

"Let's not go there." The visitor stayed hooded. "I'm only here to tell you that I'm onto your plan and have been for a while. Very bold move, and so soon after your last attempt, too. Here you are messing with the bloodline of protectors again. The Absolute's sleeper cell, so to speak. Will you ever learn?"

"You do not have the power to stop me, hypocrite, when you are as estranged from The Absolute as I am. You're the Unworthy One. Our brothers made sure of that when they cast you out. You waste all your power protecting the pitiful souls they all keep sending your way to Xibalba."

"Some of what you say may be right, for now, but know this, little brother, you most minuscule of all the gods, I have a plan. That plan will allow me to stop you and get Father's attention. The Absolute will not forever ignore me. The end of my long banishment is coming. And truthfully, I have you to thank for it."

"Me? I would sooner help Inti or Mithras."

"If they still existed, you mean. Nevertheless, you did help, dear Difatos. Your actions re-kindled the fire of the bloodline—*you* woke them. They will help me re-ascend to my rightful seat next to my brothers. Once I help them take care of your little insurrection, that is."

Difatos growled and lunged, but his talons struck nothing but the fading mist left behind as the intruder disappeared.

CHAPTER
TWENTY-ONE

JESSICA HARDLY STOPPED crying all the way back to Pine Creek. They left her bike in St. Catharines as she and Robert made the drive in his SUV. After Robert explained everything to her, she was in no shape to make it home on her own. She didn't want to be left alone in her emotional state, anyway. On the way home, the space between her cries was filled with questions. Her feelings moved from disbelief, to sadness, to anger, to denial, and back again. She vacillated between despising and loving the man sitting next to her. The man that until three hours ago she had spent her whole life thinking was her father.

Jessica was surprised at how easily Robert remembered the way back to Edward and Elena's farm. He had told her the last time he'd set foot on this property he wasn't even Robert Benitez yet.

Robert's Chevy Trailblazer eased onto the property and crunched up the dirt and stone driveway. He came to a stop in front of the doors to the prairie barn. He put the car in park, turned off the ignition, and let his hands fall onto his lap. Jessica wondered if Robert felt as alone as she did. Even with the man who'd been her rock her whole life sitting next to her, she had never felt more helpless. Without a word, Jessica placed her hand over Robert's and gave it a squeeze.

"Thank you."

Jessica exited the vehicle. She hoped he knew enough to stay back, giving her time and space.

CHAPTER
TWENTY-TWO

ERIC PULLED HIS Chevy Laguna into the driveway at the farm. Filled with both excitement and apprehension, he knew there was a long way to go before this thing was solved, but he was buoyed by the visit to Andy Pontillo and the prospect of meeting Dr. William Dirk.

He found himself wanting to share everything with Jessica and wondered when she would be back from her visit with her dad. At first, he didn't notice the SUV with Ontario plates. He brought his car to a stop and climbed out, gun in ready position. He looked around and didn't see anyone. Then a man appeared from behind the house, eating an apple and not paying much attention.

"Don't take another step!" commanded Eric.

Robert stopped in his tracks and slowly raised both hands. "Whoa, son! Hold up, I'm not the bad guy." Robert cocked his head to one side. "Wait ... Eric? Is that you? My God, it is! It's been so long. It's like I walked back in time 30-years. You're the spitting image of your dad."

"So I've been told." Eric didn't relent with the gun. "You seem to have me at a disadvantage. I don't recall anyone from Canada that would pop in unexpectedly on my parents."

A voice: "Eric, stop! What're you doing?"

He recognized the voice as Jessica's. *Why have I been calling her Jessica?* "You know this gentleman?" He glanced in her direction, keeping the Glock partially raised.

She quickened her pace and came upon the two men. "Of course I do. This is my dad."

Eric holstered the Glock.

"What she means to say is that I'm the man that raised her. This isn't the most ideal situation. Not at all how we planned to tell you—"

"You know I'm getting awfully sick of everyone being so mysterious the last few days. If you have something to say, say it!"

"I'm your Uncle, Roberto dos Vidas, your mother's brother. I'm sure your parents never mentioned me. After Jessica came to me about this case, well, I knew it was time to reveal everything about all these damn secrets."

"You ... you're my mom's twin that my dad talked about in his journal?" Eric turned to Jessica. "Is this your Dad? My uncle is *your* d—?"

"Pay attention, idiot, your dad is my dad, and your uncle is my dad, and my dad is my uncle … keep it straight."

The newly-revealed Roberto dos Vidas started rubbing his chin. "Any chance we could find a comfortable place to talk?"

Eric shook his head as if coming out of a daze. "Sorry, I'm just a bit confused and tired of playing catch-up." Eric turned and faced Jessica. "Didn't you go home to see your dad?"

Jessica walked over to Eric and took him by the arm, leading him toward the deck at the back of the house. "I did, Eric. I went home to see my dad and came back with my uncle."

"Well that didn't really do anything for clarification purposes."

CRIC, JESSICA, AND Roberto took seats around the patio table. The umbrella was tilted for morning shade, just like Eric's mom left it. He had seen her perform the morning ritual countless times.

"Must be fate, the only furniture left that's not been destroyed." Eric looked through the blasted patio doors into the house, then back at Jessica and Roberto. "You know Mom always had her cup of morning coffee out here. It's funny … so many details, events, and actions that we see and take for granted, only missing them once a person's gone."

Eric sat back, slumped a little, laced his fingers, and rested his elbows on the arms of the chair. He shifted his gaze between Jessica and his *new* uncle.

The awkward silence was broken by Roberto. "Safe guess your dad's journal told you of the events in Campeche 30-years ago?"

Eric gave a few nods and continued to listen.

"Okay, then, there are a few blanks I'm sure need to be filled in. None of us wanted to let each other go—ever. We we're family. But after the events at the dig there was no other way. The first thing we needed to do was make our way here, to Hurley County, to inform John Pontillo's family what happened and to turn over the man's personal items."

"That's when you met Andy?"

"Yes, we made fast friends with Andy, and he went to work convincing your parents to stay in the area. In short, we found out your mom was pregnant, so I stayed with her and your dad until you were born. We made arrangements to part ways after you were born. I took your sister and moved to Canada. I only made contact with your parents a few times over the years, just to let them know we were still okay."

As Roberto was speaking, Eric pushed back his chair, stood, and turned around to survey the field beyond the porch. He whipped around, astonished at the words that filled his ears. "Did you say *sister*? What sis—" He looked at Jessica, who was slowly nodding. Eric stumbled backwards. Roberto jumped up to help him, but Eric waved him off as he slumped to the ground along the porch railing.

All of the oxygen had been sucked out of the world; Eric's lungs wouldn't inflate. His brain decided to take a ride on the merry-go-round and no one was there to stop it. It just kept going faster. Tears welled. He buried his face in his hands. "What the hell's going on?"

Jessica moved to Eric's side. She slid down the porch railing, sidled up to him, and wrapped her arm around his shoulder and pulled him close.

Eric was a child looking for comfort, he nestled his head into the crook of her arm and shoulder.

Tears broke and flowed freely down their cheeks.

CHAPTER TWENTY-THREE

A SHADOWY FIGURE, insubstantial, misty, emerged at the edge of the barn. He observed the newly-anointed family members deal with their emotional struggle. He longed for the days that his family had shared those kinds of moments.

The bringing into existence of new and wonderful things at the hands of The Absolute was always such a joyous event for him and his brethren. Now, one rogue sibling threatened to destroy all of the beauty that remained on Earth. He could not let that happen.

The creatures he and his brothers had a hand in creating and guiding did not deserve the fate Difatos had in store. He was impressed with Difatos's ambition. This was his second attempt at claiming this planet and its inhabitants as his own, but the Absolute's natural laws forbade such an action by his children. That didn't stop them, though. They had fought over the souls of mankind for millennia. This was not how it was meant to be. Now, because the higher gods were too busy with one another, Difatos was going to swoop in and claim the forbidden prize.

That would not happen.

"Besides, these amusing monkeys are far better

with the Devil they know. I'll help these ancestors of the ancient bloodline." The King of Lies started to dissipate.

"I have to."

CHAPTER TWENTY-FOUR

THE TEARS STOPPED, but the silence remained. Hallmark didn't have the right words for this situation.

"I'm sorry you two had to find out this way. There was never going to be an easy way to have you two meet … hell, to have all of us meet." The man gripped both of their hands. "But keeping you apart was safer—ugly or not, and it *was* and *is*—that was our reality."

An eerie din drew the three new family members' attention to the barn.

Eric turned. "Did you both hear that?"

"Like someone"—Jessica came to her feet—"talking through a creepy howling wind."

"Exactly." Eric shaded his eyes, looking into the field beyond the barn "What the *hell* is that? Smoke? Mist?"

The trio sat, silent, watching the field.

Standing at the porch railing, Roberto turned back to his nephew and *niece*. "Craziness your parents and I hoped to avoid. There's power in our bloodline. We'd learned of a lineage of twins dating back to antiquity. This has been our family's charge. Some might think of it as a curse, but that would be wrong. It's our history, and our duty."

"Legacy, destiny … whatever name you give it, Eric and I have to deal with it."

"You both need to be ready for the eventual return of Difatos."

"Eventual? What if this damned thing is already here? Look at this place?" Eric gestured towards the house and barn. "But for now, forget about the damn demon-god. How could this have been a good idea? We all lost so much. Decades with our sisters. And we didn't have time to be uncle and nephew." Eric waved towards Roberto, then at Jessica. "She never got to know her real parents. How did you choose who went where?" Eric shook his head. "How do we get that time back? How's any of this been fair."

"The answer's simple, nephew, even if frustrating: Life's not fair. Staying separated made us less of a target. All signs pointed to the male being most powerful. Your father thought it best if you stayed. Both of them could better protect you. As for the time, no, we don't get it back."

Jessica slapped her knees and stood. "We have to move forward and take care in the time we *do* have, no matter how long or short."

"I *really* need some time to process all of this." Eric started pacing the length of the deck.

"We *all* need some time." Roberto slapped his knees and stood. "How about I get us some food?

Jessica smiled. "The old Benitez way, when the going gets tough, the tough get food."

Roberto: "Is the Case & Clark Deli still open?"

"You know that place? Mom and Dad loved it. It's open, the owners' sons are running it. A lot of odd stories come out of their: mob hits, celebrity sightings, occult activities, ghosts."

Jessica: "One of my first days on the job, they were being investigated for using the store as a front for selling cigaweed. It turned out to be some ex-wife or girlfriend with an axe to grind."

The conversation volleyed back to Eric. "I've heard stories the store sits on an old Indian burial ground."

Roberto chuckled. "I didn't know that. Thankfully, though, none of that stuff has affected the quality of the food, and especially their monster-sized subbs." His smile grew even wider. "Your parents and I were fixtures there."

"Didn't know it's been open that long! Damn, *that* list of mine is getting long."

"I'll be back in a little bit." Roberto made his way to the SUV; the reunited siblings followed. "We can put our heads together and figure out what the best course of action is."

"You are taking all of this surprisingly well. I feel like an ass for all the breakdowns I've had."

"I guess I'm just the strong one." Jessica punched Eric in the arm. "But, listen, I know I should be going bat-shit crazy. I was raised by our uncle. We didn't know about each other until half an hour ago."

"Our parents are dead at the hands of a Mayan god-king. Let me say that again, *Mayan god-king*. Let's not forget, we're part of an ancient muthah-flubbin' bloodline that is supposed to defeat it, and there's a shit-ton of cards stacked against us."

Jessica's fingers flashed a V. "Two decks' worth, but tell you the truth, I feel calm."

"I'm nauseous."

"About six months after getting hired, I met y— our, *our* parents. Before long, I was stopping by once a week to spend time with your Mom.

"*Our* Mom."

*"*Yeah, wow, that's weird to hear." Jessica held Eric's hands. "Instead of being left to wonder what if, I at least have those moments. I'm going to have to take comfort in that. Better to have those moments of joy than one long stretch of nothingness. Maybe, deep down, she knew who I was the whole time."

"She may have. They were magical people. What did Roberto tell you?"

"Told me my mom passed away during childbirth."

Eric's eyes widened.

"You look like I *felt* when I found out. Dad said that was the easiest answer. If he would've said she just took off or that I was adopted, I might have wasted time looking for her later."

"Practical and calculated, that plan has my dad written all over it. It does make sense, but it doesn't make it any less of a cheat."

"I won't say that I don't *feeeel* cheated." Jessica tousled her hair with both hands. "But I couldn't have asked for anyone better to raise me."

"You're managing this just like Mom would. Like water off a duck's back, she'd say."

MAYBE WHAT ERIC said was true. Jessica figured it was more likely he was just saying it to be kind. At any rate, she appreciated his efforts to comfort her. It added credence to the thought she might have misjudged him.

She walked over and gave him a big hug.

Eric and Jessica wandered around the property sharing stories of their childhood spent apart. Eric told her everything he could about their parents and what it was like growing up on the farm. Jessica found the more they compared tales of growing up, the more similar their upbringing. Whether it was Eric's adventure vacations or her adventure camps, gymnastics, martial arts, outdoor (survival) schools, or countless other activities.

The reminiscing was put on hold as Roberto pulled up with the food. Jessica thought it took a bit too long for him to get back, but wasn't surprised that Roberto would have built in extra time for her and Eric to get acquainted.

Back at the patio, they ate their custom Case & Clark foot-and-a-half long subbmarines, SUBBS SO BIG, IT NEEDS TWO B's. Against the pall of their surroundings, Roberto said, "These are just I remembered, worth their weight in gold."

"Growing up, these things were a staple in my diet." Eric pointed his stuffed-to-overflowing heart-stopper at Jessica. "You?"

"Since moving here, you can damn well bet I've had my fair."

As they finished cleaning up from their meal, Roberto started the after-dinner conversation. "Let's get down to brass tacks. We need to get our asses to Dr. Dirk."

Jessica then pulled Elena Archer's necklace from her pocket. "I couldn't log this in as evidence.

Something compelled me to hold onto it." She held it out. "Here."

"Thanks." Eric looked at the inscription: HE WHO HOLDS THE KEY CAN UNLOCK MY HEART. "Mom and I had a tradition. Every year on our birthdays we were to fit the key and heart together." He removed his paracord bracelet. "I'd like you to have the necklace. We could start the same tradition."

"I … Eric, really?"

"It's right. You should have it."

"Hey, kids, cement the thought by doing it now."

Jessica positioned the heart-shaped pendant on her palm so Eric could join the pieces. Then, astonishment: The heart shone like a star. The engraving elevated off the pendant as the inscription was rewritten into a different message. "Tell me, *tellmetellmetellme* you're seeing this?"

Eric nodded as he read the message:

To my
extraordinary
children,
I bestow upon you
a piece of me,
that it might
protect you from
what comes. May
you find strength
in each other.
All my love,
Mom.

Tingles shot up Jessica's arm, and she saw auras of black, green, and purple dance around their hands.

"Holy *THATRACEDRIGHTTOMYSHOULDER.*" Eric's hand, arm, and shoulder was shaking.

Then it stopped.

"There's no question now. This belongs to you." He adorned his sister with the necklace. "Now I know why I was staring at you the night we met. You look just like Mom."

Jessica caressed her new heart. "Thank you, Eric."

"What happened with you guys?"

Eric and Jessica responded, "We don't know." Then they showed Roberto the joined pendants and its new message.

From Eric, "I think we received a—"

"Blessing from our mother." Jessica started to laugh. "I don't know any more than that, but it was a—"

"Something wonderful." Eric grinned as Roberto looked at the pendant.

"According to her message, the blessing you two received might have a bit more of a punch to it." He glanced at the pendant's message again. "Have you two ever been flashed?"

Eric gave his uncle a strange look. "That's illegal, isn't it?"

CHAPTER TWENTY-FIVE

"SO, YOU'RE SAYING, with flashing, we can transfer information, abilities, and strength between each other, and even inanimate objects?"

"That's about the gist of it, PJ, though it's a bit more complicated. Depends on how deeply one connects to their life force. As Eric said earlier, your parents were magical people. In fact, we all are, according to the prophecy. Nonetheless, even magical people are people, and have different skill-sets that they develop.

"Personality, interests, all that and more come into play. Just like with other skills. Some people have an affinity for art, like with painting, or singing, or building stuff. What makes one more skilled than another in a specific field? Some combination of training and flight-time, but then there's that X-factor, where a person's just good at something." Roberto un-pocketed a sheathed knife. "Flashing, however, is not the only ally. There's also tools available. Special tools." Roberto unsheathed the blade.

Jessica and Eric looked at the knife. The handle looked more or less modern, or at least something one might've found within the past 100-years, or so. It was the blade that stood out, maybe seven-inches of sharp-looking, shiny black stone. This had to be one of the obsidian weapons talked about in John Archer's journal.

"Yes," Roberto handed the knife to Eric, handle first, "one of the knives your dad wrote to you about." The man watched as Eric looked the blade over. "Be careful, that thing will bite."

Jessica: "What about the rest of the stuff, a jade knife, and what, a necklace, too? Are there any other weapons besides the knives?"

"Anything can be used as a weapon."

"Yes, Dad."

Eric had almost forgotten about the Beretta that Andy had given him. "I've got something to show, gimme a sec." He sprinted to his car and returned with a wooden box. "The sheriff gave me a 9-millie. Dad had 30 special bullets made for it, some kind of composite made out of jade and obsidian."

"Well, that's new." Roberto rubbed his chin. "And I don't recall anything else that was brought back from the dig."

Eric: "Was there a specific location they needed to find? Some ritual they needed to perform? For the most part, we're flying blind and playing this by the seat of our pants. It doesn't sit well with me."

Jessica took the mahogany box from Eric and pried the gun and magazines from their molded resting places inside the box. She placed them all down and examined the case. Running her fingers along the edge of the felt-lining, about halfway down the short side of the case, a tab of fabric peeked out. "Look at this." She showed the tab and tugged. The lining pulled free, exposing the jade-and-obsidian rounds fastened to the bottom of the box. She pulled one from its resting place and tossed it in Eric's direction. "There's one mystery solved."

Eric turned the custom round between his fingers. "I don't want to get too excited, but we may have just caught our first break." He handed the round over to Uncle Roberto, who looked at it, and thunked it on his chin, before handing it back. "It's like we're in the comic books. Lots of dangerous bullets out there, but we've a common thread with this jade and obsidian. Think it's apparent these materials are like some kind of kryptonite."

"You're a geek." Jessica started handing the other rounds one at a time to Eric, who packed them into the magazine, then slid it into the grip of the gun, and racked the slide. Jessica watched as he cleared the chamber and dropped the magazine, then placed both back in the box. "We're not in a comic book. We're in a horror movie. And this shit's like silver to a werewolf, or a stake to a vamp."

Eric waved the case containing the gun. "This might not be a game-changer, but I'm hoping it puts a little shock into Difatos, if he shows up. It doesn't make us prepared by any stretch, but it can't hurt, either."

"I agree there are still too many unknowns—"

"Agreed, Dad. For example, who's getting the gun?" She pulled out her own 9mm and held it, butt out. "Want to trade brother?"

"We'll rock-paper-and-scissors for it later. Let's keep on track."

Scolding eyes and a chin-tap. "Dr. Dirk translated

a few of the tablet fragments taken from the site. We need to pray he made a breakthrough and deciphered the manuscript/codex that was found. That'll be the *real* key. Then maybe the glyphs covering the stone box, too."

Jessica: "Provided we find some clues as to where it is. The next step is to pay a visit to the good Dr. Dirk."

Eric tapped his temple and winked. "Great minds think alike. Those were going to be the next words out of my mouth."

Roberto came to his feet. "You two, get down to the university if you plan on catching Dr. Dirk in his office. I'll stick around here and make myself useful. If I start doing some repair work on the house, maybe I'll stumble on something."

Jessica motioned towards Eric's car. "Sure you want to stay here? Dr. Dirk knows you. Might be more willing to talk to you?"

"He's going to discuss *everything* with you two. He's been holding onto this stuff for decades, waiting to do something."

Eric started to jog over to his car, but then turned and came back to Roberto. He held out the mahogany box. "I'll feel better if you have this on you while we're gone."

Roberto stood straight and grimaced. "Okay … okay, now you two get going. I'll be fine. I'll be right here when you get back."

CHAPTER TWENTY-SIX

BACKROAD DRIVING AT a high rate of speed towards Chadwick Bay University, got Eric and Jessica swiftly into town. They made a right off Central Avenue onto Ring Road, stopped and consulted a large plastic-encased campus map, and located the building that housed Dr. Dirk's department. The parking lot next to Thompson Hall was nearly empty. They pulled into a spot close to the building and made their way inside.

A few wrong turns in the labyrinth of Thompson Hall had the feel of one of the chase scenes in an old Scooby-Doo cartoon. "A few more dead-ends, and we're going to run into our personal Minotaur named Difatos. I don't think he'll take too kindly to us *meddling kids*, either."

Jessica raised an eyebrow.

"Oh, don't give me that. You know you were thinking the same thing … and remember, I'm a geek."

The siblings eventually arrived at a door:

Dr. William Dirk
Professor Emeritus
Archeology and Anthropology

Knock knock knock.

No answer.

"There is someone in there." Jessica pointed at the door.

Eric knocked again and tried the handle. It was open. He shot a glance at Jessica. She mouthed *GO IN*.

He opened the door a bit more. "Dr. Dirk? Are you in there? It's Eric Archer, here with my sister Jessica … you don't know us, but you knew our parents, Edward and Elena, students of yours. It's about the Campeche Dig. We need to talk to you. It's very important."

The L-shaped room looked like the stock Hollywood version of an old professor's office: stacks of mismatched dusty old books, rolled-up maps scattered among glass-front, floor-to-ceiling cabinets that held all sorts of odd artifacts from long dead civilizations, walls covered with maps dotted with handwritten notes and pushpins marking the locations of significant finds. Jessica went over to a desk and pulled open one of the side drawers, and lifted out a flask to show Eric.

Dr. Dirk came rolling around the corner. "I'm a lush, a functional lush—but with tenure-plus."

If the room looked right out of a Hollywood sound stage, then Dr. Dirk must have come straight from central casting, a weathered elder that was the cross between Keith Richards and Peter Cushing, and a man confined to a wheelchair, legs wrapped in a Native American blanket. Long wisps of white hair formed a ring around his head from ear to ear, with but a few strays clinging to the top of his head. Day-old stubble marked his face. He wore a hound's-tooth coat with leather patches on the elbows, and a knit polo shirt buttoned to the top and a bolo tie with an ornamental Mayan glyph as its clasp.

Jessica replaced the flask back in the drawer. "I'm so sorr—"

"Think nothing of it, my dear. Even the most elite of academia must imbibe from time to time. It lightens the mood, and is good for the immune system."

"Dr. Dirk, Name's Eric Archer, this is my sister Jessica. We've come to talk to you about our parents, Edward and Elena, and the events at the Campeche Dig."

"Edward and Elena … names not heard for almost as long as I've been in this chair. Yes, the university has been more than willing to get me a more modernistic technological contraption, but this chair and I," he rolled the wheelchair back and forth, "do go quite the ways back. And they are your parents, you say. Very interesting."

Eric and Jessica started to get out identification to prove to the doctor who they were. Not that it would have cleared much up, since none of the surnames matched.

"Children, please, put away the identification. Not needed. You could hardly be anybody *but* who you say you are. Your brother, there," he pointed with a boney finger, "couldn't look any more like Edward Wolownik. And you, young lady, I noticed the resemblance to your mother as soon as I came around the corner. Now pull up those chairs and have a seat. We've a great many things to palaver about."

As they moved chairs closer to Dr. Dirk's desk, he wheeled around the cluttered space with ease, moving from pile to pile, cabinet to cabinet, gathering items on his lap, and at times conscripting Eric and Jessica to take stuff to a table. He returned to the desk and locked the wheels on the chair, signifying he was ready to begin.

Not wasting time, Jessica questioned with, "Why is it you moved to this area? You spent your whole life in the Southwest and West. Why here in Western New York?"

"You know, that is quite the perplexing line of inquiry. For the answer, my dear sir and lady, is that I haven't found the justification. Some years ago, but not more than a handful, after the spring semester, I received a communiqué from a colleague here at Chadwick Bay, a transplant from across the pond. He told me to inquire about the opening in the Anthropology department. Not to boast—because no one lauds a braggart—but my moniker carries more than a bit of gravity in the field. Of course, it was a simple matter to barter the mutual beneficence on what my being here could do for them, especially with regards to the rags. Fortunately, my particular specialization at least afforded me that much leverage. By the start of the fall semester, I was in this very office. For whatever reason, I was constrained, queer as that may sound."

"Quite honestly, with everything that's happened, it doesn't sound the least bit strange, professor."

"Then this, Master Archer, might not surprise you. When I arrived in town, I endeavored to entertain Mr Ezekiel Tyre, the colleague mentioned earlier. A professor of religious studies, I believe he was. However, there was no one by that name ever employed here, Mother England, or anyplace else, for that matter. He simply *did not*, and *does not* exist. Right now, I'm not convinced I ever really knew anyone by that name." The professor locked eyes with Eric and Jessica, and stared for a few seconds—without blinking. "Your visage betrays your shock and disbelief, but let me assure you that what I'm presenting is not the fanciful fabrication of a fabulist."

"Well, someone or something wanted you here in Hurley County. We are fortunate you decided to come here."

"Eric is right, dear doctor. It's a blessing in disguise."

"Perhaps a bit of divine intervention—or at least one can hope. Truthfully, I didn't even know your parents were in this area until I received a package from your father a few months after I relocated. To my chagrin, we never met, and it was the only contact had after the events of the dig in Campeche."

Eric and Jessica: "What was in the package?"

"With the parcel, there was an accompanying missive instructing that it was imperative to keep the notes he sent safe, and to only entrust them to his progeny. He said—and this caused no small onslaught of frustrating migraines—that I would *know* when the time was right. Now seems appropriate, and I suppose these maps and notes will also be of no small assist. But, please, inform me of what you've already unearthed?"

Eric and Jessica proceeded to tell Dr. Dirk everything they knew, starting with their respective childhoods, all the way through the deaths of Edward and Elena, to earlier in the day when Eric found out that Jessica was his sister.

Eric: "All we have in our possession is Dad's journal and the obsidian knife. Other than coming here, we are really at a loss for how to proceed."

"My, oh my, not even taking into account your independent backgrounds, you two have had quite the simple gallop—and Brutus is an honourable man!" Looking down, Dr. Dirk began to hum *A Cold Wind in August* while shuffling through the pile on his lap. Finally, he held up some papers in his tremulous hands and began to scan the pages. After some moments of thumbing, he stopped his homage to Van Morrison and held up a sheaf of papers. "A short time after the original dig, I was able to decipher some of the glyphs on the partial stone tablets we discovered. Alas, only being able to read part of the information wasn't too helpful, and each time I tried to decipher more, I found myself sharing a strange kinship with the famous smuggler, saying *I've got a bad feeling about this*, so I stopped and determined to keep it private. But it is all here in the notes. Here it is, the partial translation from the stone tablets."

Eric and Jessica leaned in closer to the desk.

Dr. Dirk: "Ruler of Xiabalba … the process begins … no death … great g[G]od-k[K]ing of man, or maybe *man* that becomes a god. Not much more will they wait … the b[B]lack r[R]oad … and *fini*." He set the papers on the desk. "As said, it is incomplete, due to the fragmented nature of the tablets. Interestingly enough, the mention of this *Black Road* is found in other Mayan artifacts, such as the Dresden Codex, and the famous Stela 6 in Tortuguero. The Mayans describe the Black Road as a place located in the heavens where a band of dust or clouds make the sky particularly dark from an earthly view. The location is approximate to where the Milky Way has its galactic center, and quite possibly where there is a massive black hole. Again, nothing is completely known. And in all this time, I have not been able to unlock the secrets of the codex. Its message has eluded me for all of these decades."

Eric: "The Campeche Codex?"

"Strictly speaking, it hasn't been named yet. There is a fondness for the name to be *The Dr. Dirk Codex*, but to my own misery, that just doesn't sing."

Jessica repeated some of Dr. Dirk's words. "Ruler of Xiabalba … man that becomes god … no death … process begins … *hmmm*?"

Eric looked at his sister. "I can practically see the wheels turning. What is it, Jessica?"

"Just hunches … could, uh, could Janab Pakal have been the ruler of Xiabalba? Is he caught in the middle of some kind of transformation? That line … what was it? 'Man that becomes a god.' That can't mean *anything* remotely good. I still don't know what part we play in this."

"I'll tell you what," Eric added. "I don't think I want to find out what happens if Difatos gets his way. I have a sneaking suspicion, whatever his plans, he needs us out of the way."

Dr. Dirk: "Despite some loose connections, it does seem plausible. As reasonable as *any* of this can sound." His laugh became a cough. He grabbed the coffee mug from the desk. The splash of liquid extinguished the irritant at the back of his throat. "Most frustrating, isn't it, not having the rest of the codex translated."

The doctor took the rest of the items from his lap and put them on the desk. Grabbing a hard leather map-case, he unzipped the side, and pulled out and unrolled a series of maps. "These are the original maps from the dig, complete with coordinates and a sketch of the chambers below." He pointed at the various spots for Eric and Jessica to examine. Next, he brought out a sealed envelope with Eric's name written in his father's hand, and with a solemn look, slid over the epistle.

Eric took the letter and grabbed a long, slender dagger from the pencil jar on the desk. Making a smooth clean cut across the envelope, he removed the contents. "More pages from his journal." Eric took a few moments and read them.

Jessica occupied herself by studying the maps the professor had brought out. Dr. Dirk wheeled himself to a filing cabinet across the room and started rummaging through it.

Eric finished reading the pages and handed them to his sister. "It tells about us, about separating us for our own safety. They had hoped to find another way to defeat Difatos, or maybe keep it searching until we were all gone. There are a few questions, though, we may have to ask the sheriff."

Dr. Dirk returned with some additional papers. He made his way to the desk and began to write on them. Without looking up, he asked, "Was there anything else of use in the pages?"

Jessica finished the letter. "The location of the necklace, jade knife, and stone box are in here. We can bring it back for you to translate. It has to give us valuable information."

"We can only hope. Maybe it's nothing; with our luck, it'll turn out to be a bridal hope chest."

Jessica shot Eric a reproving look.

"Regardless, there is a young, but extremely gifted individual in Costa Maya, Mexico, name of Eliseo Gomez. He would be the ideal man to help you with the box. He owns a touring company specializing in Mayan ruins. He is also the assistant curator at the Yucatan Ministry of Culture. A fellow with a natural affinity for the language of the Mayans, and who holds quite the passion for their sites, artifacts, and culture. There is no better point-of-contact. Though I'm loathe to say it, it would probably be best to take all of the artifacts with you, the manuscript codex, the box, the tablet pieces, necklace and knives. Better to have them and not need them, as the saying goes. Interning with me for a short time, Eliseo Gomez became a bulwark of support with any number of tasks, to and including the tablet translations—an authentic Jack-of-all-trades." He picked up the papers he had been writing on and handed them over to Jessica. "These forms and labels will allow you freedom of travel—with the artifacts—without any concerns about bureaucratic molestation, such as customs and what-not."

"You won't come with us, professor?"

"No-no-no, my dear, I am much too old to be rolling across the continent. My days of traipsing through jungles, avoiding booby traps, and cracking whips are far behind me. My place is here, and my part in all of this—despite a deeply lamenting heart—is done. I've shouldered the burden of these events for far too long. However, should *need* dictate, I will be at your disposal. Besides, I can't go too far or too fast," he smiled and tapped the side of his wheelchair, "and have no one to look after my four-legged best friend, Harrison."

Eric collected the maps and tablets as Dr. Dirk directed, then put the artifacts in a crate large enough to hold the stone box.

Jessica walked over to Dr. Dirk, bent down, and kissed him on the head. "Thank you for all of your help. We will be in touch."

The professor's face went flush. "Eric, know I have an old leather jacket and fedora? They served me well many times. You look just about the right size. It wouldn't take me long at all to dig them out."

"No, thank you. Why don't you hold onto those, and when all of this is over, I'll stop by and you can show them to me as we exchange war stories."

"Brilliant."

Eric put the crate down and extended his arm. The professor grabbed Eric by the elbow and hand and pulled him. "This is your time. Take care of your sister and put an end to this most distasteful business. The cost has already been too high."

"Will do, Dr. Dirk."

Jessica held the door open so Eric could exit with the crate. As they were leaving, they heard Dr. Dirk utter, "'The woods are lovely, dark and deep. But I have promises to keep, and miles to go before I sleep.'"

INTERLUDE III

STEPHANIE SMITH SKIPPED down the front steps of John Mancuso High School. It was a glorious June day. The year was almost over, graduation was around the corner, and she was going to be able to tell the boy she loved more than anything in the world that he was going to be a dad.

Her friends told her she was crazy to be so happy about being 18 and pregnant, but she didn't care. She and Johnnie would live the *happily ever after* she had always dreamed of, in spite of being so young, and in spite of his unstable mother. She wasn't even sure Johnnie had told his mom they were dating yet, and it had been almost six months. As far as she knew, his mom still thought Stephanie was an occasional study partner and nothing more.

When Stephanie rounded the corner, she almost ran over the very woman she had just been thinking about. "Oh, hey. Mrs. Pontillo, I'm so sorry I wasn't paying attention … kind of lost in thought. Are you looking for the boys?"

"No, no, Stephanie, I know exactly where MY boys are. You are just the person I was looking for."

"Really, looking for me? Why's that?"

"Johnnie's caught up with his brother. I know you were going to study today, so I'll give you a ride to our house."

The last thing Stephanie wanted to do was get in a car with Johnnie's mother; everything in her body was telling her to run as fast as she could in the opposite direction. *Does she know about me and Johnnie? Does she know ... oh, God, I'm pregnant? How could she?*

Only her closest friends knew about the baby.

Whatever it was, she was creeped out. *I'm going to spend the rest of my life around her once I'm married, might as well embrace the craziness.* She smiled. "Sure, thanks."

Making their way to the car, Stephanie slid into the passenger seat. Next to her, Mrs. Pontillo rummaged through her purse for the keys, started the car, and pulled out of the parking lot and headed home.

They drove in silence.

Maybe I'm being paranoid. The woman's seemed to have had a turnaround—thank God.

They arrived at the Pontillo household. Stephanie and Mrs. Pontillo entered the house. "Why don't you go into the living room? Can I get you a drink?

"I would love some lemonade."

Two waiting-for-Johnnie minutes later. "Here you go. And how are your studies?"

"My grades are great. I'm ready for graduation." Stephanie took a long drink. "I have to admit, though, algebra would have been a complete bear if it wasn't for your son."

"Imagine he has. My Johnnie is a very smart boy, but if you think you're going to be able to open your legs and take my Johnnie away, and away from his destiny, you had better think again."

"What do you mean, Mrs. Pontillo? I haven't done

anything to hurt Johnnie. In fact, I love him."

"Love? I love that boy. I have done *everything* for him and his brother, keeping them out of harm's way. And I will continue to do so. They have a destiny."

Stephanie's eyes darted around the room, there was no way to escape. *Thinkthinkthink*. "Can you excuse me? I need to use the restroom."

"Sure, I'm not going anywhere. Besides, we still need to get rid of that abomination you're carrying."

Stephanie stopped halfway across the room. "How did you know? Please, Mrs. Pontillo. I'm begging you. Don't do this." Stephanie's legs started to grow weak.

"Nonsense, the arrangements are already made. We will take care of your little problem. Then everything will be fine."

On cue, Andy Pontillo moved to Stephanie's side. Before she could scream, a rag covered her mouth and nose and Stephanie Smith's world went black.

CHAPTER TWENTY-SEVEN

ROBERTO DOS VIDAS was pulling the barn doors shut, when from behind he heard stone and dirt crunching under the weight of a car. He turned, expecting to see Jessica and Eric approaching, and was taken aback at the sight of a Hurley County Sheriff's Department patrol car.

Andrew Pontillo was behind the wheel.

It was the first time in 30-years that Roberto had laid eyes on the man, but he knew it was him. Large and imposing, even seated in a car. The years had not been kind to the sheriff, but they hadn't reduced the gravitas he exuded, either.

Pontillo exited the patrol car. "Dos Vidas, as I live and breathe. That's *you*, isn't it! I have to say, I'm not too surprised to see you here. Where have you been hiding yourself all these years?"

Roberto walked toward Pontillo with his hand out when he suddenly stopped. His smile disappeared, and the color drained from his face. "It's been a long time, Andy. I've … uh, been in Canada." Noticing the sheriff's hand was resting on his sidearm, Roberto shook his index finger. "I haven't done anything wrong, sheriff?"

"*Wrong?*" Pontillo pulled out the Glock. "No, not unless you consider being party to the murder of my brother and subsequent cover-up 30-years ago, wrong. You and the Archers ruined our lives."

"Murder?" Roberto's voice went up an octave. "What are you talking about? You know full well the way things happened in Mexico. No one murdered your brother. He was reckless, he was dangerous, he was—"

Pontillo was yelling and jabbing his gun in Roberto's direction. "How dare you? How dare you stand there and taint my brother's life? We had plans, we had it all figured out … I was on my way down to Mexico; we were going to be gods among men, and you and the Archers ruined IT.

"All your team was supposed to do was come down and remove the artifacts you found. Declare the site clear. You couldn't even do that!"

"That is all we were going to do. Then the craziness started. Elena and I got sick. The other chamber, the island … you know all this." Roberto slowly made his way, hands in the air, towards the house. "We didn't know of our lineage at the time, or how it would affect things. In our encounter with Difatos, your brother just ran off half-cocked."

"Stop with the lies and stop moving. I may be old, but I'm not dumb, and, truth be told, I'm still a damn good shot. You won't make it."

Both men were startled by the sudden sound of an approaching car. It was Eric and Jessica. Pontillo glanced over. Roberto used the distraction to get in the house. He was not fast enough. The sheriff turned back to see Roberto starting to run. He squeezed off two rounds. The first bullet ripped through Roberto's side. The force of the impact spun him in time for the second round to penetrate his right shoulder blade.

He crumbled to the ground.

€RIC COULDN'T BELIEVE what they saw as he and Jessica made their way up the drive. Eric pointed to Roberto. Before he could motion for Jessica to head over to the man, she had already taken off.

Eric made a beeline for Pontillo.

Backing away, Pontillo swung his weapon in Eric's direction.

Eric had instinctively drawn his own firearm. He stopped in his tracks. "What the hell, Andy?"

"Take that gun and lay it on the ground. Nothing funny, Eric, or I will not hesitate to put one *right* in your damn skull."

"Okay, okay, whatever you say, listen, I don't know what's bothering you, but I'm sure we can work it out." Moving slow, Eric put his gun on the ground—

"*I'm sure we can work it out*, huh? Right out of the sacred manual."

—and made his way to Jessica and Roberto. Pontillo kept his gun trained on the trio across the driveway. Roberto lay wincing in pain. Jessica's eyes met Eric's and he could tell it wasn't good.

A nauseating sticky-sweet smell of decay suddenly filled the air. The twins looked up and saw a hideous creature standing behind Andy Pontillo. Difatos had made his presence known. Eric's immediate feeling of fear quickly turned to *fear*, with the first dealing with the nightmare of this bizarre situation with a man whom he loved, but the next, with the nightmare of what was standing beside his adopted uncle.

Then Eric's fears morphed into confusion.

He watched as a hushed exchange took place between Uncle Andy and Difatos. Pontillo, however, did not take his eyes off of Eric and his family. The beast, despite its horrific appearance looked unsteady, perhaps even weakened.

Jessica let out a small cry.

Eric: "What is it? What's wrong?"

"Pain shooting through my body, damn."

"Pain? How bad?"

"Well, it doesn't tickle."

Summoning some bravery, Eric yelled, "What do you and your pet want with us, you sonuvabitch?"

"I want what I've had coming to me all these years. My kingdom. My godlike status your parents and dying uncle denied me and my brother all those years ago."

Roberto let out a small cry as he groped for Eric's hand. He guided it to the small of his back. Eric felt the grip of the weapon he had left with Roberto, pulled the gun out, and concealed it behind his injured uncle.

"You hear me, kids? Your family owes and I'm collecting!"

As the last syllable escaped Pontillo's mouth, Eric brought the Beretta around and started firing, his target lower-center, and then stitching up—his finger squeezing and squeezing and squeezing….

Pontillo dove to the ground.

But Eric wasn't aiming at him, but at Difatos.

The rounds slammed into the center of the monster's chest and upward. Eric hoped he had hit a major organ. Center Mass. The initial hits would have been a kill on a human.

The ancient god roared.

His clawed hand reached for its chest at the same time it wrapped its other slick, black scaly arm around Andy Pontillo. The sheriff had gotten back up. "I will have what's rightfully mine, and Difatos will be the GOD-KING."

Difatos chanted in a low moan, and in an instant, they were

MAINTAINING HIS SHOOTER'S stance, Eric scanned the vicinity. Convinced that Pontillo and Difatos were gone, he turned his full attention to Jessica and Roberto. He looked to be in bad shape. Jessica had already put a call into 9-1-1. She applied pressure to the wound on the right side of his abdomen. He had all the signs of shock: shallow breathing, rapid and weak pulse, and moist skin.

Eric ran to his car and retrieved a first-aid kit from his trunk and brought it back.

As he approached, Jessica spoke, her voice trembling, "I can only find one wound, but I know he was hit twice. It's what spun him around as he was going down."

Dropping to his knees, Eric opened his med-bag and pulled out a pressure bandage. "Keep the pressure on while I roll him onto his side." Coming up to her knees, Jessica kept her spread-out hands on the blood-soaked wound, as Eric maneuvered her father to his uninjured side. Next, Eric opened up his pressure bandage. "Remove your hands." Eric jammed the bandage into place, and then with Jessica's help, lifting Roberto's upper-body, got the dangling wraps snaked around the man's torso and pulled taut. Once done, Eric grabbed his second bandage and put it on top of the first one, pulled it open even wider than the first, and tied it into place. Then he quickly grabbed a few pieces of nearby firewood and placed it under Roberto's ankles, loosened his belt, and unbuttoned his jeans.

"Eric, what the hell was all of that? Pontillo and Difatos, how does that happen?"

Eric shook his head. "I have no idea. The information about John Pontillo in the journal pages we received from Dr. Dirk struck me as odd. But there is no way I expected this. Just add it to the long list of kicks to the gut that we've been the recipients of the last few days."

THE EMS TRUCK and a patrol car with Deputy Tom Deering behind the wheel simultaneously arrived at the Archer farm. The paramedics immediately made their way to Roberto. The deputy followed, stopping to check out Pontillo's patrol car sitting in the driveway, before making his way to Eric, where he stood with one arm wrapped around Deering's fellow deputy.

"Eric, Jessica, what's going on here?" He pointed

at the injured man on the ground, getting tended to. "Who's this? And where is the sheriff?"

Eric squeezed Jessica close, kissed her on the head, and motioned for her to stay by the paramedics working on Roberto. He walked a few feet away and motioned for Deering to follow.

Eric strode to the spot where Pontillo and the demon had been standing. He knelt down and began to scan the ground, running his fingers through the dirt and stone.

Deering knelt next to him. "What're you looking for?"

"Blood of an ancient god. Have any idea what that might look like?"

The deputy took his hat off and scratched his head. "Excuse me?"

"Tom, I have to tell you something that's going to sound very unbelievable." Eric held out his palms to his side. "But I swear to you I *am* telling the truth. Jessica knows all of this, too, and you know how she is. She wouldn't lie to you, and neither would I."

Tom's face wrinkled into the most incredulous look. A look Eric had seen Tom make many, many times. "You wouldn't, huh? I seem to remember a certain night on patrol when you sent me on a wild goose chase after some high school kids, supposedly partying in a field off Roberts Road. It turned out to be a herd of beef cattle. I had to throw those shoes away, by the way." He started to tick off a list on his fingers. "Or how about the time you had me climb the Portland water tower to talk down a jumper, and it turned out to be a department store mannequin that *you* put there? Or how about—"

"Alright, alright," Eric conceded. "Pranks are pranks, but I have never *lied* to you. Not even when you asked my opinion about that dog of a girl you dated a few years ago."

"That dog, as you call her, is MY WIFE *Becca*, and I thought you said that stuff 'cause you were jealous."

Eric grinned and felt his face getting flush. "Nope, never lied to you about my thoughts. Sorry, pal."

Tom Deering raised one eyebrow, doing his best Dwayne The Rock Johnson impersonation. "Just what is this that you think I won't believe?"

Eric proceeded to give the CliffNotes version of the whole mess and how they tied into the events of the last few days.

"You're absolutely right. I don't believe a word you said. My sensible mind and our history will not allow for such a thing. However, your saving grace is Jessica. She would never go along with this, if it wasn't the God's honest truth."

"Well at least I have *that* going for me. I'm glad all of those years in the department together meant something."

"Eric, buddy, I'm just pulling your leg." Deering smirked and slapped Eric on the back. "But I'm going to have to talk to Jessica first."

Jessica walked up to the pair. "Talk about what, Tom?" She turned to Eric. "They're transporting Dad to Forbes. They are still trying to stabilize him; right now it's touch and go."

Eric sighed and looked skyward. "Man, do we need to put an end to this thing and fast. Before anyone else ends up dead."

The three officers discussed how to best keep this

most recent event under wraps, and what might be the next best course of action. They decided to take Pontillo's patrol car back to the station; Tom assumed control of the situation in the county. While they were gone, he would keep Eric and Jessica informed of any odd occurrences.

Tom Deering left to see what he could do to run interference and keep alert for any strange events. Hopefully locate Pontillo. Eric and Jessica stayed to get the artifacts hidden by Edward Archer. They needed to work quickly, so they would have time to catch their flight to Belize out of Buffalo International in roughly eight hours, and then on to Costa Maya to meet Eliseo Gomez.

They walked towards the grain silo behind the barn where the stone box and knife were supposed to be.

"You know, if I hadn't talked you into stopping and making the reservations right after we left the college, if we had come right back here … Dad might not be clinging to life in the back of an ambulance."

"Hey, I thought the same thing the night I came into town when my … when *our* parents were killed. Remember what the book says?"

"We can't turn back time."

"That's right. Hell, all three of us could be dead with Difatos and Pontillo running loose, with no one but a crippled 80-year-old professor to stop them. We probably saved Roberto's life by arriving when we did. Pontillo didn't get off a clear shot because we distracted him."

"You're probably right. You *are* right." Jessica gently squeezed Eric's hand. "It's time we both show some of our Archer/Benitez/Wolownik—or whatever we should call ourselves—resolve and get this plan kicked into high gear."

INTERLUDE IV

THEY WERE STILL in their suits, top buttons undone and ties loosened. They had not uttered a word at the funeral home. They hadn't needed to. They each knew what the other felt.

They were relieved.

They had finally buried their bitch of a mother.

Her reign of terror was finished, which in the grand scheme wasn't of too much comfort. Their emotional cicatrix was way too deep and settled. Their father had passed away when they were very young. They didn't know any of the stories about their mother's hand in his death until their early teens, and even then they didn't dare confront her about it.

Andy Pontillo leaned back in his chair, fingers laced atop his head, wondering where his brother came up with his ideas. John sat across from him at their mother's kitchen table, back straight, forearms flat to the Formica, fingers drumming as he waited for Andy's response. John raised both eyebrows, pressed his lips together, and suddenly banged his knuckles.

"Explain this again. Why do I need to go to Mexico—with you?"

John spun the Lazy Susan on the table. "There is an old-ass manuscript that tells of an old-ass god-king that will manifest itself and rule over—"

"RULE OVER THE WORLD." Andy grabbed the Lazy Susan, and spun it in the other direction. "I know all this. Whether it's real or not is something different."

"I believe it. And you believe it, too. You're just wanting to give mom the finger. You have to help, Difatos needs us—*both* of us. Plus, what've we got to lose, besides everything, as in *every*-thing?"

Andy shook his head. "And just be under someone else's control?"

"It wouldn't be like that, and you know it. We'd be his kings."

"We're finally free, John. We don't need any gods or curses."

"Trust me, Andy. No one and I mean *no one* will ever have control over us again, if we do this."

"The only person who ever did is where she should be, rotting in the ground. And even if Hell doesn't want her, there's no way she is coming back. She can't bother us again. We are finally free."

John leaned in. "She may be gone. But there is always someone else, someone who tries to control you. I'm talking about never having to answer to anyone again. I'm talking about being gods among men."

CHAPTER TWENTY-EIGHT

THE PAIR REAPPEARED deep in the woods after a second jump. Pontillo fell to the ground and vomited. He hated teleportation. He looked up to see Difatos tending to his wounds.

Pontillo approached the being.

"That weapon harmed me! Their *ki* was there for the taking, their blood, the power of their lineage would've been mine."

"Listen, Difatos, aren't you a god?" Pontillo answered with a bit of venom. "Don't glare at me like that. Those bullets can't kill you. Merely flesh wounds. Besides, a modern weapon hardly fits into the ceremony that could banish you. I gathered the blood-ancients, and they're close to retrieving all of the artifacts. You still need me as much as I need you.

"Okay, okay, let's not fall apart now. We've both waited a long time for what is within our grasp. You a bit longer than me, but still." Pontillo had taken to checking and reloading his Glock. "I think it's time we pay the good Dr. Dirk a visit. I'm sure he has some wonderful insights as to what the twins may do next."

Difatos howled as he dug out the last of the bullets Eric had put in its chest. "Yes, let's finish this and we will both enjoy our reaping."

PART IV
VOYAGE OF DISCOVERY

CHAPTER TWENTY-NINE

THE SLAB OF concrete concealing the limestone box, necklace, and jade knife slid back into place with a loud thud. Eric collapsed to his hands and knees, breathing hard. Edward Archer had dug a 10-foot-deep, six-by-six chamber under the silo to house the artifacts.

Outside, Jessica had finished packing all the collected artifacts in the crate from Dr. Dirk. She was hammering the last of the nails into the top as Eric emerged from the silo, wiping his hands, brow, and the back of his neck with the T-shirt he had been wearing.

"The old man sure didn't make that easy, did he?" Eric remarked. It had taken several hours to uncover the exact spot where the concrete lid was, and then extract the artifacts. "These things better be worth the trouble."

Jessica threw her brother another T from the car. "Just hope this Eliseo Gomez person is as helpful as the professor let on. That chest is covered in glyphs. There *has* to be useful information on it. I can't believe it's all just decorative."

"There's that look again, Jessica."

"What look?"

"Spill it. There's something you're not telling."

"You're my brother for all of 15-minutes and all of a sudden you can tell when I'm hiding something, is that what it is, as if you know me?"

Eric moved to hug her, and she started to rebuff him, when she changed her mind and welcomed the comfort. Eric patted her back. "I was going to chalk it up to masterful detective skills and my ability to read people. But, those weren't on display as far as Pontillo was concerned."

Jessica stepped back. "All right, it's the box. I get the same burning sensation through my body that I had when Difatos appeared. And I had flashes of being able to translate a few of the glyphs on the lid."

"So, my brotherly instinct was spot on." Eric snapped his fingers and pointed at Jessica. "I'm sure it means something. We need to get down there and meet Mr. Gomez. Be nice to know what we're up against, especially under our time crunch. There's a reason for Difatos to appear after all this time."

"I wonder if we're missing the 800-pound gorilla."

"What would that be?" Grabbing a bottled water held out by Jessica, Eric rinsed off his hands and took three long gulps.

"This *is* the year of the end of the long Mayan calendar. The end date isn't until December, but what if this is the beginning?"

"If you would've said that to me last week, I would have hauled you off to the psych ward for an evaluation. Of course, last week I didn't know I had a twin, and had never emptied a mag into an ancient Mayan god before. So, anything is possible. That kind of information is what we need from our man down in

Mexico."

They loaded the crate into the trunk of Eric's car.

SITTING ON HER couch, looking at the box of salvaged mementos taken from the Archer's—*My parents. Oh, God, this whole time I had parents*—house, Jessica was glad Eric was in the shower. She needed this bit of time to be alone.

Then she stopped.

Closed the box.

She'd have to look through the stuff later, the photos and bric-a-brac and keepsakes. For now, the only thing on her mind was her daddy. She need to get to him, to stand by his side—*Fuck, he's in in-ten-sive fucking care*—to comfort him like he's always been there to comfort her, to guide her, to teach and bless and just fucking be there ... and she could see it, so much of it, him teaching her to ride a bike, to swim, to drive, her going to prom, and how proud he'd been, and now all this, and the look on his face when she'd graduated *again-and-again-and-again*, from high school, college, the academy, and then all this, all this bullshit, and him *poofing* into an uncle, which was a bunch of crap, 'cause he was her dad, and always would be, her daddy—her rock.

Then Eric walked into the room and her sorrowful trance was broken.

"Hey, ready when you are." Eric noticed that Jessica was standing there in the middle of the room. Walking over, he squeezed her shoulders, bending his neck a bit to make human contact. She looked to the floor. Eric lifted Jessica's chin. "What is it?"

As she brought her eyes up, Eric could see the tears ready to burst.

"It's nothing, just thinking too much." She wiped away a tear before it could flow down her cheek.

Eric held his gaze. "We're going to get through this. Roberto is going to get through this. There is a reason why this happened the way it did. Everything we've known to be true in our lives, not the minutiae, not the details, but the really true stuff, is still with us. And for me, just a bit ago, I thought I was orphaned, but, instead, I've gained new family. I have you and Roberto and I'm going to fight like hell to keep it that way. I'm not going to lose any more family to this *Thing*."

"I'm getting sick saying this, but I know you're right."

"Knocking the doubt outta that head o' yours?"

"I guess. Just promise if you see me like that again, you'll give me a swift boot to the keister."

"As long as you do the same for me. Now let's get to the hospital."

CHAPTER THIRTY

TOM DEERING ANSWERED his cell on the first ring. "Deputy Deering?"

"Hey, Tom, it's Eric. Jessica wanted me to call while she finished getting ready. How are things down at the hospital?"

"Your uncle's still in recovery. Surgery was tricky, something about the bullet being lodged close to the heart. The doctors, though, are confident he'll pull through. I don't think Jessica is going to be able to see him before you guys leave."

"That's not going to sit well. We'll still stop by on the way out of town, anyway. What about Pontillo or his wife?"

Deering let out a bruised sigh. "Nada. Patrols have gone by the house, but it's deserted. His patrol car is still back at the station and he hasn't called in."

"And he won't. Whatever you do, don't confront him, because that thing won't be far behind. And even if it doesn't show, remember, the man's my Uncle Andy, and he bore down on me. Observe and report and wait for us to get back from Mexico."

"Don't have to tell me twice. The sheriff's intimidating enough on his own. But you know as well as I do, if there's innocents in danger, I'll have to act."

"Stay frosty. We'll see you in a few minutes. I think Jessica is almost done."

Eric stood tapping the cell phone to his lips, thinking out loud, "God, please don't let them have to confront Pontillo and Difatos while we're gone. We don't even know if we can handle it with the artifacts, and these guys have nothing."

Jessica entered the room, overnight bag slung over a shoulder. "Talking to yourself?"

Turning with a smile, he tossed the phone in her direction and started to walk out of the room. "C'mon, let's get to Forbes."

CHAPTER THIRTY-ONE

ELISEO GOMEZ WAS intrigued by the correspondence received from his old professor.

Newly-discovered Mayan artifacts were always exciting. "Discoveries" outside of Mexico were made every so often, as pieces illegally removed from the country popped up in private collections. Sometimes they made their way to museums and were turned back over to Mexican authorities. The second bit of news, however, almost made him jump out of his skin. An un-translated manuscript was like finding the Holy Grail.

He couldn't wait to see it and meet the people Dr. Dirk had sent with the items. He knew the professor would not be able to make the trip himself. He hadn't heard from his old mentor, since leaving as the man's T.A. and taking up the position of Assistant Curator of the Yucatan Museum of Natural History.

Born in a small village nestled between the many Mayan ruins, Eliseo became something of an expert on Mayan culture and even worked for a tourism company as the youngest guide on record. Eventually, his family moved to Alaska, when a position opened for his father on one of the big fishing vessels, similar to the ones on

The Deadliest Catch.

In a stroke of fortune, one of the preeminent scholars on Mayan history taught at the University of Anchorage. Never lacking confidence, Eliseo visited Dr. Dirk and explained his background to the man. The professor, so impressed with Eliseo's knowledge that he became his academic advisor, had guided Eliseo from the enrollment process straight through to his appointment as a teaching assistant.

Now here he was, many years later, Assistant Curator, of all things, and part owner of The Native Pride Travel and Tourism Company.

But the thing still lived for was the rush gotten from the discovery of new Mayan artifacts and decoding their puzzles. Friends wondered when he was going to settle down. *Settle down?* It wasn't that he didn't have an interest in women, or they in him. Quite the contrary. Here, he fit the classic bill of tall, dark, and employed.

He enjoyed being a workaholic.

It got things done.

CHAPTER THIRTY-TWO

JESSICA ALWAYS ASSOCIATED hospitals with healing and blessed events, like the birth of a child, a place where good things happened. That was until she started her career in law enforcement. Now, whenever she was near a hospital, the only images that came to mind were blood, broken hearts, and shattered lives.

As she and Eric approached Forbes Memorial, she felt her anxiety rise like a cascading wave.

Eric parked the car and they made their way across the crowded lot, weaving in and out of the rows of cars waiting for their drivers to return with looks of joy or sorrow. As they took a few steps onto the sidewalk, the automatic doors slid open. A silent welcome into what in Jessica's mind was a hostile environment. The medicinal, sterile smell reminded her this place could be the savior or the destroyer of the man she had grown up knowing as her father. She and Eric strode shoulder to shoulder down the corridor toward the Intensive Care Unit, with her fully aware that conversations halted and eyes were averted as they passed. Despite best efforts to suppress the information, rumors had started to circulate about the events of the last few days, and news traveled fast in a small town like

Chadwick Bay.

They reached Roberto's room.

Jessica reached for the door handle and hesitated. She stared through the window of the door at the motionless figure lying on the bed. She could hardly believe who it was and what had happened.

Eric stood behind and placed his hands on her shoulders. Gently squeezing them. "Go ahead, it will help him to hear your voice."

Jessica took a deep breath, blew it out, and pushed down on the door handle and walked in. The hiss of the ventilator and the beeping of the heart monitor resonated in the otherwise silent room. The number of tubes and wires attached to Roberto's body rendered him a surreal medical marionette. The only movement emanating from the bed was the slow and shallow rise and fall of his chest.

Pulling up a chair beside her father, Jessica sat, resting her elbows on the bed, fingers clasped as though she were about to pray. She spoke calmly, like she knew Roberto would want her to. "You were right about the professor. But then, when aren't you, right? He really did help a lot. Eric and I need to go to Mexico to meet an ex-student of his. Things are moving in the right direction. I can feel it. We should only be gone a few days."

Her voice trailed off when she finally took a serious look at Roberto. She could hardly recognize the man she had grown up with. His skin was pale, face gaunt, and eyes accented by deep dark circles. "I don't care what has happened in the last two days. You are *always* going to be my father. Everything that makes me, *me*, is because of you. I'm only strong because of you. I know you can hear me." The dam had burst. Tears streamed down her face. "Everything is going to be all right. You just need to remember the same lessons you taught me."

She held Roberto's hand while stroking his forehead, and *whisss*-pered, "Benitez's don't give up. We don't back down. We find a way." She gritted her teeth, then *whisss*-pered more forcefully, "And you *will* find a way back to me, back to me and Eric."

She laid her head next to Roberto's arm and allowed herself to sit there and silently cry.

INTERLUDE V

THE FLIGHT TO Mexico was fine. Even the ride through the backwater towns was tolerable, but hiking through the god-forsaken rain forest, that's where Andy Pontillo drew the line.

"What the hell are we doing out here, John?" With a stream of profanity, he swung his machete into a nearby tree. "I'm sick of this heat." He smacked himself on the back of the neck, squishing some tiny winged-monstrosity. "And these Frankenstein bugs. Damn it. This is not my idea of a vacation."

John was ahead of him on what could only optimistically be called a path. He stopped and took a drink out of his canteen. "Stop being a bitch! You've done nothing but complain since this morning. We're about a quarter of a mile from something that is going to change our lives forever."

"You keep saying that."

"And you keep denying it. Why? 'Cause of Mom? She's gone. And good riddance. Bitch was a monster, and I loved pissing on her grave as much as you did. But what she never was, was a liar. You've read her journal, handled her research just like me, and it's all led us to this place and time. We didn't survive that ogre for nothing. It's time to take our due."

The foliage parted.

Andy's jaw dropped.

Two large glyph-covered pillars rose out of the

ground. Between them were half a dozen stone steps leading up to what looked like an altar. As they approached the structure, Andy could feel what could only be described as waves of heat and cold pulsing through him. His brother smiled, and punched him on the shoulder before motioning for him to move to the front of the pillar on his right.

"Oh, John, you were right. I was such a bitch."

"Soak in the energy, Andy, just let it in and be happy." John placed his palms on two sigil-less spots on the pillar in front of him. Andy did the same. After a few moments, their bodies began to shake. They started to read the glyphs out loud. They understood them and the directions they gave. In a trance, they moved in unison up the steps to the altar. As they knelt before the raised stone slab, they removed the machetes from their sheaths. Taking hold of the hilts in their right hands, they pulled the hardened steel blades across their forearms. The cuts were deep enough to start blood pouring out of the wounds. As they chanted in a low tone, two small circular spaces opened in front of them. They placed their arms up to their elbows in the apertures and let the stone close around their arms. Blood flowed to somewhere, to somewhere … beautiful.

Andy looked at John, and he at him, and the both of them smiled wide, as they each saw the other's milky, swirling, shiny black eyes.

Moments went by, hours, maybe years, and the top of the altar—*CRAAACK*—split with a loud crack and the sound of stone grinding, and busting, and fighting, against stone. From their knees, they could not see into the opening. They did, however, witness a slab ascending from the center. When everything stopped moving, their arms were released.

John was the first to stand.

Andy sat back on his heels, motionless with incredulity.

"Andy, get up here! You have to see this!"

Andy pulled himself up next to his brother and stared at the stone slab. He shook his head. "How … how can I read this? It's not possible."

"And to think you doubted? This is incredible. Don't you see now that I was right? We're are on the right path. This *is* happening."

Andy stretched out his arm, ran his fingers across the carved glyphs, and read:

THE EMISSARIES WILL OPEN THE GATE IN THE CHAMBER OF CONVERGENCE. ENEMIES WILL HOWL. INNOCENTS WILL DIE. DIFATOS WILL LIVE AGAIN.

FOLLOW THE PATH OF THE LOWLANDS TO THE MEETING OF THE GREAT AND BOUNTIFUL TREES. THERE YOU WILL FIND THE KEYS TO HIS UNLOCKING. ONLY THOSE WITH THE VISION, ONLY THE SACRED TWO WILL COMPLETE THE DUTIES.

THE FEW WILL BE FOUND ON AN ISLAND FILLED WITH THE MAJESTY OF DIFATOS AND ALL HIS KINGDOM HAS TO OFFER. THE EMISSARIES WILL RISE.

REWARDED FOR THEIR SACRIFICE, THEY WILL RULE OVER THIS REALM FOREVERMORE.

As the last word slipped off Andy's tongue, he and his brother looked at each and bumped fists.

CHAPTER
THIRTY-THREE

MEMORIES CAME RUSHING back to William Dirk as the unmistakable smell of sweetness mixed with decay filled his office. He didn't need to look around. Difatos had come to exact his revenge.

The professor calmly opened the top left drawer of the antique oval partners desk in front of him. Inside was a small tin. He removed the single white pill from it and bit down hard, releasing the fine white powder into his mouth. He picked up the coffee mug used earlier to hold down the edge of the maps displayed for Eric and Jessica. A figure emerged from around the corner.

"So, you're the famous snobby prof who *murdered* my brother."

"Andy Pontillo, I presume?"

Pontillo nodded.

"My dear man, you have things mistaken. John's own actions caused his demise—and at the hands of that abomination you prostrate before." The professor jumped a bit in his chair; he wasn't sure if it was the effects of the pill or the sight of Difatos appearing behind Pontillo.

Difatos growled as he moved closer. "I remember

your stench as well, old man."

"We just came for information." Pontillo took off his hat and played with the brim. "This can be easy or hard. Don't try anything stupid. We can be as civilized about this as you want, doctor, I may even accept a cup of coffee." Pontillo pointed his hat towards the Professor.

"Oh, this?" Dr. Dirk held up the mug. "It's nothing, just washing down a little preventative medicine, provided by the kindest of apothecaries. The kind used in all of the old spy movies. Once I—

"Fuck me."

"—smelled that distinct stench, I knew Difatos was here. I'll be damned if after all I've been through, anyone else determines my fate. The best thing about this," he held up his mug, "parting salutation, is that it works quite quickly."

COUGH COUGH

He struggled to bring a plaid handkerchief to his mouth as his muscles started to spasm, and was able to wipe away a bit of the frothy bile that had formed around his lips. "Yes, quite quickly. Enjoy your time in the darkness for ... I am traveling into ... the light." His voice got weaker, gasping for air with each word. By the time he finished his sentence, the professor was slumped in his wheelchair, eyes staring.

DIFATOS SNORTED IN defiance.

Pontillo punched the wall next to him, then turned to the ancient god and pointed his finger. "And don't *you* say a thing. How was I supposed to know the old coot would have the rocks to commit suicide?"

"This does not help us find the blood-ancients and the implements we seek. We can gain nothing from this disgusting human husk."

"Whoa, hold on a minute. Just because the old man is gone doesn't mean he can't be of any help." Pontillo moved to the dusty underused PC in the back of the room. The professor was still signed in to the university network. A few minutes of rooting around the computer, Pontillo determined that Dr. Dirk had arranged the paperwork for a large crate to be shipped to Belize. He also learned from an e-mail that he was in contact with one Eliseo Gomez. A check of his e-addy gave the sheriff all the information he needed. Eric and Jessica would be heading down to the Yucatan. if they weren't there already. Pontillo turned to Difatos. "It looks as though you're going home. The twins seem to think the old stodgy doctor found someone who can help unlock the secrets of the glyphs and weapons. How nice of 'em to gather in one spot, and somewhere we were going to end up, anyway."

Difatos began to pace.

"Not that I'm looking forward to it, but will you be able to teleport both of us to Mexico?"

"Yes."

"If that's the case, let's head back to my house where I can gather what I need, contact my people in Campeche, and then we can POOF. I'm sure Julia must be home by now."

Without a saying a word, Difatos moved closer to Pontillo, wrapped his arm around him, and in an instant, they were

CHAPTER THIRTY-FOUR

"LADIES AND GENTLEMEN, we have just been cleared to land at the Philip S.W. Goldson International Airport." The pilot's voice crackled over the intercom. "Please make sure one last time your seatbelt is securely fastened. The flight attendants are currently passing around the cabin to make a final approach check and pick up any remaining cups and glasses. Let me be the first to welcome you to Belize, *Mother Nature's Best Kept Secret*."

"Mother nature's best kept secret, huh? I probably would've gone with *Belize it or not* as my slogan." Eric eased his seat into the proverbial upright position.

Jessica turned her head, dropped her chin, and looked at Eric through her brow. "Really? *Belize it or not*, how very punny of you."

"Punny? Did you say punny?" Eric let out a laugh. "Now you're starting to catch on, sis." He gave Jessica a light tap on the arm.

AFTER A SOFT touchdown, the plane taxied to a

stop. There were a few more informational announcements, and then the mad rush to the overhead compartments and de-boarding the aircraft. Eric scanned the passengers for anyone who looked out of place. He wondered if they had been followed. Most of the crowd was made up of young professionals in their late 20s and early 30s. They looked like they had money to burn and were eager to do it in a tropical paradise.

"Let's not fight the crowd. We still have an hour and a half ride to Costa Maya before getting to Mr. Gomez."

They made their way down to BAGGAGE CLAIM and Eric spotted the signature red and blue double A's with the eagle between them emblazoned on the window and door of the American Airlines office. Their precious crate would be arriving there for pick up rather than being thrown onto the regular conveyor belt.

They took their claim check to the desk and the large crate from Dr. Dirk was soon again in their possession. It took almost 20-minutes for the crate to arrive at the office. Eric, talking little, was now in full police mode. He noticed Jessica had done the same, scanning the crowd and on high alert for anyone suspicious. Once the crate arrived, Eric pulled it and their backpacks on a four-wheeled flatbed provided by the airport. They needed to find transportation to Costa Maya.

As they emerged from the terminal into the thick warm morning air, a large, dark, curly-haired, barrel-chested man dressed in the loudest Hawaiian shirt bore down on them. Eric instinctively got into a defensive stance. As the bull of a man approached, he smiled widely and put his hands up, waving his palms back and forth. He started hitting himself in the chest with one hand and spoke in a thick accent: "Paco ... Paco."

"I have no idea what to make of this immense native man approaching us. Any guess? Friend or foe?"

Out of the side of his mouth, without taking his eyes off the man, Eric whispered, "Did he just say *taco*? Is he trying to sell us tacos?"

"*Paco.*"

The man stopped in front of the pair. "Paco take ... Paco take, come ... Senor Eliseo."

Jessica questioned the man in near flawless Spanish. "Senor Eliseo? Do you mean you're going to take us to Eliseo Gomez? Do you work for him at the tour company?"

He nodded. "Eliseo send Paco. Paco take you Eliseo. Come." He took the handles of the cart and started off in the direction he had come from.

"I guess we're going with him." Eric jutted a thumb in the man's direction. "So Paco's his name. And where did that Spanish come from?"

Jessica started after their new acquaintance. "Good assumption, detective, and remember, I spent three years down here in the Peace Corps. I picked up the language and worked on it since then."

"In Hurley county, that's got to come in handy. I wonder if Paco will let us stop for some tacos. Kind of hungry after that flight."

"You can think of food at a time like this?"

"Can't help it if I'm hungry."

"Jeez...."

As they approached Paco, he was already loading the crate into the back of a late '90s Subaru Forester. Painted on the side of the door was *The Native Pride Travel and Tourism Company* with its company logo, a jaguar paw print behind the name. Paco came around to the passenger side and escorted Jessica to the front seat and opened the door. He waved his hand in the direction of the back seat, motioning to Eric.

"Guess I know where I am at on the pecking order." Eric climbed into the SUV. Jessica turned, looked over her shoulder, smiled and chuckled.

Paco wasted no time taking off. Quicker than understanding Paco's broken English, they were out of the city and traveling on the Northern Highway.

As they traveled, their very accommodating driver explained their surroundings and his background to Jessica, who in turn translated for Eric. Born and raised in Costa Maya, he had for the last six years worked for Eliseo Gomez, who treated him as family. He enjoyed it because he got to tour the countryside and meet many people. He was the company's official driver, delivery man, and informant.

Not only did he know all the shortcuts and streets in the eastern half of the Yucatan, but he knew which people to trust and which to avoid. Day or night, he knew the safest places in the city. He was not happy about the increase in tourism over the last few years, but it was a double-edged sword. More people meant more work for the company, but it also meant more change for the sleepy little fishing village. It already had docks for a few of the smaller cruise lines. Paco hoped that Costa Maya never reached the concrete nightmare status of Cancun, which had become a commercialized American tourist trap. Tall, modern buildings ruined the beauty.

He said they had lost the soul of Mexico in gaining all of the excess of America, all the things that wasn't Costa Maya. He was buoyed by the fact the tourism board in the government had made plans to push ecotourism, hoping to bring in divers, bird watchers, nature lovers, and all those travelers who love the Caribbean, but hate the ugly commercialism to the northeast.

The trip from Belize City to Costa Maya was rife with exotic landscape. Jessica picked up a tour book from the middle console. She started to read selected pieces of information. "The Yucatan is home to a subtropical climate, which includes a hot and a rainy season. The warmest weather reaches into the mid-80s and bottoms in the 60s. There's no shortage of amazing examples of native flora and fauna, from Mangrove swamps to pristine rainforests. Many small farms struggle to keep from being choked off by the fast-growing plants."

Eric asked about an upcoming large body of water.

"Must be the Hondo River. Says here it makes up miles of border between Belize and Mexico. We should be coming up to a Unites States-sponsored military drug checkpoint."

"Another fine use of American money in the decades' old war on drugs. When's the government going to cut the cord on that loser of an initiative?"

They came to the checkpoint and crossed without issue.

The next town they drove through was the City of Santa Elena. At the mention of their mother's name,

Jessica turned her shoulders, reached back, and squeezed Eric's hand.

The tension eased when Paco made mention to Jessica that the town was the home of the famous *Laguna Negra* or *Black Lagoon.*

Jessica confessed to knowing it was here that the name of the legendary creature from the old Universal Studios monster movie came from.

Eric: "We're in the middle of our own horror show, minus the cheap special effects and rubber suits."

Real blood had been spilled and the danger they faced was grave. As the three of them turned onto Federal Highway 186, they entered long stretches of desolate rainforest.

Along the way, howler monkeys shrieked at their arrival. They caught glimpses of a few cat-like animals meandering along the road. After consulting the tour book, Jessica was sure they were margays or ocelots. One had even ventured across the highway in front of them. Paco mentioned they were two of five indigenous cat species in the Yucatan, the sacred jaguar being the most well-known.

Another turn took them to Mexico Highway 307. They passed through several small towns, Xul ha, Buena Vista, and Pedro Antonio Santos. They stopped at a PeMex in Bacalar, which was the largest town they had seen, where they filled up on gas and some *authentic* Mexican fast food.

After leaving Bacalar, Paco made a left onto a small, two-lane road. A green and white road sign with PUERTO COSTA MAYA and an arrow on it let them know they had arrived at their destination. Within minutes, they were pulling into an attached garage at the rear of *The Native Pride Travel and Tourism Company.*

As they exited the Subaru, they right away noticed Eliseo Gomez, looking every bit the part of a tour guide, with khaki shorts, hiking boots, and a knit two-button short-sleeved polo that bore the company's logo.

He met them with open arms. "Eric and Jessica, how nice to meet the both of you." He stopped when he laid eyes on Jessica, took her hand between his, and kissed the top of it. "Welcome to our little tropical paradise. Glad you made it here in one piece."

"That doesn't inspire confidence. Paco, here, says he's the best driver in the area."

Eliseo moved in closer to Eric and dropped his voice to a whisper, "Oh, Paco is an amazing driver. I was referring to any local trouble you might have had. There has been a suspicious car out across the street for several hours. I think someone knew you were coming here, my friend."

As Paco and Eliseo moved the crate into an office, Eric nonchalantly looked around and saw the suspect car and its passengers. He wracked his brain wondering how anyone could have known where he and Jessica were going. They had not told Tom Deering. Then he blurted, "Oh, my God!"

"What is it?" Jessica turned, saw the car, and felt a tingle run up her spine. "Oh, God, they got to Dr. Dirk."

"They got to Dr. Dirk."

Trying to be inconspicuous, Eric stood in place and stretched a bit from the long flight and car ride. As he did some trunk twists and stretched his arms, he glanced at the men in the car. He was sure one of them had taken out a cell phone. "The *suspicious* car Eliseo mentioned, who else could it be?"

"Do you really think Pontillo's got that long a reach? That much influence? How would he have people that he could contact down here on such short notice?"

"He's hanging out with a demon, anything's possible, plus, he used to vacation here all the time. I mean ALL the time. Every vacation he and Julia took was to the Yucatan." Eric cupped a palm over his face and rubbed his chin. He let out a small laugh. "It all makes sense now. He was researching, building a network. Trying to make sure this plan with Difatos came to fruition. He must have been bringing his wife here under the guise of a tropical vacation and continuing the work he and his brother had started."

"Unless she was in on it, too."

Eric hated to think of sweet Aunt Julia as part of this plan to empower an ancient god. A plan that had put one person in the hospital and killed four others, including his parents. Of course, his father's supposed best friend was the mastermind behind it, so all bets were off.

The twins made their way inside and found Eliseo Gomez in a back office of the building, leaning on the desk next to the crate they had brought to him.

"You two must be very special to Dr. Dirk to have him trust you to bring these items down here." Eliseo patted the crate.

"Well, our parents were special to him. We're just picking up the family business, I guess you could say."

"YOUR PARENTS? SO, you two are brother and sister? How great is that!" He found himself drawn to Jessica. He couldn't quite place the feeling, but he wanted to be near her. Then he noticed her cheeks starting to flush.

Jessica glanced down. "I think it is pretty great, Mr. Gomez."

ERIC TURNED HIS head, pausing a few moments in each direction to try to make sense of what was developing. He looked at them both as if they were each growing a second evil head. "Hey, before running off to Vegas and getting hitched by Elvis, I think Eliseo ought to get filled in and what may be at stake."

Eric knew what was coming. Jessica gave him *The Look*. Eric put his teeth together and smiled a cheesy smile. She waved him off and returned her attention to Eliseo and the crate.

"I think before we do anything else we need to get this crate and its contents to my workspace in the museum where they can be properly studied. Then maybe you can tell me the rest of the story."

"You don't really have to use kid gloves with this stuff, Eliseo, it was kept in a concrete bunker, hardly a sterile environment."

"Understood, Mr. Archer."

Eric put up his hand. "Please, it's Eric. We're gonna be spending a lot of quality time together, far too much for formalities."

"Good then, Eric, it's just a much safer environment in which to work. There is quite the black market for Mayan artifacts, and they seem to find their way illegally out of the country more often than not. There are a lot of prying eyes in and around these streets. Especially since people know that I am a curator. When they get to thinking there might be something of value around here, they would just as soon kill us as they would to have it handed over nicely. Not to mention our new acquaintances across the street."

CHAPTER THIRTY-FIVE

IT TOOK A little time, but Eliseo, Eric, and Paco were able to cobble together a reasonable facsimile of the crate containing the artifacts.

Eliseo turned to Eric. "Jessica and I will wait here while you and Paco take off in the Subaru. You will have the decoy. Once the gentlemen across the street follow you, Jessica and I will use the company's Jeep to transport the real crate to the museum. We have a guard going in for the nightshift we're going to pick up and who'll help with security."

"I'm glad someone around here has been thinking ahead. The only problem is that I can't communicate with Paco" Eric jerked his thumb over his shoulder. "She can."

"Paco knows enough English to get by. Besides, if you run into any trouble, he knows the streets and alleys. And quite honestly, Eric, who would you rather have by your side in a fight? Me or Paco?" Eliseo smiled widely.

Eric cocked his head, and raised an eyebrow. "Alright, we'll do it your way. But from now on, let's make these decisions together."

"Didn't mean to step on any toes. I just wanted to get the artifacts to the museum ASAP so we can start examining them. I still don't know why they are so important, but I'm sure you two will fill me in."

Jessica had kept tabs on the car across the street. Paco had placed the crates in their respective vehicles and then got behind the wheel of the Subaru. He fired up the engine and revved it a few times.

"I think someone is anxious for me to climb into the passenger seat. Paco must be warming up to me."

"Maybe that is the case. He can be impatient at times. The ride to the museum is about 35-minutes, and a bit longer for you since Paco is going to lose the gentlemen across the street. Jessica and I won't leave until we know there aren't any more prying eyes to worry about. With any luck, we'll see you at the museum in about an hour."

Eliseo walked to the driver's side of the SUV and relayed some instructions to Paco. Eric entered the passenger side. As soon as Eliseo was done, Paco eased the Subaru out of the garage and onto the street. It didn't take long for the dark green Chevy Nova to pull out of its spot and follow the car with the fake crate.

PACO HAD TAKEN a few evasive turns to try and shake the tail. Eric was impressed not only with Paco's driving, but his thought process regarding how best to elude their pursuers.

"Paco, get behind their car. I want to corner them and see if we can get some information."

The burly driver nodded and hit the gas. He made

a few sharp rights and lefts that took them into one of the many partially developed parts of town. Paco then pulled quickly into an alley and backed into an open loading dock and killed the lights on the SUV. They didn't have to wait long to see the Nova creeping past the alley. At the third pass, their pursuers pulled in. They didn't know it yet, but there was only one way in and out of the alley. Paco pulled the SUV out of its recessed spot, turned on the headlights, and blocked their exit.

The sight of headlights must have made the driver of the sedan jump, because the car jolted to a stop. There was no way for them to turn around in the narrow space between buildings.

Paco opened the driver's side door and crouched behind it, brandishing a .22 caliber rifle that the company kept in the SUV for scaring off wildlife on the various tours they ran. Eric exited the passenger side, reached to his hip, and then decided against pulling his gun, his traceable detective's gun. He looked over at Paco, who was furrowing his brow at Eric.

"Paco, tell them to get out and throw down their weapons. We want to talk to them."

Paco barked out some very forceful words in Spanish. Eric could only assume it was what he had asked. Two men emerged from the car with their hands in the air. Eric and Paco moved from behind the cover of their vehicle. Paco still trained the rifle on the men.

"*Habla ingles*?" Eric shouted as they approached the men. He shot a glance at Paco along with a thumbs up. Paco just shook his head. "Tough room," Eric muttered. At that instant, Eric saw a flash of silver in the hand of the smaller of the two men in front of them, as the larger rushed Eric. He heard Paco cry out in pain as a throwing knife speared his right quad, causing him to drop the rifle. The second man, with a face that looked like he was walking into a 90 MPH windstorm, was about as tall as Eric and twice as wide, closed the gap between them in a hurry. Going into defensive mode, and jamming the thug charging him with a side kick, doubling the man over, Eric immediately threw a spinning heel kick that connected with enough force to nearly take his attacker's head off.

He turned to see Paco finishing off the other thug. The man's own knife piercing through the soft skin under the mandible and entering the brain. The henchman's lifeless body slumped to the ground. Having several defensive wounds on his hands and forearms, Paco started administering self-aid, while Eric went to check on the man he'd kicked in the head. Eric checked his opponent for a pulse. There was none. The man's temple had been caved in. *How could I have possibly kicked that hard?*

Paco hobbled to their assailants' car, put it in neutral, and rolled it as far back in the alley as he could. He then motioned to Eric to help him lift the man he had rendered inert. They carried him over to the sedan and dropped him behind the car. Paco popped open the trunk. They lifted the dead weight into the trunk and rolled him back so there was enough room for the second man. Hugging the side of the car, Eric rolled up the windows and locked the doors and wiped the car clean of fingerprints, the best he could. Once the second man was in the trunk, Paco threw the keys in and slammed it shut. They made their way to the

Subaru and cautiously exited the alley. Paco drove carefully through town to highway 307 and they headed to their rendezvous point in Merida.

After minutes of silent driving and well out of town, Eric was the first to speak. "Good job back there. Quick thinking, too, it's almost as if you had done that kind of stuff before." He glanced at Paco, looking for any kind of response. There was none. Paco just drove. Eric could see that the gravity of Paco's actions weighed on him like a two-ton chain. "We should stop somewhere and clean up those wounds. I noticed a first aid kit in the back earlier." Eric motioned to the rear of the SUV. Paco just shook his head and waved Eric off without averting his gaze. "Okay, then, I'm guessing it's just a silent ride to the museum. I hope Jessica and Eliseo haven't had any trouble."

CHAPTER THIRTY-SIX

THE YUCATAN MUSEUM Of Natural History sat on 10-acres of prime real estate in the city of Merida. Jessica thought it looked as though the city had sprung up around the museum. It was a three-story building done in traditional colonial style. Five major roads intersected at the structure, creating the illusion that the building was the center of the city. Due to the pattern of the streets, the road surrounding the museum became a large round-about. To Jessica's relief, they had arrived without incident. Once inside the employee parking area, the security guard they picked up along the way helped them unload the crate.

Deep in the bowels of the museum was an artifact inspection and preparation room, where Eliseo and Jessica started to unpack the crate. The first item lying on top was Edward Archer's journal.

"Maybe you should read this; it's the book I told you about. It recounts his encounter with Difatos at Campeche." Jessica handed the journal to Eliseo.

"Edward Archer? Don't you mean your father?"

"He is, but it's a little strange using that term since it was only a day ago that I found out he and Elena were my parents." She paused and sniffled a bit. "Is there a restroom close? I think I need to freshen up a bit."

"Let me draw you map."

JESSICA BOUNDED BACK into the room with a vigor she had not previously shown. "So, have you had a chance to get through the journal? There's some amazing stuff in there, right?"

Eliseo couldn't do anything but agree. "This, uh, Island of the Dead fascinates me. There are archeologists down here that have been looking for evidence of such a place for decades. The place has almost become a myth on the level of Atlantis. The story goes that the island was manmade, built by the highland Mayan kingdoms as a place for Difatos to rule over the Maya when he would return to Earth. He was supposedly trapped there by some non-believers. In some stories, these people were warriors who actually saved the Mayans from an existence of servitude. These non-believers/warriors were purported to have bound Difatos, and they with him, so they could watch over him for all time. The island is said to now only appear to descendants of those warriors, and only in a time of crisis."

"An island invisible to all but a few people; I can't wait for Eric to hear this one." As she started to pull out more packing material, Jessica let out a cry as a wave of pain rippled throughout her body. It shook her so much she had to grip the end of the examination table with both hands to keep from falling.

Eliseo rushed to her side. "Are you okay?"

Jessica grunted. "Ugh ... I'll be fine." She wobbled. Her legs felt slightly sturdier than cooked spaghetti.

"Maybe you should sit down for a minute." He took her hand and placed his other at the small of her back as he led her to an office chair along the wall. As her pain subsided during the walk across the room, it was replaced with comforting warmth. Eliseo left her side to get a bottle of water from a small dorm-sized fridge, and the pain came back, though not as strong.

Gawd, what an odd sensation.

Eliseo returned and handed her the water, their hands touching briefly in the exchange. That feeling of comfort washed over her again. She thought it was too much of a coincidence. "This is going to sound strange, but did you feel that?"

Eliseo looked nervous. "Yes, but I assumed it was just me. I wasn't going to say anything. I don't know ... what's wrong with me."

"There isn't anything wrong with you. I think you have some kind of connection to these artifacts and these recent events."

Jessica proceeded to tell Eliseo everything that had transpired in the last three days: Difatos, the Mayan King Janab Pakal, and the artifacts. "Now put that together with what you read in the journal, and you can see why Dr. Dirk wanted us to come down here."

"That is an amazing story, just amazing."

Jessica took a drink from the water bottle.

"Oddly enough, I seem to remember bits of stories from my childhood that are very similar. I had a great-great-grandfather who was a Mayan shaman. We were told that he was lost defending our people from Difatos. He's like the bogeyman to kids down here.

Warnings about not wandering off into the woods, making sure we didn't anger the underworld gods or we would disappear without a trace, all very surreal stuff to try and grasp as a kid. It scared us all for sure."

"Well, this is as real as it gets, Eliseo. We have to figure out how to stop this thing, or many more people's lives will be in danger."

"I don't doubt the sincerity of anything you have said. I just wonder where I fit into all of this. How are you feeling, ready to tackle the rest of those artifacts? I'm itching to get a look at the limestone box."

Jessica made her way back to the table. "I'm fine. I was in pain earlier today, too, after touching the box. I want to know why that is. As well as figuring out just what the hell we are supposed to do with all this stuff."

THEY WORKED IN tandem, removing the broken slabs and the manuscript. The crate was taken apart one side at a time so they didn't have to lift the limestone box. As the last side was lowered, Eliseo became entranced by the glyphs covering the box. He moved furiously around the table, studying each side. He jumped up on the table to study the lid of the box, running his fingers over the markings like he was reading Braille. It, like the rest of the box, was covered in beautiful ornate Mayan glyphs. He motioned to Jessica to join him on the table top. They stood there kneeling over the box as new parents would stare at their sleeping infant in a crib. A look of pure joy came over Eliseo's face. He looked at Jessica and mouthed the word *amazing*.

Jessica rummaged around for a legal pad and a pen.

WITHOUT REMEMBERING SHE had moved, Jessica found herself on the table next to Eliseo. The warmth she felt earlier returned. The meanings of the symbols started to crystallize.

She was entranced, directed by some beckoning invisible force.

She felt the connection radiating between her and Eliseo.

The translations flowed from him. She felt the words enter her body, coursing through her soul to be released to the paper in front of her. The translations were now coming more rapidly. Jessica and Eliseo's bodies swayed and rocked in unison, their movement in sync with the pulsating hum emanating from the box.

Pushed to exhaustion, they continued to pour over the symbols. The translations came even faster. They moved around the table, almost floating together. The world around them swirled. As they reached the final side, they experienced a surge as the box revealed the last of its offerings.

Both participants collapsed onto the box, sweaty and breathless, with no more to give.

Jessica was breathing heavy. "What the hell was that?"

"I CAN'T BELIEVE what is written on this box, and that it has been hidden all these years. We need to double-check what is written. Make sure we have the translation correct." Eliseo waved the notepad in the air.

"Let's get to it."

The pair resumed in the same spot as before, meticulously double-checking. Then they triple-checked.

The yellow legal pad lay across Jessica's crossed legs and she leaned back, arms extended behind her. "This is a pretty big deal?"

"You can't begin to understand what an amazing find this is!"

Jessica grinned and slapped Eliseo on the leg. "Yes, I can."

"It's like finding irrefutable proof that Christians or Muslims or Jews or whomever are the ones who got their story right."

"Maybe all of them are right."

"It very well could be. It refers to gods in the plural, to competing forces. It also explains why the Mayans disappeared. No one has ever known why these people vanished—and now we do and we can't tell a soul." Eliseo was beside himself with excitement, practically jumping out of his skin. "This is just so incredible. Archeologists and anthropologists dream of a discovery like this."

The door to the room swung open and they both

shot up and turned in its direction.

Eric and Paco.

"I appreciate your enthusiasm," Eric pointed at the pad on Jessica's lap, "but does it tell us how to stop Difatos? Because I think things are going to get hotter for us down here real quick."

"Eric!" Jessica jumped from the table, ran over and threw her arms around his neck. "We were so worried about you two."

He returned the hug. "I'm not going to lie, there was a tussle. But, it's safe to say Pontillo's goons won't be following anyone else ever again."

Eric recounted in detail his and Paco's meeting with the men in the mystery car. "Does this stuff tell us how to defeat The Big Ugly?"

Eliseo was still shaking with excitement. "It ... uh, not exactly. We need to go to the ruins and match these fragments with their counterparts. There isn't enough information in these pieces. But it is clear there is a plan to stop him. There has to be. Anything else is unthinkable."

Jessica moved closer to Eliseo and put her hand over his, hoping their previous encounter that had *calmed* her down would have the same effect on him. *Or at least as much as a hand is capable of.* "Eliseo, there are a lot of ruins. Where do we need to go?"

"Kohunlich, we need to go to Kohunlich. It's a couple hours' drive. We should pack all of this up and go. I know it has been a long day of travel for you, but if we leave soon enough we'll be able to get to the ruins before daylight and any tour groups. I'll explain everything along the way."

"Let's get to it then." Eric grinned. "Maybe we can

catch a little shut eye on the drive. Power naps have always done me wonders."

PART V
THE BELLY OF THE BEAST

CHAPTER
THIRTY-SEVEN

THE SUBARU SPED down the nameless dirt road.

Eliseo had Paco stay near the CB radio and a cell phone in case they needed him. "Cell phone reception at the ruins is at best unreliable. The radio in here could turn out to be our only means of communication."

As they drove, Eliseo shared that the village he was born in was nestled between Kohunlich and Campeche. The ruins there were the first he had explored as a child, and later in his formative years, served as a tour guide. "From what we deciphered from the box and manuscript, the ruins must hold the final clues to Difatos's plans and the key to stopping him."

Eliseo beamed like a kid who just caught Santa in his living room. His excitement boiled over in the form of an impromptu lecture on one of the world's greatest mysteries. "Recent findings regarding the Mayans show there was, in fact, no Mayan empire. Throughout the Golden Age, from 250 BC – 900 BC, the Mayan lands were filled with independent city-states, much like that of Greece. The similarities continue, in that they all spoke a common tongue, had a common religion—that consisted of a pantheon of more than 60 deities—and other cultural aspects, such as being in a constant state of war with each other. The city-states could be divided into two territories: the highland area and the lowland. It is the fate of the lowland area that has caused much consternation between archeologists, anthropologists, and historians. The rapid disappearance of the inhabitants of the lowland area has perplexed these experts for years. Over a relatively short period of time, the lowland people simply ceased to exist. They vanished without a trace—just like Roanoke, but on a grand scale. Competing claims blame conflict and/or diseases for the demise and eventual disappearance of these civilizations. The northern highland areas continued to prosper after the abandonment of the lowland city-states. This made the event known as *The Great Mayan Collapse* all the more puzzling."

Eric cut in. "Boy, do you remind me of someone back home. What you're saying is many of our blanks have been filled in."

Eliseo continued as he pieced together the information gathered from the box and manuscript. "Yes, indeed, they have been. The god we know as Difatos inhabited the body of Janab Pakal on more than one occasion. He needed a host to inhabit when he wanted to visit our physical world. Janab Pakal was the leader of a small Mayan lowland area. His kingdom, Ciscinuhual, was constantly squeezed by the larger ones around it. In true Mayan tradition, he performed a ritual involving sacrifice and bloodletting to gain the attention of the Mayan gods. The story goes that Difatos reached out to Janab Pakal. Bent on keeping and expanding his power, he sacrificed his family, which included two sons, a daughter, and a wife in order to impress and appease Difatos. He was so taken by Pakal's dedication, he offered him a special reward. The king then started down the path to becoming the earthly vessel for Difatos. Difatos tried to rule over the *realm of man*, meaning Earth. The upper gods grew stronger with every soul sacrificed. Difatos was a lower god entrusted with collecting and sending them souls. The souls were sent to the Mayan underworld named Xibalba, which loosely translates into *Place of Fear*. Pakal stayed loyal even when Difatos inhabited his body. They helped him orchestrate wars between the surrounding kingdoms. The armies of the other city-states didn't know why, but as the Ciscinuhual fought, they wouldn't kill their opponents. Instead, they would leave them maimed and wounded. Their screams of agony on the battlefield, and those that originated from the torture of innocents, were like a symphony to the senses of Difatos. He would come along and inhale their ki or soul energy while they clung to life. In some cases, the body disappeared and left only a charred mark in its place."

"Holy shit, the night I got back into town and investigated our mother's ambulance accident with Pontillo, we saw her gurney. All that was left was a burn mark and the necklace that Jessica has on. In our father's journal, he described the scene when they found the clothes of the missing locals. Scorch marks burned into the ground near their clothes."

Eliseo nodded. "Well, that makes sense with what else is in the manuscript. It states that Difatos wiped out all of the lowland kingdoms, even his own. The men loyal to him were the last to go, but they also met their demise, and had their souls devoured just like the other inhabitants. Next, he moved on to the highland city-states to continue wiping out the Mayan people. These wars that historians thought were ceremonial more than anything, we now know were waged so Difatos could collect the ki of the combatants and innocents. Instead of redistributing the ki to the upper gods, as he was supposed to, Difatos kept it for himself."

"Difatos took over the body of a *man*." Eric stared at the two. "Men can die! Men can be killed." Eric leaned back against the seat with his hands behind his head, fingers laced, crossing his ankles as he put his feet up between the two front seats and closed his eyes in an attempt to get some sleep. "We already know he bleeds. So, to quote Arnold Schwarzenegger: *If it bleeds, we can kill it.*

CHAPTER THIRTY-EIGHT

THE PASSENGERS IN the company SUV were so involved in figuring out their mystery, they failed to notice the door-less Jeep Wrangler trailing them since they left town.

"Stay back, Carlos!" The man leaned forward and smacked the driver in the head. "Let them lead us to the treasure. The more the element of surprise is on our side, the better." As he spoke, he loaded slugs into the semi-automatic Remington 12-gauge that lay across his lap. "They *have* to be heading to the ruins; it'll will be easy to track them there." He tapped the man sitting next to the driver. "Call the boss and let him know we have a positive ID on the museum curator, and we are in pursuit. Ask him if he has anyone else on this job."

The man in the back of the Jeep stopped giving directions and racked a round into the chamber of the shotgun.

CHAPTER THIRTY-NINE

ERIC AND JESSICA woke up as Eliseo maneuvered the SUV onto an access road just before the main entrance to the parking area for the Kohunlich ruins. He punched a code into the number pad on a pedestal and the iron gate swung open.

Eliseo's position as assistant curator carried with it the ability to close any ruins to public viewing for the purpose of archeological study. It was early enough in the day that the first of the touring groups had not yet arrived, and he would make sure it stayed that way. Parking the Jeep, he proceeded into the small building that served as an office and break area for the guides. As he went inside, he propped open the door that read AUTHORIZED PERSONNEL ONLY and urged Eric and Jessica to follow.

"I think it would be better if one of us stayed out here with the artifacts. Jessica will be right behind you."

"Sure, sure, volunteer me. You just want to get some more sleep."

"Do you really think I would do that? Besides, I figure you and Eliseo wouldn't want a third wheel around."

"Whatever, I'm heading inside." Jessica jogged the

short distance to the building and entered the small control room.

Eliseo was at a PC. "I'm sending e-mails to the various tourist companies letting them know that the ruins will be closed for at least the full day today and to make arrangements to reroute their groups to other sites."

Jessica looked around the room and fixed her gaze on the monitors for the closed-circuit cameras that surrounded the park. "Could there be a group of tour guides coming in this early?"

"There shouldn't be anyone around for a few hours. That's the reason I'm sending these e-mails, to keep everyone away. Why?"

"There's a Jeep in the parking lot." She pointed to one of the monitors. "Three guys total. Two have gotten out and they're checking the gate. One's stayed in the back seat."

Eliseo hit SEND and rushed over to the monitor. "They aren't anyone I have ever seen. They could just be eager sightseers."

"At 5:30 AM? And they just happened to pull up minutes behind us? I doubt it, Eliseo."

"More of the sheriff's people, perhaps?"

"Eric and I will find out. You stay glued to that monitor and call if anything drastic changes."

It didn't take long for her to reach Eric, who was already at the corner of the small building in a crouched position, gun drawn. He waved for Jessica to get down. As she did, she pulled her own weapon out.

"Three men pulled up in a Jeep right after you went in the building. They came to the access road gate first, and then moved on to the main gate. It looks like they want to get in here in the worst way."

"Eliseo and I saw them on the monitors inside. I was coming out to tell you. Are they more of Pontillo's men?"

"Who else'd be following us? There must've been a team scoping out the museum. Shame on us for not noticing them on the ride over. We can't make that mistake again. If we even get the chance to. I want to get a look at the back of that Jeep. It bugs me that one guy hasn't left it. He's hiding something, protecting something, or talking to someone. Can the cameras inside zoom in?"

Jessica shook her head. "It's a pretty rudimentary system that uses fixed position cameras."

"Damn, guess we get to do this the fun way. Okay, here's the deal, I'm going to head back down by the access road and come up along the rock wall. It's too high and too smooth for them to scale. But there are some spots on our side where I can get high enough to see the Jeep. You just keep an eye on them. Let me know if I need to get flat or get out in a hurry."

"Just remember the whole twins-thing is important to stopping Difatos and Pontillo. That means both of us need to be present to send Difatos back where he came from."

The pair switched positions along the wall, and as Eric silently found his way toward the back of their vehicle, he winked and nodded. "I'm always careful."

"Just get going." She kept one eye trained on the men at the gate as she watched Eric maneuver to the park wall.

Eric was able to quickly and quietly make his way near the main gate. He found a service ladder and climbed it until he reached a small ledge which allowed him to perch in a way that he could see the Jeep. He looked back and punched a thumbs up at Jessica, then looked down in time to see the men who were at the gate pulling back the tarp covering the back of the Jeep.

This shit is about to get real.

CHAPTER FORTY

RAUL GUZMAN HATED waiting.

As a young man fending for himself in the streets of Puerto Rico, Raul always took what he wanted. He didn't give a damn about what other people thought or felt. But, he had never been promised a payday like the one the boss-man on this job was offering. So, he stalked his prey, instead of pouncing. He had two more men coming from the west to meet him at the Kohunlich ruins. He, Carlos, and Ed had hoped to slip in behind their quarry quietly and take them by surprise, but it didn't look like that was going to happen.

Raul wished that the other men would hurry up and get here so they had a numbers advantage.

Carlos jogged back to the Jeep. "Hey, man, there is no way that we can get into the ruins. We would need some climbing gear to get over these walls. Neither of us saw anyone moving around inside, either."

"I'm sure they're in the admin building. We could wait for the park to open, but I'd like to do this without any witnesses. These places are crawling first thing in the morning, while it's still cool out." Raul stepped out of the Jeep for the first time.

Edwin and Carlos made their way to the rear of the

Jeep and threw back the tarp, exposing their own shotguns, which were clones of Raul's. As they loaded the guns, they heard noise coming from the other side of the entrance gate.

ELISEO GOMEZ WALKED toward the gate. "Hello? Hello? Who's is there? Can I help you?"

Eric couldn't believe his eyes. *Funk me.* He instantly motioned for Jessica to move to the wall, and made a secondary motion of holding up his gun and pointing at it, and then to the men outside the fence, telling her they were armed.

RAUL FELT LIKE a spider with a fly in his web.

Eliseo Gomez was coming to him.

The only question was the whereabouts of his earlier passengers. He'd better play this cool. He left the shotgun on the floor of the Jeep and walked towards the fence, motioning to his counterparts to stay put.

"Eliseo Gomez? You are Mr. Gomez, right?"

"You have me at a disadvantage, my friend, do we know each other?"

"Ah, no, but who lives around here and does not know the most famous Mayan tour guide?"

"Thank you for the compliment. Unfortunately, for today, the Kohunlich ruins are not going to be open to the public."

"That is unfortunate. My associates and I were hoping to get a look at the *new* artifacts we have been hearing about. Pretty hush-hush. We didn't even know about their arrival until just hours ago. Maybe you can make an exception for us?"

OVERHEARING THE CONVERSATION taking place at the gate, made Eric uneasy. These guys *were* working for Pontillo. Jessica was just few feet from Eric's position. He crouched down even lower and whispered, "The guy at the gate's unarmed. The other two are hanging by the back of the Jeep. We need to take these guys down. I can take the two in the back. When you hear my signal, pop out around the corner and get the drop on the guy at the gate. Get him secured, somehow."

"What's your signal?"

He held up his gun. "You'll know it when you hear it."

Eric climbed to the top of the rock wall and hovered above the two guys at the back of the Jeep. They were both relaxed and leaning over the back gate. *Please, let 'em stay right there.* He put his gun in the holster and shuffled into position. He leapt off the wall and landed with his full weight on the backs of both men. They crumpled when the concentrated force of Eric's 200-pounds hit them. Each man let out a sudden loud grunt as their sternums bounced off the back edge of the Jeep. Eric heard ribs *craaack* over the noise they made. Hearing them starting to choke, he figured their diaphragms must have collapsed.

He wished he could just kick them into unconsciousness, but he'd be just as likely to kick them into the hereafter. Making his decision, he grabbed a shotgun, "Sorry, guys," and broke their shins—definitively.

JESSICA HEARD THE men's screams. *The signal!* Coming around the around the corner, she surprised the third man. "Get your hands through the gate now! Eliseo, use your belt to secure him."

Raul Guzman protested as Eliseo tied him to the bars of the gate. "You don't know what you're doing! We are just sightseers."

"With shotguns? That's a novel idea."

"One cannot be too careful in the jungle."

"Tell it to the judge."

SECURING THE OTHER shotgun, Eric cleared the Jeep for any more weapons, happy that the doors had been removed, happy to see another shotgun in the back, and happy that the keys were in the ignition. Then he looked up, saw two motorcycles approaching from the west. "Two more party crashers, Jessica. Get out here pronto!" Eric moved towards the gate with all three Remingtons.

Eliseo unlocked the gate. Jessica opened it just enough to slip through, and looked down the road just in time to see the motorcycles stopping, thinking the riders might be assessing the situation.

Eric looked at Eliseo. "Hey, contact *la policia* and get 'em out here."

"I can do that. What do we do in the meantime?"

"YOU are going to stay and cover these assholes." Eric handed one of the pumps to Eliseo. "If one of them struggles to get free, shoot him." Eric handed Jessica one of the weapons, who checked and cleared it. "Jessica and I are going to have a chat with the motorcycle boys over there." Eric started towards the Jeep. "Come on, sis, we have some interrogations to conduct."

The roar of the motorcycle engines drowned out Jessica's response as she got in the vehicle, and, like Eric, set her shotgun between her leg and middle console. The tires spun, slipping on the pavement damp with overnight dew. Smoke bellowed from the rear of the Jeep and it lurched forward onto the main road, fishtailing as it sped away. Eric, gripping the steering wheel, called out to the bikers in a low tone, saying, "Try all you want, but you're getting grabbed and tagged," wasted no time trying to catch the motorcycles.

Jessica buckled in and retrieved her sidearm from her hip. She slid over as far as possible in her seat and tried to get a bead on one of the bikes. The layout of the road did not cooperate. There were too many twists and turns that the bike riders were familiar with. Eric needed to keep up their speed to avoid losing them in one of the curves. The Jeep came dangerously close to tipping several times. The guys on the bikes fought their pursuit like the third monkey trying to get on the ark.

When the road straightened, Eric pushed the pedal to the floor.

Jessica was leaning out of the vehicle. "WE'RE NOT CLOSE ENOUGH FOR ME TO GET A CLEAN SHOT."

Bike rider number one slowed, braked, and abruptly turned to face the Jeep. He fired two quick rounds, neither of which came close to hitting their mark ... but the shots forced Eric to swerve, exposing the wide side of the front passenger tire.

Then the cyclist emptied his clip.

Several of the rounds hit rubber and steel.

Eric overcompensated and they went careening off to the side.

The brakes locked as their vehicle spun. The Jeep's front end, hitting the dirt edge of the road, flipped, launching them into the air, where they went end over end before coming to rest on the roll bars and sliding down into a large culvert, Eric and Jessica screaming, holding hands, and—*FLASHING*.

€RIC'S HEAD THROBBED, but there was—

—*no pain, no blood.*

Instinctively, he released himself from his seatbelt and hit the ground. He canvassed his head for any sign of injury. When he pulled his hand away, it was dry. Still disoriented, he started to crawl toward the back of the Jeep. As he did, he saw Jessica lower herself out of her seat. She stayed under the cover of the Jeep and was feeling around the ground.

"Dammit, I can't find my gun."

My God, she looks ... she looks fine, just fine. Eric wanted to say something, but the words wouldn't form quickly enough in his mouth. He focused his energy on reaching the rear of the Jeep, and when he did, he smiled weakly at the sight of the deerslayer that belonged to one of the thugs incapacitated back at Eliseo's. He braced himself against the back of the Jeep and gave the Remington a function check. He had not heard another sound from Jessica, but knew the ruffians on the bikes would be coming back for them.

Eric rolled away from the Jeep and came up on one knee. He saw the bike and rider at the precipice of the ditch. He took aim and fired, hitting the bike in the gas tank. The gas poured out and caught fire as it touched the scorching head pipe.

Fuel sprayed the rider and caught him on fire.

JESSICA HEARD A motorcycle fading off in the distance. One was still near. "Stuck around to finish us off, huh, buddy? We'll see about that." She knew if they emerged from the wreckage, their dance partner would be ready to take them out. She spotted a shotgun some yards away, its pistol grip the only part of the weapon that wasn't submerged in the sludge at the bottom of the culvert. She hadn't gotten a response from Eric and didn't think there was much time before the bike rider dismounted and came after them.

A split second before hearing a shotgun slug fired from off to her side, a slug from the Remington she had recovered disintegrated everything from the neck up into a misty red cloud of polymer, bone, and brain.

Out of her peripheral vision, Jessica saw Eric take a few steps up towards the road. Gripping her weapon, she rushed to him. "Eric! I heard the other bike take off." Her turned and faced her, and she started to look him up and down. Then, laying down her shotgun, she grabbed him by the shoulders and spun him in a circle, pausing a moment to look at the utterly destroyed jeep. "My God, Eric, you look, um, freaking amazing!"

Eric hugged her. "You do, too."

She could hear the second motorcycle screaming back down the road—heading back *their* way.

Eric and Jessica—*CLAACK CLAACK*—hit their bolt releases, and moved into position by the side of the road, and the smoking motorcycle and decapped bad guy, hiding behind the overgrowth.

As the motorcycle got bullfighting close and started to gear down, Jessica charged. She wished she could see the look of shock on the man's face as he saw the butt-end of the shotgun heading straight for him. Jessica's timing was too good and it was too late for the rider to change direction or stop the bike.

The stock knocked the man off the motorcycle as it hit him squarely in the throat. The bike and the man's body continued, but the man's head snapped forward and then backward, hitting the road and then ping-ponging between his neck and the pavement. Jessica was on top of the still form as soon as he landed, the man's head resting cattywampus to his shoulders.

Taking to her knees, Jessica started rifling through the man's pockets for intel.

"Remind me never to piss you off."

"I don't take too kindly to someone trying to kill me." Glancing up, she noticed the strange look on Eric's face. "What?"

Eric started to laugh.

"What?"

Eric turned and pointed. "Look-it *that* Jeep!" Eric started to laugh again. "We should be dead, like effin' dead."

Jessica started to laugh.

Still staring at the Jeep that looked put together by Salvador Dali, Eric said, "Let's get out of here. I need to get some attention."

"Medical attention? But we're fine—we flashed, we actually *flashed*."

Eric stayed facing the Jeep. "Don't need medical attention, but laundry attention."

"What?"

Eric chuckled. "Look-it my pants."

CHAPTER FORTY-ONE

ANDY PONTILLO SHOWED no emotion as he finished tying his naked wife to the bed they had shared for more than 35-years.

"What is going on, Andy?"

Andy, also bare—62-years showing itself in his folds of fat, chapped skin, that mole he hated, his penis, with just its head peeking out, which had always been more than long enough, looking like it was hiding in its nest of graying hair, the scars on his knees from when he'd had his caps replaced—staying silent and straight-faced, bent down and gave her a chaste kiss on the forehead.

"Why're you doing this … my beautiful man, you-you love me?"

He had no answers, not for her.

The childless woman's eyes welled over with tears, an expression of impending, soul-crushing betrayal *blitzkrieging* across her face, and she knew, *knew* she was doomed.

In utter hopeless panic, she started the futile process of screaming and struggling against the ropes.

The only words Andy offered the woman he had spent over half of his life with, were, "Till death do us part."

The sticky sweet smell of decay filled the Pontillo's bedroom. Difatos appeared in the far-right corner, out of Julia field of vision.

A naked Andy Pontillo picked up a thin-bladed obsidian dagger. He continued to ignore the tortured screams of his wife. "I am ready for the ceremony." Sweeping his arms crosswise, palms out, Andy presented his wife to the demon. "I willingly offer this innocent as tribute to you, Lord Difatos."

He moved to the side of the bed as Difatos moved to the foot.

It was then that Julia caught her first glimpse of the demon, and with a voice now gone hoarse, she let out some pathetically begging rasps. She shot Andy a desperate look as he stood with an impassive stare. Mascara had streamed down Julia's face. Between her sniffling and gasps for air, she tried over and over to get out the word *Why?*

Andy quickly went into the adjoining bathroom and came back in with some baby wipes and cleaned Julia's black smears away. "I know how much you like to be put together, and for this, I promise, you'll be looking good."

In keeping with Mayan traditions, all parties involved in the ceremony must partake in ritual bloodletting. Pontillo was tasked with making the initial incisions. With the obsidian blade directly over Julia's heart, Andy's hand perfectly contoured across saggy bosom and weathered skin the lightest of lines in the shape of an eight-pointed star, the same kind of which he'd practiced on paper, matted and then framed throughout the house since nearly his honeymoon.

At the same time, Difatos began to chant in his low

gravely tone. As he recited the nearly-timeless words, the skin around the coring splayed open, forming a bloody flower with fleshy petals.

To the extent that Andy's care had been properly rendered, the proffered star would open her ki to Difatos, so that he would be able to draw the greatest amount of virtue and sweetness—gifted to all of The Absolute's earthly children—from this pure sacrifice. The god continued to chant as Pontillo now stood straddling his wife.

Andy pierced his testicles, sending drops of blood into the weeping flower blooming on his wife's chest. Instantly, the room was engulfed in a smoky turquoise hue. The mystical energy surging through the air catapulted Andy across the room and onto the floor.

Difatos stretched out a hand, and extended a single obsidian-clawed digit, and with its fine needle point, began to decorate Julia's body with arcane glyphs. He started at her shoulders and worked down both sides of her body, his single razor yielding the essence of her ki. Unlike the pattern effortlessly drawn by Andy, just piercing beneath the skin, Difatos's ministrations cut deep into her soft flesh, and then deeper still, far far deeper than Julia's mere physicality.

The pain was so intense that Mrs. Pontillo—never to lose consciousness, until all was completed—lost all awareness of her surroundings.

When Difatos finished, he lowered himself to the floor at the foot of the bed and raised his bloodied finger into the air. As he sat, he chanted a repetitive phrase, and the turquoise smoke/mist mixture emanated from the incisions in Julia's body, and found its way to Difatos, where he breathed it deeply in, taking it all.

Andy looked at his wife.

Her wounds were cauterized.

The room filled with the repugnant odor of burnt flesh.

Julianna B. Pontillo
Born: June 6, 1952
Died: August 20, 2011
Beloved daughter, sister, wife.
IN DEATH, SHE DID PART

CHAPTER FORTY-TWO

AS JESSICA AND Eric approached on the motorcycle, several local police officers spun with raised weapons. Eliseo came out running. "No! No! These are the friends I was telling you about. Captain, please get your men to put their weapons down."

The captain complied and his men lowered their rifles.

"Thank you, thank you so much."

The pair got off the bike and Eric immediately took off for the building.

"Dios Mio, I was so worried about you." Eliseo took Jessica in a tight embrace. She surprised herself by returning the gesture and letting it linger for a moment. Eliseo's hand trailed along the outside of Jessica's arm until he hooked his hand into hers, and led her over to a picnic table at the edge of the parking lot inside the walls. As they sat, a police officer came over to them looking for answers to the questions Eliseo could not provide. Jessica, however, was able to fill in most of the information the officer was seeking.

Eliseo's connections were proving to be invaluable. He knew all of the local law enforcement from having grown up in the region. It didn't take much persuasion to get the police to believe the story and take their assailants into custody. But even if it had, being known, being liked, and having cash, would've still been able to bridge the gap. After all, these were Mexican police.

"The police will be taking the two remaining men to the station house and will try to get them to talk. If they know anything about this Pontillo fellow, we will know about it shortly."

Eric suddenly appeared. "Two? Who's missing? There were the two guys I jumped and the guy secured to the gate. I'm no rocket scientist, but that makes three." He was cleaned up with a new pair of NATIVE PRIDE employee's pants and a bit of restored dignity.

"Yeah, I wasn't even thinking. It should be three, shouldn't it?"

They both turned and looked at Eliseo.

"Well, the guy we secured to the fence apparently wasn't so secure. After I called the authorities, I checked on the guys that Eric jumped, and when I got up to check the fence guy, he was gone." Eliseo pointed at some cops. "There are two officers inside the park now. He couldn't have gotten far."

"DAMN. WELL IF they are Pontillo's men, it would have gotten back to him sooner or later, anyway." Eric was slightly annoyed with Eliseo, but tried not to let it show. "But I would have preferred to have as many bargaining chips as possible and take as many of his men out as possible. The more shorthanded he is, the better. I was hoping to've had this thing figured out before he got down here."

"Sorry, it was a bit more excitement than I'm used to in my profession. Besides, I don't think I could have fired your gun if I needed to, anyway."

"Don't beat yourself up over it." Jessica moved closer to Eliseo and took his hand. "You were put in a tough position and did everything you could. Your contacts with the authorities have been a tremendous help. I mean, think about it. The mess Eric and I made down the road. We should be in custody, but thanks to you, we are free to go about doing what we need to, to stop Pontillo and Difatos."

Eric put his hands up as if surrendering. "I think that knock on the head was harder than I thought. I wasn't crucifying you, buddy, just lamenting our position out loud. Either way, we need to get back to the task at hand and figure out what we need to do to get rid of Difatos."

CHAPTER
FORTY-THREE

DRENCHED WITH SWEAT, Raul Guzman slipped deeper into the jungle, quickly moving away from the ruins, still trying to piece together what had happened. The fate of the other men he was working with really wasn't his concern, but this simple snatch and grab had now become personal. That bitch at the fence had put a gun in his face—in *his* face!

No one did that to him, least of all a woman.

Whoever she was, she'd pay for that transgression. This wasn't about the artifacts anymore; he would teach her a lesson. If it didn't get in his way, he would *still* try to find a way to get out with the artifacts. It sounded like they were pretty rare. *First things first, waiting out the local police*. They wouldn't travel too far into the wilderness before giving up. Raul knew if there was one thing you could count on in this part of Mexico, it was that the local law enforcement quickly lost interest if something looked like it was going to be too difficult.

It was a truth he was counting on.

CHAPTER FORTY-FOUR

A SHORT TIME later....

"The men we encountered earlier are sticking to the story of being simple treasure hunters. They said they scope out the docks and local airports and *my* museum waiting for something valuable to show up." Eliseo flipped his cell phone shut. "They contend they have never heard of Sheriff Andrew Pontillo, but the cell phone they had on them had several New York numbers in it. They are all locals who grew up in the region, and they are being detained for the foreseeable future. The man who went missing is named Raul Guzman, apparently the brains of the operation."

Still quasi-groggy from the hit to the head and the tumble in the Jeep, if not physically, then psychologically, Eric sat up from the couch. "At least it's good to know we've stunted Pontillo's efforts. But damn, he has a long reach, and it's extended as far as we feared. Hopefully, we spooked this Guzman guy and he won't cause us any more problems."

Jessica entered the room with her face buried in a guide book. "*The Face of Fangs*? That is the translation of Kohunlich? We really need to go to a place called Face of Fangs?"

"Don't worry about the name. The Mayans loved

violence and the macabre."

"I know, I've seen *Apocalypto*."

"Well, uh, this particular name—"

Eric grinned. "I've seen *Apocalypto*, too."

"Fuck *Apocalypto*." Eliseo broke a pencil in half. "Everybody thinks they're a goddamned expert on the Mayans because of that stupid-ass movie." A pause. "Anyway, the name's derived from the carvings around the main entrance of the temple. When you stand back and take it all in, it looks like a large, menacing fanged mouth, nothing really sinister."

"Hope this is one of those cases where looks are deceiving."

"Again, don't worry, and if anything happens, I've got your back." Eliseo broke into a wide smile.

Eric caught the knowing smile Eliseo had just shot at Jessica. "Unless you need to shoot my gun."

Jessica smiled. "Or we plan on watching *Apocalypto* tonight."

Eric was hoping the perceived flirting between Eliseo and Jessica was just a part of his imagination, but he figured he couldn't be that lucky. "Okay, then," Eric let out a long sigh. "Let's get moving, it seems to be getting a little hot for my liking in here."

Eliseo led the way out the back door of the guide building.

Jessica leaned in toward Eric as she passed him. "One of these days I'm going to knock that damn smirk off your face."

"Many people have said that to me on multiple occasions, and for too many years to count. Hasn't been done yet."

THE TRAIPSING-TRIO made their way up the steps of the Kohunlich temple. Jessica led the way with rappelling gear and floodlights in addition to her backpack. Eric and Eliseo were left to struggle with the limestone box and all it contained. After several excruciating minutes, they were at the top of the temple steps. They plopped down on the box, exchanged weak high-fives, and pulled bottled water out of their respective packs.

Eliseo guzzled his, then doused his head with the remainder. The men's respite was brief; just moments after they sat down, Jessica poked her head out from inside the temple. "What's taking you guys so long? C'mon, get a move on!"

The men looked at each other, grinned, rolled their eyes, and then bent down to pick up the box. As they lifted, both exhaled and muttered *weemen*.

ABOUT 20-YARDS distant, Raul Guzman stood camouflaged at the edge of the jungle. "The temple—with only one way in and one way out." A hunter's smile split his face.

"I might still pull this off."

CHAPTER FORTY-FIVE

"I'M INTRIGUED BY the fact the glyphs led us here." Eliseo and Eric started setting up floodlights around the chamber. "I've been in and around these specific ruins as long as I can remember, know them like the back of my hairy hand. To think there's is something new to discover is … it's amazing."

"And less than a day ago you thought Difatos was the bogeyman, a threat parents used to keep their kids in line?"

"Got me there, Eric. There have been a lot of things that have opened my eyes in the last 24-hours." Eliseo glanced in Jessica's direction.

"Can you hit on my sister *after* we save mankind from eternal enslavement?"

"Hey!" Jessica walked over and *poke-poke-poke-poked* a finger in Eric's chest. "You-Cut-It-Out. Your sarcasm isn't getting us any closer to solving this puzzle, either, buddy!"

"You two are starting to carry on like some high schoolers. There's already enough tension without adding your sexual *crushing* to it."

Jessica glared at Eric, freezing his next statement. After letting out an annoyed breath, she strolled over to Eliseo, took his face in her hands and *kisss*-ed him in a way that would make a man forget every other kiss he had ever or would ever experience.

Eric's jaw dropped.

"There." She turned to Eric. "Is that good enough for you? No tension in the air now. It's all out there." She snapped back around toward Eliseo. "Great kiss, wasn't it?" And then she strode out of the temple.

Eric could see Eliseo's flushed cheeks. He alternated between watching Jessica walk out and Eliseo looking like he needed a smoke.

Once she was gone, Eliseo looked at Eric, held out his palms and shrugged. "Weemen, huh?"

"The strain of all this nonsense is finally getting to me. I should go after her."

"Maybe we should give her a moment alone?"

Eric stopped in his tracks and glanced back. "You're probably right."

"Hey, *mi hermano*," Eliseo winked. "I think I got the best end of this whole deal."

Eric wanted desperately to change the subject. "What is it we're looking for in here, anyway?"

Before Eliseo could answer, Jessica's voice … she was yelling!

But neither of them could make out what she was saying.

Eric and Eliseo took off in a dead sprint for the temple entrance. As they reached the top of the temple steps, Jessica's words became clearer.

"Eliseo! Eliseo! Paco's on the CB. He has some important information. But he'll only tell you."

Passing Jessica on the temple steps, Eliseo trailed a hand across the woman's back.

Emerging from the temple, Eric started to feel shiver-ing in his spine. It sent him into full cop mode. He scanned the perimeter. "Something's not right, Jessica."

"What do you mean?"

"I can feel it." Eric continued to look around. "I've got a bad feeling about this. A bad, bad, feeling."

"Okay, Dr. Spock, whatever you say."

Eric walked to the left of the terrace outside the temple's entrance. "Dr. Spock is the guy who ruined a generation of kids with that stupid book. Mr. Spock is the *Star Trek* character. My line was from *Star Wars*."

"I know."

"You know what?" Eric was making a second visual sweep, when, *There it is*, he caught movement. He stared at the jungle foliage to the left of the temple. He fingered for Jessica to join him.

"I know the difference between *Star Wars* and *Star Trek*. It is highly illogical to think that Mr. Spock said *I've got a bad feeling about this*." Jessica was now looking in the same direction as Eric.

"Glad you still have your sense of humor and your heart hasn't taken over all of your emotions."

Jessica punched Eric in the arm.

"*Owww*, you don't know your own strength."

Jessica walked down the temple steps toward Eliseo.

Eric kept his eyes roaming in the general area where he'd seen movement, waiting for whatever it was to again draw his attention. "I feel like I'm looking for the Predator when it's camouflaged." He felt relatively reassured nothing was there, at least not anymore, but that *funny* feeling was still with him.

It crept into his stomach and hunkered in.

RAUL KNEW HE had been spotted moving back into his hide. A few more minutes and the woman would have been his.

He wasn't worried.

She would get what was coming.

There was time, plenty of time.

CHAPTER FORTY-SIX

"JESSICA AND I will be spending a day out here alone." The twins approached as Eliseo's conversation with Paco ended. He was sitting sideways facing out of the passenger door of the Subaru.

Eric: "Where am I going to be?"

"The office back in Costa Maya received a call just a bit ago from a Deputy Tom Deering."

Jessica: "He's our colleague from the Hurley County Sheriff's Office, keeping track of Pontillo and Difatos for us."

"Yes. Well, he couldn't get through to either of you and called the office. He said there's something dreadfully wrong at the Pontillo house, and he didn't know how to handle the situation. He's asking for you to come back and help. I took the liberty of having you booked on a flight back to the States. Instead of a straight flight to Buffalo, you will stop in Raleigh, and take a small commuter plane to Jamestown Municipal Airport. It is a bit more expensive, but gets you home almost two hours earlier. Deputy Deering will be waiting for you at the airport."

"It must be something really big for Tom to pull me away. I don't like the idea of splitting up. Are you sure you two will be okay out here without me?"

Eliseo took Jessica's hand. "Yes … and we've been fine so far with the translations. Might take days to find anything new, artifacts don't just pop out of thin air. It will take Paco a while to get here, anyway. We can go in and get started. If something happens and you can't leave, we'll just get word back to Deputy Deering that you may be delayed."

Jessica: "It's settled then. You know Tom wouldn't have called if it wasn't important. I'm just surprised you haven't made some comment about it being a ruse so Eliseo could get me alone out here."

Eric eyed their clasped hands. "The thought did cross my hand."

Jessica chucked the canteen she had just taken a drink from in Eric's direction and walked off toward the temple. He deflected it away from his head with a quick swat, sending it tumbling to the ground. "Just kidding, just kidding, jeez, women are so sensitive when you bring up their love life."

Eliseo picked up the canteen as he walked by. "You don't know when to quit, do you?"

Eric patted the man's back. "Not often enough, but it's helped keep me alive."

Within minutes they were back inside the main chamber with the battery-powered floodlights on.

"Something special? Something out of place?" Eric ran the flashlight up and down the wall in front of him. "Anything weird or different?"

"I've been here so many times you two will have to be the ones to spot it. Walking in here is like walking into my living room. I'm so familiar with it, nothing looks special."

They worked silently for a few minutes and then

Jessica looked up. "Hey, Eliseo, take a look at this crack. It's smoothed on both edges. And fits together, like a puzzle piece."

"Huh, that was never here before. At quick glance, it looks like a crevice in the limestone." He ran his hand along the space, reaching to his limit. "Eric, bring one of those floods over here, would you? Angle it up the wall."

Eric knelt on the floor, adjusted the light, and something caught his eye at the base of the wall. About a foot off the ground was a marking that looked eerily similar to the glyph on the necklace from the box. "Umm, guys, you may want to come down here."

Jessica and Eliseo kneeled next to Eric.

"Look right here." Eric crawled over to the wall and brushed away some dirt and cobwebs. "This symbol is the reverse of the glyph on Jessica's necklace." He traced his finger along a groove in the stone extending out from the marking. It made a circle that completed itself back on the other side of the reverse glyph.

"The necklace," Jessica commented as she slipped it from around her head. She leaned in and started to fit it into the groove in the stone. The piece with the glyph fit as perfectly as the rest of the jade and obsidian beads did in the grooves. She was just about to press the glyph into place when Eric spoke up.

"Do not be one of those Indiana Jones booby traps. I would really hate for someone to find us with 1000-year-old poison darts sticking out of our necks or crushed under a huge boulder."

They all glanced slowly upward.

"Okay, no boulder. But that doesn't mean no

poison darts."

Jessica shook her head. She pressed the glyph into place and the chamber filled with the noise of grinding stone. Then the noise ceased and nothing else happened. She pressed the rest of the necklace into the recessed spot. More grinding and the sound of stone cracking, then again nothing. The three sat back and stared at the necklace pressed into the wall.

Eric: "That was less eventful than imagined."

Just then two circular pieces of stone fell from either side of the necklace and in their place were two perfectly round, hollow holes. Eric moved to the wall and tried to see into the opening with a flashlight. "Should I stick my hand in there, Eliseo?"

"Go ahead."

"If this thing crushes my hand, I hope you get testicular ebola."

Eliseo chuckled. "It's a deal."

Jessica brushed Eric's hand away. "Fine, big guy, if you're too chicken to stick your hand in there. Let me at it."

"I didn't say I was chicken. I've just watched a lot of adventure movies and I'm thinking it's a 50/50 shot I come out of this without a hand."

"Well, Indy, are you going to or not?"

"Okay, okay." Eric squeezed his eyes and eased his hand slowly into the hole. It went in to about mid-forearm. "There's a lever of some kind." He grunted. "I can't move it." He kept his arm in the hole to the left of the necklace and shimmied himself into squarely facing the wall. He tried to put his right hand into the other opening, but it was too small. "Can't even get my hand in that one on the right. Like it's meant for a smaller hand."

Eliseo and Eric looked at Jessica.

"Can't be that simple?" Jessica stuck her hand in the opening. It slid right in. "A lever's in this one, too."

Eliseo's hands came to his face and he fell onto his backside. "Warrior twins … *warrior twins, warrior twins* … just a legend, but here they are."

Eric looked back. "What the hell are you stammering about?"

Eliseo shook his head. "Warrior Twins, *guerreros de doubles*, you two … it's all coming together. There is a legend. We were told many stories as kids about hero warrior twins sent by the righteous gods to protect us in our most desperate times of need. Always one boy and one girl. And it all fits going back to your mom and Uncle Roberto. You two are the next in line, the twins of legend. You're here now because you *have* to be. You found each other because the fates determined you would. Unbelievable or not, considering all we now know."

"Okay so we are these *Wonder Twins* you're talking about."

"Warrior twins," Eliseo corrected.

"Whatever." Eric motioned his chin towards his arm stuck in the wall. "What are we supposed to do now?"

"Umm, I don't know. Try turning the levers at the same time."

Eric looked at Jessica and smiled. "On three? One, two, three and then turn the levers, or are we turning on three, like one, two, then turn?"

"Why does it matter?"

"Come on, sis, tell me you have never seen the

Lethal Weapon movies … ugh, you're killing me."

Eliseo: "I've seen them. Mel Gibson and Samuel L. Jackson right? Great movies!"

"Yes, Samuel L. Jackson, because he's in everything."

"This conversation is asinine." Jessica locked eyes with Eric. "One, two, three, then turn, okay, Murtaugh?"

"You've seen them." Eric smiled. "And if I'm anyone, it's Riggs."

The pair counted and the levers moved, grinding from one position to another. They pulled their arms out. The rock wall slowly slid backward, grinding along the floor, tearing away years of cobwebs and filling the air with a cloud of fine dust.

Eric made his way to the opening, trouble-light in hand. Cool, stale air wafted into his face as he stuck his arm and head around the other side of the rock. Eric lit up the open space. He looked down. "There's stairs. Grab one of the floods, and whatever else you think we need. I'm going down."

Jessica took her backpack and another flashlight and headed for the stairs.

Eliseo stopped her.

"We may need this." The necklace had popped out of its resting place as the wall opened up. Eliseo moved behind Jessica and re-attached her necklace. "For luck, if nothing else."

She turned and kissed Eliseo on the cheek. "Also for luck." She entered the stairwell.

Eliseo followed.

Eric waited for his partners to join him. "What would you guys say? Looks like a 12x12 room to me, and check out the corners, the room's square, but there are no seams anywhere."

"These walls are unnaturally smooth. It's odd they are clear of any markings."

Jessica illuminated the middle of the chamber. "Our luck hasn't run out yet. Look at these chunks of limestone. They match the pieces in the box upstairs. We need to get that down here."

"Hey, Eliseo, I think when my sister said *we* just now, she meant me and you. Typical."

ERIC AND ELISEO retrieved the box. They unloaded the tablet pieces and took a rest while Jessica matched the pieces together. No surprise that the sections of tablets turned out to be exact matches to the ones Eric and Jessica had brought with them from Dr. Dirk.

"These add even more rich detail to the story Jessica and I uncovered deciphering the glyphs on the box. And now I see where the codex will be useful."

Eliseo and Jessica worked in tandem translating the reconnected slabs of limestone. Eric wandered around the chamber looking for any other signs that might help.

"Eric, were done with the translations. We just need to organize what we wrote."

Eliseo started to read. "It was only when he moved on his own to the highland city-states that the other gods took notice of his actions. Once the extent of the carnage in the lowland city-states was realized by The Absolute, He set His plans in motion that would rid the realm of man of the scourge His creation had become."

Eric was confused. "The Absolute? *Who* or *what* is that?"

"Much like the Greeks, Romans, and numerous other deities of past religions, they liked to mettle in the lives of humans. This information points to a God of the gods, the All Father. And it seems as though He didn't take too kindly to one of His own directly interfering with the lives of the Mayans."

Jessica took over. "The Absolute created weapons that when placed in the right hands would stop Difatos. These would send Difatos on the Dark Road or the Path to the Void. During a time of need, warrior twins of the sacred bloodline will appear."

Eliseo: "See, the tools, at least some of them, have been placed in front of you. We just need to figure out *how*, *when*, and *where* to use them. There isn't any more about the twins in here. The rest deals with Difatos and his claims to power."

Jessica: "All can be put in place to rule Xiabalba. The process begins with the eradication of the ancient bloodline and the implements of Difatos's destruction. Once he has vanquished the twins, and removed their blood from the pool of life, no death can touch the great god-king of man. The other gods, not much more will they wait, as they are sent one by one to the Black Road. Soon none will be able to stop Difatos. He will serve at the right hand of no one, and all mankind will bow to his power."

Eliseo paraphrased the last little bit. "If the most righteous and powerful of the other gods had bothered to interfere, they could have neutralized the threat of Difatos in one fell swoop, but it seems as though they had other things to worry about."

"Other gods? What the hell does that mean?"

"As we dig deeper into this mystery, Jessica and I have come to realize that the Mayans believed there were many different gods on several levels of importance. The Absolute created a bloodline bestowed with special powers and responsibilities."

Jessica motioned between Eric and herself. "All signs point to you and I being part of that bloodline."

"And what, we're tasked with stopping Difatos, or any other god that steps out of line?"

Suddenly a grayish mist swirled in one corner of the chamber. It appeared and disappeared within an instant.

"You guys see and hear that?"

"I saw the mist, like what we saw back at the farm."

Eliseo nodded. "I saw it, but what did you hear?"

Eric: "Like someone trying to talk in a windstorm. Faded in and out, but it said: *You are on the right path, keep pushing, complete the task.* What was that?"

Eliseo shook his head. "Maybe the gods are talking to you."

"What? Like, *Are you there, god, it's me Eric?* Come on. What makes me and Jessica so special."

"Seems frustrating now, Eric, but think of it as an investigation. All of the evidence doesn't just jump into your lap. I'm sure Eliseo would tell you it's that way with archeology and anthropology, too. It will come. There has to be more and we will find it."

Eric was about to speak when he stopped and cocked his head. "Now, do you hear *that*? Damn gods talking again?"

A faint beeping.

"Damn, look at the time." Eliseo checked his watch. "That has to be Paco. We've been down here for over an hour."

They all grabbed a light, made their way to the stairs, and rushed out of the temple to see a relaxed Paco leaning on his car outside the service gate. As they made their way, Eric wondered if he was doing the right thing in leaving Eliseo and Jessica. They got to the gate and Paco beckoned Eric to hurry.

Eric turned to Jessica, looking for an answer.

"It's going to be fine. I will be fine. Nothing is going to happen to me while you are gone. You're not getting rid of me. Besides, I've got Eliseo."

Eric dropped his head to one side and raised a brow.

"I didn't mean … ugh, you are so difficult."

She leaned over and kissed him on the cheek. "Make sure you come back in one piece, too, mister. Warrior twins doesn't work as a title if there's only one of us. And I promise, no Indiana Jones stuff until you get back."

"Sounds good, be safe." Eric climbed into the jeep next to Paco.

RAUL GUZMAN WAS sure that in the group's hurried state they had not noticed him. When he was sure the adventurers were not coming back, he stepped from the shadows. From what he caught of their conversation, only two of them were coming back. There were stairs somewhere inside; he was sure he heard them mention that.

If he could find a place to hide, he might be able to take them out one at a time.

Raul found himself in need of a weapon. It didn't have to be anything special. If he couldn't handle that woman and the archeologist nerd, then he should get out of the business and go back to hustling money from tourists.

Raul turned his attention back to the chamber; it was well lit. He could see the staircase the others had talked about. Heading in that direction, he grabbed a flashlight from one of the backpacks left behind, descended the stairs, and noticed the box the two men had struggled with earlier.

There must be something in there of use.

Peering into the box, he noticed the glyph-covered partial slabs of stone. Those would fetch a fair sum, but then he noticed something even more needed at the moment—a knife. Granted, it was unlike any other he had seen. It had a beautiful ornate handle and a striking green blade.

Jade!

It would do.

He found a small recessed area behind the stairs, where he could wait for that bitch and her friend to return. *This is going to turn out all right for me after all.*

He cut the power to the flashlight.

PART VI
END GAME

CHAPTER FORTY-SEVEN

TOM DEERING WAITED patiently next to the squad car. He fidgeted with the brim of his campaign hat. Snapshots of life clicked in his head: high school sweetheart, marriage, career, house, and a baby Jeremy.

He loved the quirkiness of Hurley County, but this sheriff and the demon stuff was too much, and he was tasked with keeping a lid on it. *This place lives for gossip, regular as the rising sun.* If what he thought was true at the sheriff's house, Eric needed to take the lead. Deering hoped Eric had some answers for him, and was close to finishing whatever it was he and Jessica needed to do.

"Tom, Tom, over here." Eric exited the terminal building of the county airport.

"Thank God, you're finally here. Don't know how much more I can handle."

"Tell me about it on the way." Eric climbed into the passenger side of the squad car. They pulled out and drove down Airport Hill and made a left onto Route 60, heading north. "We're making some headway down in Mexico. A few hiccups, but Jessica and our contact, Eliseo Gomez, are going to be able to crack this thing wide open. That reminds me, I wouldn't mind stopping by the professor's office. I'm sure he'll be impressed."

Deering kept shooting glances at Eric, waiting for his turn to contribute to the conversation. "Seeing Dr. Dirk is going to be out of the question."

"Why? It's not out of the w—"

"You're not following. The professor's gone. Ricky Mack found cyanide in his system. Why would the old man off himself?"

"Andy." Eric pounded the dashboard with his fist. "The doctor held onto my parents' secret for so long. It's not right. At least he went on his own terms. Good for him."

"It might get much worse. Strange reports coming to us about the Pontillo place. Looks normal, but no one has seen the Pontillos the last two days."

"What reports?"

"Peculiar noises, weird colored smoke, strange smells. Nothing good. Nothing normal."

"He couldn't be sick enough to have hurt his wife. Not Aunt Julia. He loves her."

"He loved your folks, too, Eric." Tom instantly regretted the words.

"We're burning daylight. Let's get out there ASAP." Eric checked his Glock. "We may have the element of surprise, hopefully his men weren't supposed to make contact yet. He won't know I left Mexico."

Deering didn't need further instruction. He flicked on his lights, pressed the pedal, and headed toward the Pontillo residence. Eric may've been a pain in the ass to work with, but Deering never doubted his skill or instinct. They made the turn off of Route 60 onto

Lakeview Road.

"I want you to park down a ways from the sheriff's house and wait for me."

"Wait for what?"

"For me to get back. I'm going up to the house."

"That's a bad idea, wrapped in a shitty concept, covered in scheme."

"You brought me back because things were getting weird. Weird is my new normal. Julia could be hurt, or worse. Pontillo and Difatos could have set this strange stuff up to get me and/or Jessica away from Mexico."

"There are too many unknowns."

"You know me, can't stay away from a mystery."

"I know. I just don't like it." Deering pulled the patrol car into a parking area of a scenic overlook.

"Half hour tops, then call for backup, grab that riot gun, and come save me."

"I got your six."

Eric responded by giving Tom a shug."

"Thirty minutes, then I'm right behind you. Good luck." Tom set a timer on his digital watch.

"A timer? You are efficient Deputy Deering." Eric disappeared into the woods which morphed into the tree line that ran along Andy Pontillo's property.

Tom Deering stepped to the rear of the patrol car and popped the trunk. He donned a Kevlar vest. *Hope this day doesn't turn out like Danny Glover's in* Predator 2.

He strapped on a bandolier that held 25 shells. He made sure the Heckler & Koch FABARM FP6 was fully loaded, then racked a round into the chamber. "Hope to God you come walking out of those woods in less than 30-minutes."

CHAPTER FORTY-EIGHT

JESSICA AND ELISEO walked back to the temple.

Did you mean what you said about not being able to shoot Eric's gun?" She took out her sidearm and cleared the chamber. "If you want, I can show you. You'd pick it up in no time."

"May I?" Eliseo held out his hand.

"Safety's on, chamber's cleared. Get the *feel* of it."

They entered the outer chamber of the Temple. As they approached the stairs, Eliseo stopped and moved to the side. "Ladies, first."

Jessica brought her flashlight to life. "Ever the gentleman."

"It is easy to be that way around you." Eliseo followed her down the stone stairs.

Jessica made her way to the center of the room where the limestone box stood and the broken tablets lay pieced together. "We really did a lot here, didn't we?"

Eliseo reached the bottom of the stairs and sat down. "As much as we have uncovered, Eric is right about the fact that we are no closer to finding out how to use the weapons to get rid of Difatos."

"Wow, never thought I would hear you say you and Eric were on the same wavelength."

"His heart's in the right place, even if his head isn't all the time." A pause. Eliseo looked away. "Huh, that's weird." He moved from the steps and backed away from Jessica. "The room looks round from this angle. The walls, almost windswept. There seems to be some indentations on the floor, just a foot or so away from the wall. I didn't notice any of this earlier. Come here and take a look. Tell me if you see the same thing."

THIS WAS HIS chance.

The tour guide was standing within striking distance; once he took him, he would grab the woman and teach her a lesson. He waited for her to make her way over to Eliseo, and then he moved from behind the stairs, and struck, slashing at Eliseo's leg just above the ankle, just missing the Achilles tendon. He had hoped it would send him to the ground, but he just stumbled towards the center of the room. Eliseo screamed and grabbed for his leg as he started to go down.

Jessica, confused, instead of looking to where an attack might come from, turned all of her attention to Eliseo. Raul slid in from behind, hooking his left arm inside hers, and pulling her close as he brought the knife to Jessica's throat.

"Hey, bitch, remember me? You shouldn't have stuck that gun in my face. It's time to pay up."

Jessica could barely let out a scream with her head

pulled back and the jade knife ready to open her throat.

"Not so tough now, are you?" Raul tightened his grip on Jessica and put more pressure on the skin of her neck.

"What the hell, man? Do you realize the trouble you're?" Eliseo tried to steady himself while raising Jessica's gun. As his weight shifted, pain shot up his leg, and he could feel the warm, spreading wetness soaking through his sock.

"Oh, so the one-legged tour guide is going to save his damsel. Tell me, how accurate do you think you can be without being able to put pressure on that leg?"

"Just let her go and I can make sure the charges placed on you are not that severe."

"Wow, you would do that for me? I'm honored. Didn't realize you had so much pull with the police around here." Raul pulled the knife in a tad closer while grabbing Jessica's right breast. "No, what you are going to do is put that gun down on the ground and slowly push it over to me. Then I'm going to shoot you and teach the *chica* here what happens when you stick a gun in the wrong person's face." He licked Jessica's ear. "And I'm going to have fun doing it, too."

"Do you really want to bring that kind of heat upon yourself? I mean it really could be much easier for you."

Raul Guzman was becoming agitated. "Don't tell me what I do or don't want to do! Just put the fucking gun on the ground already!"

JESSICA COULD FEEL Guzman's grip on her loosening as he grew angrier. He was losing control. *Just keep doing what you're doing, Eliseo.*

"No need to yell, Raul. We'll do it your way. Even if it's wrong." Eliseo knelt, placing the gun on the floor of the chamber.

"Now back away." Guzman inched forward. "Kneel down, bitch."

Jessica knew Guzman wanted to get that gun in his hands, but he was going to have to loosen his grip on her to do it. She readied herself to move the moment she felt any slack in his hold. She did as instructed and lowered herself to her left knee, but at the same time straightened her right leg backward—between Guzman's legs. He pulled the knife away from her throat, but tightened his hold of her arm as he reached out to take the gun. Eliseo had retreated a few feet, but Guzman didn't notice he had positioned his good leg under him, coiled so he could leap at any moment.

Eliseo's eyes caught Jessica's, and without a sound they both sprang into action.

Jessica kicked hard and fast, catching Guzman square between the legs. His grip instantly went slack and she pushed herself. Simultaneously, Eliseo leapt forward, grabbing Guzman's wrist, and twisting the attacker's arm behind him before letting the momentum from the leap carry them into the wall of the chamber.

Blood splattered on the wall as Guzman's nose broke from the force of the impact. Eliseo raised Guzman's arm, and before it broke, drove him to the ground. Eliseo straddled Guzman and started wailing on his head—"Piece of shit! You-Goddamned-Piece-of-Shit!"—sending their assailant on the bullet train to Unconscious-Ville.

Eliseo fell to one side.

His chest heaved, his body shook, and he stared at his hands.

Jessica was there in an instant with the medical kit from her backpack and nylon rope. She tended to Eliseo's leg as best she could. Then they both secured Guzman by hogtying him with the climbing rope.

"I was so worried." Eliseo held on to Jessica. "There was no way I was letting him leave this room with you. I just didn't know what to do."

"You were perfect. Calm. And you waited for him to lose control and made your move. It all worked out."

Eliseo stood and helped Jessica to her feet. He leaned in and returned the kiss she had given him hours earlier. He pulled away slightly, his hands cupping her face. "I won't ever let anything bad happen to you. I couldn't stand it."

"YES, YES, DIEGO, I know this is the most we've talked to each other in years. I was hoping it would be under different circumstances as well. Thank you for sending your men out so quickly. Of course I will catch you up on all of this as soon as I am able." Eliseo hung up the phone and returned to Jessica. "Guzman will be on his way to police headquarters in a few minutes. My friend Diego assures me there will be a laundry list of charges following him."

"Nice to have friends in high places. I think we've

had enough excitement for one night, don't you? I could use a beer and someplace comfortable to sit."

"Then let's retire to the plush environ of the BREAK ROOM."

Eliseo secured the outside door of the administration building. Jessica scrounged up some food from the provisions they brought. They both cleaned up in the washroom as best they could and sat down to what might as well have been a five-star meal.

"I don't know about you, but I still feel jittery."

With the grace of a magician drawing a rabbit from a cap, Eliseo emerged from the other side of the refrigerator door with four Dos Equis. "This fine Mexican beer might be just what the doctor ordered to take the edge off." Eliseo opened two beers, handed one to Jessica, and sat down next to her on the couch. "You know, I grew up with all of these fantastic stories about the bravery and courage of the warrior twins, and how they were perfect beings. You certainly fit the bill."

Jessica batted her eyes at Eliseo. "Awww ... I bet you say that to *all* the girls."

He laughed. "I'm serious. This is some mind-blowing stuff we're dealing with. What we know proves the existence of gods."

"Not just god, singular, but gods, as in more than one. Think about what that will do to the world."

"Amazing and frightening at the same time. I surely don't want to be the one to let that cat out of the bag."

Jessica touched her index finger to her nose and smiled. "Not it."

"Well, thank you for throwing me under the

proverbial bus."

Jessica lightly tapped Eliseo on the arm. "You can handle it, big guy. I have faith in you."

"I appreciate that. But you know, it's equally amazing for me to be in the presence of one of the warrior twins. I really feel blessed, but at the same time I'm questioning why I am the one who gets to have this experience." Eliseo absentmindedly ran his hand up and down Jessica's leg, over and over tracing its outline.

"Wow, you really know how to lay it on thick." Jessica slapped away a wandering hand. "Those are some very cosmic pick-up lines."

"Nothing of the sort. You're part of my heritage. You're here in the present, but at the same time you are a legend, a *living* legend."

Jessica put down her beer and took Eliseo's from his hand and placed it beside hers. She turned to face him, stretching one leg on either side. "You are adorable." She leaned in and pulled him by his shirt down on top of her. "Well, Mister, I'm questioning my existence. Have you ever slept with a living legend?"

INTERLUDE VI

ANDY PONTILLO WALKED along the picturesque path at the edge of the meticulously manicured green space of Forest Hill Cemetery.

What a waste of prime real estate. Why do we continue this idiotic ritual? He reached into a plastic trash receptacle and pulled out a bunch of wilted, dying flowers. The ribbon attached said TO GRANDMA, WE LOVE YOU. Andy tore the piece of cloth off. "She doesn't even know you bought this, fools."

At the end of the path, he stepped onto the grass, walked down two rows and five gravestones in, and stood between Johnnie and Mother. He pulled a full pint of Knob Creek from his back pocket, cracked the seal, poured some on his brother's grave and took a long swig. He replaced the cap and leaned the bottle against the granite memorial, a tradition he started the year Johnnie died.

"I brought her flowers, John." Andy tossed the garbage bouquet at the base of Mother's headstone. "Won't ever understand why you wanted to do this every year, but this will be the last one. I'm so close, I can taste it, my dear brother. Everything you believed is going to happen." He turned his attention to the grave next to John's. *Those are better than anything you deserve, bitch.*

Zzziipppp.

Andy proceeded to water the flowers marking Mother's grave.

CHAPTER
FORTY-NINE

€RIC DIDN'T LIKE the feeling he was getting as he moved out of the tree line and closer to the Pontillo house.

His gut instincts had served him pretty to this point in life, and they were screaming at him to turn and run. He pressed on knowing that he had to get to the bottom of this long strange trip he had been taken on.

He quickly and quietly ambled through the wooded area that surrounded the Pontillo residence until reached the house. Eric's spine started to act up as he moved in closer. It was the same empty feeling he'd had driving up to his parents' house the day after the murders. The house seemed devoid of life. He peered in a few of the downstairs windows and tried to open them.

Locked.

"Screw this." He decided to try the front door. Not surprisingly, he found it unlocked. The people in Hurley County rarely if ever locked their doors—a practice that might change in an instant if the true story of all that had transpired over the last few days ever got out.

Every fiber of Eric's being screamed at him to rush

into the house, but the years of training took control and he opened the door with caution. A putrid smell hit him in the face like Buford Pusser's Big Stick, the smell of decaying, burnt flesh filling his nostrils. He backed out of the doorway and wretched. He kept from vomiting, but barely. His mind instantly went to the night his parents were murdered and tears began to well. He brought his hand up to the bridge of his nose and pinched, squeezing his eyes shut. He took a moment, then another three, before gritting his teeth and forcing a long deep breath past his lips.

The pro-fessional, *the* cop doing his job, was back in charge.

He made his way past the front door and rested his hand on the banister of the open staircase. He formulated a plan and started combing the house for any signs of the Pontillos or Difatos.

A quick scan downstairs produced no results.

He circled around and was back near the front foyer and standing at the base of the stairs that led to the second floor. "Damn, this is always when the bad stuff happens in the movies. At least I didn't actually say *I'll be right back* to Tom.

Moving to the stair, back pressed against the wall, he started to ascend, Glock at the ready. He vacillated between looking up to the unknown and checking back down the stairs. The closer he got to the second-floor landing, the stronger the odor first smelled as he entered the house.

The stench of death led his nose to the master bedroom.

Keeping his gun high in one hand, he opened the door and stepped inside. The air was thick and rancid.

He could see Julia Pontillo's lifeless corpse tied to the bed. Dozens of the same carvings and glyphs that covered his father's body were carved into her skin. He couldn't help the tears that streamed down his face.

Looking at Julia's desecrated naked body, he imagined the horrific pain she and his parents must have endured. There was a sheet folded on a chair in the corner of the room.

Eric made his way over.

Holstering his gun, he picked up the sheet and spread it out over the top of the husk that used to be Julia Pontillo. "Don't worry, Aunt Julia, I promise, Andy will never hurt anyone again."

Eric exited the room and started to descend the stairs. He paused when he heard a voice from below, one that he knew all too well.

CHAPTER FIFTY

"THERE IS NO one here. The blood-ancients, as you call them, are in Mexico, which is where we need to be."

"I needed time to infuse the energy gained from the innocent. And one of the spawn of the ancients is in our vicinity. I can smell it, *feel* it."

Eric appeared at the door of the study, where just days ago he'd had a conversation with Andy Pontillo. "I'm right here, Difatos, and I have something for you!" He emptied the clip of the Glock 37 and sent Difatos reeling. Pontillo dove behind one of his chairs. Eric knew his old boss was there, but his focus was solely on the demon. He ejected the magazine, slammed in another, racked the slide, and fired again.

A few rounds into the reload, Eric saw Pontillo in his peripheral coming at him with something in his hand. Before he could react, Pontillo swung a fireplace poker, bringing it down on Eric's gun and knocking it from his hand. Eric grabbed the poker, shifted his weight, and was able to throw the sheriff over his hip, sending him flying. Turning back to Difatos, he saw the demon starting to recover from the barrage of bullets he'd sent his way.

Wanting to press the advantage, Eric scanned the

room, but couldn't locate his gun. Andy kept a .308 Winchester rifle in the garage, if he could get there. Difatos stood in front of the French doors leading to the deck, Eric's straightest and quickest shot to the building outside.

"You've reached the end of your existence, chosen one. Once the ki of you and your sibling is mine, no one will be left to stop me. My conquest of this realm will be complete. I'll hold The Absolute's greatest prize and all of my brethren will bow to me."

Eric used the reprieve Difatos's monologue provided to focus and energize the decorative medieval shield he pulled from the wall. With uncanny power, he launched himself at Difatos. As he slammed into him, the force of the blow sent both of them crashing through the double doors. Eric rolled over the top of his enemy and sprinted for the garage. Difatos leapt and tackled Eric from behind. He raised a clawed hand, poised to strike. "Your essence will give me great strength."

"Stop, Difatos, don't kill him, not yet!" Pontillo approached, stepping over broken glass and splintered wood. Difatos grabbed Eric by the shoulders and forced him to kneel.

"Everyone has a fatal flaw, guess yours is this little neck of the woods. And coming here alone? I thought you were a smarter cop than that."

"Always thought of you as a good cop and a friend to my parents, guess we disappointed each other."

"I was NEVER a good cop. Remember, there are two types of people that go into law enforcement, those who genuinely want to help others, and people who are power hungry control freaks?" Pontillo closed in, pulling out the same knife used to incise his wife. "I played your parents from the beginning. This was always about *me*, always. I pushed your parents to stay in the area, convincing them it would be best for you and your sister. I wanted to keep you two together, but your mom and uncle had different ideas. Eventually, I acquiesced, keeping track of one of you would be good enough, the other would eventually show. Fate has a funny way of working things out."

Searing pain ripped through Eric's punctured shoulders. "You planned this. That's not fate, and it'll be your downfall."

"Regardless, your damn father made it much more difficult than need be. He wouldn't confide in me where the box and the weapons were hidden."

"Foresight, sensed a Judas in his midst."

Andy scowled. "Rather than just being able to kill you, you had to be brought into the circle. The shock of their deaths and the revelations in the journal should have broken you, made you easy to take down. Don't you see? You never had a life of your own. You've been a pawn in a much greater game, used by me, used by your parents."

Eric grimaced. "That's where you're wrong, Andy. If you had gotten into chess like Dad and I, you would know a pawn CAN take down a king." He threw his head back, motioning to Difatos. "You and your smelly pet."

"Always the charming smart-ass? Your time in the sun is just about up. I'm surprised to see you here, instead of in Mexico with Benitez trying to figure out a way to stop us. The only thing not being here does is prolong her life for another day. Too bad, she won't be privy to this little secret." He leaned in, inched the blade closer to Eric's face. "There's no way to stop us once your bloodline ends. After that, it's simple clean-up, destroy the weapons, Difatos ascending in the pantheon of the gods, and then *me*, taking my rightful place at his side."

"Enough of this mindless prattle! The spawn of the blood-ancients have eluded me for long enough. I will savor the taste and feel of your essence as it is pulled from you. Take solace in that your demise will greatly nourish me. Soon death's icy touch will be nothing but a fable."

"Hope you choke on my essence."

$HIT, ERIC. DON'T be mad at me for being early to the party.

Tom Deering emerged from behind the hedgerow and sprinted around the corner of the house. He rushed toward the combatants, praying it wasn't too late to help. As he closed in, he emptied the gun into Difatos's back. He stopped a few feet away, dropped to a knee, steadied himself, reloaded, and fired again, and kept firing until the last shell ejected.

Difatos reared up and growled—a little more than stung by the rounds—Eric fell to the ground. He used the distraction to lunge forward and grab Pontillo's hand clutching the knife. The two began to grapple. Eric bent the sheriff's wrist back towards him, driving the blade into his rib cage. Pontillo screamed. Eric pulled it out, grabbed the man he once loved like a second father by the shoulder and drove the knife to its hilt into his carotid artery, twisting the blade. "This is for my parents, you sick son of a bitch!"

Difatos, recovered from the barrage of slugs, stumbled towards Eric and Pontillo. He wrapped both of them in his slick, oily, scaled arms, and chanted. A blinding light and swirling smoke appeared as they were disappeared.

Tom Deering was launched backwards by the energy generated. He sat up, shading his eyes from the dissipating light. "Godspeed, Eric, and good luck."

CHAPTER FIFTY-ONE

ELISEO'S EYES POPPED open; he had the feeling something terrible had happened. Just as suddenly, he was comforted by the fact Jessica's head was still resting on his chest and her naked curves nestled. One arm and leg lazily draped over his body.

He didn't want this moment to end.

Of all the amazing occurrences in the last day and a half, the consummation of their relationship ranked at the top—there was no second.

They had talked before drifting off to sleep and agreed the experience was like no other. Their connection was evident from the moment they met. No matter what the rest of this adventure entailed, Eliseo made a promise to himself, that he would do everything in his power to keep Jessica safe.

As if on cue, Jessica started to stir. She lifted her head, smiled and kissed Eliseo's chest, and then moved upward and kissed him, sucking in a lip before nibbling on his tongue. "What time is it?"

"Not nearly time for us to get moving, but something tells me we should."

He grabbed various parts and squeezed and nuzzled and found hair to stroke. "It's about 3:00 A.M.

I'm going to send out e-mails again about the ruins being closed. Then I think we should get back to the chamber. I've an idea about the indentations I saw before all of the unpleasantness with Mr. Guzman."

"Unpleasantness … that's one way of putting it. Well, you can go send your e-mails as soon as you help me find all of my clothes." Jessica smiled as she pulled her shirt from between the couch cushions, then smiled even broader when it came in her hands in two pieces. "Eliseo, got another shirt?"

CHAPTER FIFTY-TWO

AS QUICKLY AS possible, Eliseo and Jessica returned to the chamber discovered the day before. It still had mysteries to reveal. They went into full investigation mode as they searched for more clues.

"Look here. What I started to show you yesterday. These indentations near the wall. They look like they're supposed to hold something. Help me move one of the tablets over here."

They moved the first tablet they translated into the spot. It fit—perfectly. The chamber floor between the tablet and the wall started to move. The stone flowed, looking like mercury spilled on a tabletop—moving, creamy liquid, re-a-ranging, re-forming … into new glyphs to be translated.

"Holy shit, add that to the list of things never seen before. Let's get these other tablets into place."

Without a word, Jessica moved to the next one. She and Eliseo worked to get them all into place. As each stone was set, glyphs appeared between it and the wall. Once they were all in place, the pair made their way back to the first tablet and began to decipher the glyphs.

"It looks like we're going to have to rely more on the codex and manuscript this time around, and not so much by feel."

"Were I a lesser man, I would make some kind of base comment about how figuring it out by *feel* is much more fun, but I won't."

"Here I was thinking you weren't a typical guy."

"SO ONE OF the warrior twins is always more in tune with the metaphysical side of things, while the other is a beast of earthly power. If the former is a blade, the latter is a hammer."

"Hammer-head. I've only known my brother for a few days, but I have a feeling he's been called worse. He'll probably just tell you that you messed up the translation somehow."

"I wouldn't doubt it. Anyway, from what this says, Difatos has tried to usurp control of the realm of man on three other occasions. Each time he has been defeated by the twins. With each attempt, he grows more powerful. That must account for the shortened time span between his intended coups. The prophecy proclaims, 'When the gods are defeated for the last time, the cycle of the warrior twins will be broken.'"

"With the rising number of conflicts around the world, and the increasingly selfish, uncaring, and apathetic nature of man, it's no wonder my parents, and now Eric and I, have been called on to face Difatos for the second time in just 30-years. He is thriving on man's hatred and mistrust of each other. I'd bet he uses it to grow stronger."

"It is a distinct possibility. I find it odd these

newest translations don't mention Difatos by name. They just keep saying gods, like it doesn't have to be Difatos that the warrior twins face."

"Maybe there isn't a need to use his name anymore. Where is this Island of the Dead that holds the implements needed to send Difatos to the Black Road? I mean we already have the twin obsidian and jade knives, but what about the jaguar pelt, the staff with a jaguar claw at one end and an obsidian orb at the other, and the all-seeing jade mask? These aren't things we can pick up at the local market."

"I know where the rumored location of the island is supposed to be, but I have no idea how to actually travel there. Maybe if go to the spot along the coast where it's supposed to be, the island will appear. After all, you are a blood-ancient."

"Then we pack up and go. We get word to Eric and he can meet us there."

"That'll be easy enough to accomplish through Paco."

Jessica stood and stretched, cocked her head to one side. and stared at the markings around her feet. "Were these on the floor before?" Jessica pointed to a series of glyphs ringing the box in the center of the room.

"They most certainly were not. But they look like gibberish from here." Eliseo walked over and stood within the circle of the glyphs. "I'll be damned. Come here and look at this."

As soon as her second foot landed inside the circle, they felt a vibration in the floor and heard a low steady hum.

"What is that?"

"Your guess is as good as mine." Eliseo turned his

attention to the glyphs and started to read them, turning to follow the circle around. "These words don't make any sense in the order they're in. It's like they can't be translated. All that comes to me is the Mayan pronunciation. Why don't you try?"

Jessica started to read the glyphs. "Same thing, it's just the Mayan pronunciation that fills my head. It's like I can't think of anything else."

"Try again. This time vocalize what comes in your head."

"Sure." As Jessica started to speak, the vibrations felt earlier got stronger. The hum, almost deafening. She looked at Eliseo. He urged her to continue. Jessica looked down at the floor and didn't notice that the walls were now spinning, but Eliseo did.

"Ay, *Dios Mio!*"

They both felt the shake and clatter of the chamber. It spun faster and faster as Jessica finished reading. A greenish-purple haze filled the area and there was a flash of light, and then another, and another and anotherandanotheranotheranother

Eliseo and Jessica's screams were drowned out by the loud crack that followed the final enormous starburst.

CHAPTER FIFTY-THREE

BY THE TIME the room stopped spinning, Eliseo and Jessica were on the floor holding on to the limestone box like a life preserver.

"That would be one hell of a ride at Disney."

"I'm not sure I ever want to do that again. Look at that." Eliseo pointed to where the staircase had been. There was now a large opening. He started walking towards it.

Jessica ran to catch up. "You aren't going anywhere without me."

They stepped through the opening and found themselves in a corridor filled with ornate carvings and artwork. Six large pillars, three on either side, were spaced between the artifacts. As they walked through the corridor, it veered off to the left and they saw daylight, sand, and water. Jessica ran ahead, out to the water's edge. She could tell they were on an island. By the time Eliseo reached her, he was able to surmise they were off the coast of Campeche.

"We're on the Island of the Dead."

"How … how did we get here? And how are we going to get Eric here?" Jessica looked around in amazement.

"The warrior twins must have been given a way to

travel back and forth. What is more vexing is that back in there"—Eliseo jutted a thumb over his shoulder—"I counted glyphs and carvings from no less than five other civilizations, including the Greeks."

"So, this bloodline thing isn't just related to the Mayans? Let's get back inside and see what we can find. There has to be something in there telling us what to do next."

As they entered the corridor and rounded the corner, Eliseo and Jessica came face to face with two warriors carved into the pillars they had walked past just moments earlier.

"My God, that female warrior … she looks just like you, and *look*, she's holding the staff mentioned in the glyphs. The male's face is blurred, it might look like Eric, but it's hard to tell. He does have the pelt and jade mask, though." Eliseo moved in and gathered the items from the statues. "See if you can read the glyphs at the bottoms of the pedestals."

"These tell what Eric and I have to do to start the process. There's an incantation, and we have to carve the glyphs for power and knowledge, it's a bloodletting."

"Quite the common practice, as far as antiquated societies are concerned. I would have been surprised if there wasn't."

The pair made their way back to the inner chamber and laid the items on top of the box.

"What is the next step? Find our way back to Kohunlich?"

Before Eliseo could answer, a loud crack and boom filled the chamber inside the temple. It was the loudest thunderclap Eliseo had ever heard. It was followed by a blinding flash of light. Eliseo and Jessica both closed their eyes and shielded them.

In an instant the light was gone.

"That was eerily familiar."

"I'm seeing spots. What was that all about?" Eliseo rubbed his eyes, trying to get them back in focus.

"I hate to be the bearer of bad news, but I would bet the house that it has something to do with Difatos."

DIFATOS, PONTILLO, AND Eric slammed into the beach near the water. Eric scrambled to distance himself from the demon. Disoriented from the teleportation, he kept trying to run, and kept stumbling every time until he stopped and vomited. The soft footing of the beach added to the level of difficulty and to his confusion. Finally, he caught his balance. Not understanding how he was on a beach didn't stop him from taking off in a mad dash. Eric saw what looked like the mouth of a cave up ahead.

Get to shelter and get away from Difatos.

Eric's legs worked overtime, moving faster than his mind. He slammed into the wall and bounced off. He fell and got back up and rounded the same corner to the inner chamber that Jessica and Eliseo had just passed. He was stopped dead in his tracks by what he saw.

"Tell me I'm not hallucinating? Are you really standing in front of me, Eric?"

"Jessica, Eliseo, where the hell did you come from? Where are we?"

DIFATOS FELL TO all fours as they landed.

The stress of transporting three bodies rather than two left him weak. Difatos made his way to Pontillo and drew the last bit of life from his dying body. "You have completed your last act as a good servant. Your sacrifice will help me defeat the blood-ancients."

The god raised his arms to the sky and began to chant. He knew that in a short amount of time he would be well enough to pursue his prey.

CHAPTER FIFTY-FOUR

"WE ARE ON The Island Of The Dead."

Jessica hugged Eric. "The chamber we found is some sort of vessel for transportation. How did you get here?"

"The last thing I remember is sticking a knife in Pontillo's neck and that demon grabbing a hold of the both of us. Then we all hit the beach and I just scrambled for cover." Eric looked back to where he'd come from. "Jesus, he could be right behind me. What do we do?"

"I'm pretty sure teleporting the three of you that distance has taken a toll on Difatos. We have a little time, but let's work fast all the same."

"So, what have you figured out? What do we need to do?" Eric looked over the jade mask and jaguar pelt. He put the mask up to his face. It was shaped like the mask worn in the *Phantom of the Opera* as it covered Eric's forehead, one eye, and a cheek. As soon as it touched his skin it adhered to him. Through his left eye, he could see Difatos kneeling near the water's edge. Not moving. He pulled the mask off. "I could see Difatos meditating on the beach."

"That's called the *Mask of Second Sight*." Eliseo

pointed at the blades. "The knives, which seem to be the actual things that send Difatos away, stay with you and Jessica. The staff is used to seal the box, and the pelt lines the inside of it. The stone box itself is needed to open the portal to the Black Road. You and Jessica each play a part in the process of opening the portal. She will perform the bulk of the ritual, reciting the incantations the glyphs spell out. The male twin's role in each of the conflicts has been that of a powerful physical force, the hammer to the other's finesse."

"You sure this is going to work, Eliseo?"

"Of course I'm sure. I got it out of my *Vanquishing Mayan Demon Kings for Dummies* book."

"Oh, I see, now everyone is trying to get in on the funny." Eric shot back a smile. "Where do we need to lead Difatos?"

"We have to get him in here." Eliseo pointed into the limestone box centered in the room.

Eric looked at the box and back up at Eliseo. "I don't think he's going to fit."

Eliseo and Jessica rolled their eyes.

"There is some sort of transformation that happens during the ceremony. He needs to be struck simultaneously with both knives. The prophecy, just like many, is not exactly crystal as to *how* or *where* he needs to be struck. Our best guess is that you both are needed to strike him, and that when you do, it will start the events in motion that send him on the way to the Black Road. It is commonly thought that this Black Road refers to the galactic center of the Milky Way, and possibly to a massive black hole."

"You would think the *For Dummies* book would spell it out a bit clearer."

Jessica and Eric kept their respective jade and obsidian knives. Jessica   picked up the staff and twirled it a few times, going through some staff forms.

"Wow, sis, I didn't know you were a baton twirler in the marching band."

Jessica gave a halfhearted smile and proceeded to finish the form she was performing by smacking Eric across his backside. "You never miss a chance to be a world class smartass, do you?"

Eric shrugged and held out his hands, palms up.

Eliseo donned the Kevlar vest Eric was wearing when he teleported to the island. He checked the Beretta and then put it into the tactical holster Eric had given him to wear. "Once the ceremony is started, Difatos is bound to appear, probably drawn here by your blood."

"Well, let's hope those jade/obsidian bullets hold him off until Jessica and I complete the ceremony."

Eric moved over to the box and arranged the jaguar pelt inside as Eliseo instructed. Meanwhile, Eliseo and Jessica met a few feet away and held each other's hands.

Finally, Jessica looked up. "No matter what happens, promise you won't put yourself in any unnecessary danger trying to save me. Because I have to think that whatever happens is *meant* to happen. That's the definition of destiny, right?"

"I told you yesterday. I won't ever let anything bad happen to you again, so I can't in good conscience make that promise. I care for you too much."

As tears came up in Jessica's eyes, she leaned in and kissed Eliseo on the lips. "You know you could have said you loved me. It wouldn't have been too soon."

"Demon NOW, room LATER."

The twins moved to their designated areas at either end of the box. Jessica   laid the staff at her side and Eric did the same with the jade mask.

"No going back once we start this. Are you ready?"

Jessica nodded and knelt across from her brother. She brought the jade knife up to her outstretched forearm. Eric did the same with the obsidian blade in his possession. Jessica carved the glyph for knowledge into her arm at the same time Eric carved power into his. Jessica chanted the incantation found at the base of her statue. The small amount of blood spilled seemed to grow in volume as it coursed through the carvings on the side of the box. The carvings began to glow and pulsate. A distinct droning could be heard. Eric and Jessica began to rock slightly from side to side, their arms still extended in front of them.

ᴇLISEO POSITIONED HIMSELF at the doorway to the chamber, waiting for Difatos to arrive. Only Difatos didn't appear there. Difatos's familiar sticky sweet smell of decay filled the room as he materialized in the *back* of the chamber across from Eliseo's position, and behind Eric and Jessica. They were not aware of his appearance because they were still entranced by the ritual. Difatos let out a low growl and instantly moved towards the twins in the center of the room. Eliseo screamed at the top of his lungs, hoping to gain Difatos's attention. However, the ancient god had his own deadly agenda, and was not deterred or distracted.

Eliseo ran forward, drawing the Beretta from his holster.

He stopped and steadied himself, bringing the gun to the shooting position Jessica had taught him and gave the trigger three quick pulls.

The sound of the gun discharging did not phase Difatos.

Eliseo finally managed to get his attention as the first of the three rounds hit. The jade and obsidian bullets had a damaging effect on the monster, with the first bullet hitting him in the shoulder and sending out a spray of turquoise blood. Difatos flinched and growled, but kept moving. The next two rounds were much closer to center mass, where Eliseo had initially aimed.

The olden god now yelped, sounding like an overgrown wounded dog. The bullets ripped into his scaly flesh just left of the center of his chest.

More blood vacated the demon's body in spurts.

He was stopped in his tracks.

A clawed hand moved to investigate a wound and then he looked up, Difatos finally acknowledging Eliseo's presence, and letting out a deep guttural growl. Eliseo stood his ground and fired his final four rounds into the chest and abdomen of Difatos. The force of four shots hitting him in rapid succession sent the ancient god stumbling backward. Quickly, he swapped out the empty mag.

"C'mon, guys, break out of the trance."

Eliseo's plea went unanswered and his respite from Difatos was short-lived. The demon coiled his back legs, and in an explosive jump, leapt the width of the room. In a panic, Eliseo emptied the gun in his direction. Difatos swung his large scaly black clawed hand as he landed and struck Eliseo, sending him reeling, where the man bounced off the wall and slumped to the floor.

JESSICA BROKE FROM the trance just in time to see Eliseo slammed into the wall.

She screamed and moved to attack Difatos with the staff. Eric had already rolled and come up with his knife in an overhand grip. He turned to face Difatos.

Jessica ran at the back of Difatos, propelled herself through the air with the staff, and flew over the top of the demon, the clawed end of her polearm gouging and plowing the length of his back as she did.

He howled in pain.

Eric took advantage of Jessica's distraction by driving the point of his knife into the back of the demon's knee. Keeping the knife lodged in its leg, Eric opened up a large gash as he moved behind their adversary. Difatos mule-kicked with its good leg and caught Eric in the ribs, the shot propelling him across the chamber, where he landed and gasped for breath.

Difatos turned its attention towards Jessica.

Jessica parried each of the ancient god's attempts to strike her. Sparks flew as the obsidian claws clanged off her staff. Difatos was relentless. Jessica started to tire. Her moves became purely defensive and her reactions slowed. She found herself backed against the wall, her arms weakened with each passing moment.

She couldn't hold out much longer.

Eric gathered himself and jumped on Difatos's back. He held on to his thick scaly neck and stabbed with his knife over and over, puncturing several holes in Difatos's thick hide and causing his turquoise blood to flow. Difatos screamed in pain and shrugged his powerful shoulders.

The reaction sent Eric flying off his back.

Rested, Jessica took her turn and went on the offensive. She brought the staff between the beast's legs, hoping that since he was once a man it might have some effect. Difatos howled again. "You men are such babies."

With unnatural quickness, Difatos reached down, and in one motion, grabbed the staff from Jessica's hands and sent it flying. She reached to her side and drew her knife. Before she had a chance to act, she, too, was tossed across the room. The knife skittered across the floor in the same direction.

In the corner, Eliseo started to stir, but did not yet fully regain consciousness.

Jessica landed near a large chunk of debris that had fallen from the vibrations caused by the ritual.

Eric made his way over to his sister. As he drew near, the jade and obsidian knives were drawn to each other and merged into one knife. The weapon instantly pulsed and glowed in Eric's hand as he picked it up. Power surged through the newly-joined weapon. "Well, shit, why didn't I think of that earlier?"

For the first time since the battle ensued, a look of apprehension and fear ran across Difatos's face.

Eric smirked and glanced back at Jessica.

"Eric, no, don't, you can't take him by yourself."

"Hey, I'm the blunt instrument, remember? Stay covered." Eric put the jade mask up to his face, and it adhered just like before. In a flash, Difatos's body was marked with foggy green ovals. The mask showed Eric where to attack the demon. "Alright, Big Ugly, it's just me and you now. Let's do this." Eric moved with a speed never before possessed. The mask not only showed him where to strike the demon, but it also allowed the warrior twin to know Difatos's every move split seconds before they happened. He lashed at the demon and avoided his blows until all but one glowing mark remained. The blows positioned Difatos directly in front of the glowing, pulsating box.

With a guttural animal scream, Eric leapt at Difatos and drove the joined knife into his chest and sent him crashing backwards into the box as the portal opened. A bright flash, swirling turquoise, purple, and black smoke all led up to an implosion that engulfed both of the combatants as they were sucked into the box.

Eliseo crawled to the box and struggled to fix the lid on top of it.

Jessica lowered the staff into the semicircle groove in the top of the box.

The stone took on the same kind of fluidic quality as the chamber floor had. It moved and reorganized itself, locking the staff in place and securing the lid to the box.

The noise and light that had emanated from the box were gone.

The chamber grew deathly silent.

Difatos and Eric had disappeared into the void.

Battered and beaten, Jessica and Eliseo leaned on

the box. Jessica caressed it as tears streamed down her face. "Eric."

Eliseo moved to his knees, and laid his arms on his thighs. He breathed heavily and stared at the box in front of him, still trying to comprehend what had happened. He eventually crawled over to Jessica and pulled her off the box. He wrapped his arms around her, pulling her in tight. She fell limp, burying her head in his chest and continued to sob, with Eliseo joining her.

Difatos was banished.

The victory rang hollow.

EPILOGUE NEXT

FOUR MONTHS AFTER the final events in Mexico....

Eliseo stood by his new bride's side, holding her hand while she positioned herself on the examining table in the obstetrician's office. They waited anxiously for the results of Jessica's most recent check-up.

"Are you sure Dad will be fine being alone at the house for this long?"

"He will be fine. I doubt your father's going to run a marathon while we're gone, but he's now almost fully-recovered, and knows his limitations. We'll be home soon enough."

The doctor entered the room, closing the folder in her hand and smiling ear to ear.

"I'm guessing from the look on your face that everything is okay with the baby, Dr. Schaffer." Jessica shifted her weight. "He or she is healthy, and we are on track for a normal pregnancy?"

"Well," the doctor responded. "The answer to that is *yes* and *no*. You came in today wanting to know the sex of the baby, correct?"

Eliseo nodded. "Yes, we were hoping to get started

on the nursery soon."

"You may want to rethink your plans. He *and* she are both very healthy developing babies. Congratulations! You're going to have *twins*, one boy and one girl."

The newlyweds looked at each other, shocked expressions on their faces as the prophecy reverberated in their heads: *The cycle of the warrior twins will be broken when the gods are defeated for the final time.*

EPILOGUE II
LIGHT AT THE END OF THE TUNNEL

AN INDETERMINATE AMOUNT of time after the defeat of Difatos.

A flash of bright light and a swirling multihued cloud appeared in the sky, a mixture of green and tan smoke-like clouds that swam wildly in all directions. A blackish gray point developed as two objects were expelled from its center. A jade-and-obsidian knife and mask fell and were lodged into the sand.

Then something else was cast from the vortex in the sky—a body, which crashed onto the rocky beach. The figure lay face down, in tattered clothes, cut and bleeding … it slowly rose to consciousness.

Eric Archer weakly lifted his head, his face looking like a prize fighter that had gone the distance with Ali; he looked around and could tell he was on the Island of the Dead.

He managed to utter, "Not, again, I did not buy a return ticket," before his head dropped to the sand.

A figure shrouded in shadows walked towards him. Eric heard a voice that was barely audible. It sounded like waves crashing on the shore inside his head.

The figure spoke.

The upper half of Eric's body was lifted by some unseen force. He was dragged away from his resting place. The figure's voice became clearer.

"I wasn't sure you were going to make it. You accomplished your task well. The Absolute was wise to choose your bloodline. You can rest now, until you are needed again. Soon, all of this will make sense. Your emergence on this side will cause the other gods to take notice. You need to be ready. Your family needs to be ready. This has just begun."

Enjoy this sample from the first chapter of: "Blood of the Ancients, Book II: Difatos Ascending," Coming this fall/2017 from Tim A. Majka and Devil Dog Press

CHAPTER ONE

SERGEANT HOWARD "HUSTIE" Hustelange's feet were chewed up bubble gum. The Blue Knight program started almost four damn long years ago would be the death of him.

Why the hell'd I let the chief talk me into this? 'Cause you'd be out of a job, dipshit.

Chadwick Bay's Second Ward walking beat would ensure he'd have the flattest arches in Florida's Del Boca Vista phase five retirement community. Seriously hamper already dreadful golf game.

The neighborhood, covering a half-square-mile on foot, made it a two-and-a-half-mile loop, that his feet knew intimately. It ran east to west from Main Street to Central Avenue. Lakeshore Drive ran along the northern border, with Third Street the southern. Hispanics now made up a majority of the 14,000 residents.

I'm too old to learn Spanish.

The boardwalk's shops and bars came alive during the summer season, bringing the most activity to the shift, especially when local legends, Uncle Ben's Remedy, rocked the stage during the weekly *Music on the Pier*.

His proudest moment was when he stopped an attempted robbery in front of Sheik's. As a reward, first drink—free for life.

Most nights however, were *boorrrinnnggg*. Never pulling out his piece and only half-threatening to inflict baton justice on curfew breakers. Sergeant Hustelange figured on another garden variety night.

He was gravely mistaken.

JOHNNY MORTON WHINED, "C'mon, Billy. How long can it possibly take to find a baseball?"

"Yeah, man, not cool! So not cool!" Jaxson Smith kicked the ground. "It's almost time to go and all of us haven't batted."

All five kids were frustrated: "Biiillllyyyy!"

Sergeant Hustelange traveled down Rutledge Street. His planned loop around the Emerson/Wright Park bike path was waylaid. Young, frantic voices pierced the night air. He jogged over to see the kids facing a wooded area, at the edge of the ballfield. "If you boys carried on any louder, you might wake the dead. What seems to be the problem?"

Jaxson Smith stepped towards the man in uniform. "*Ummm* … uh, officer, you see our friend—"

"*Your* friend, none of us even like him. We just needed an even number of kids to play."

"What-*ever*, Trev. You don't always have to be a jerk."

"Okay, okay, let's all calm down." The officer

knelt to look at Jaxson Smith. "Why don't you finish what you were saying?"

Before Jaxson could reply, a boy's agitated, screaming voice escaped from the wooded area. "Stop! Leave me alone! Help!" and a whimpering sound, like a scolded dog.

The sergeant jumped up and sped off into the woods in the direction of the screams.

As he ran, he yelled to the other boys to get home. Glancing back, he thought he saw the evilest of smirks appear on their faces. Momentarily confused, he stumbled over an exposed tree root, lost his balance, and fell to the ground.

The sergeant frantically ran his hands through the rotting leaves and sticks searching for his gun.

He crawled a few feet and the tops of two small gym shoes appeared. He looked up to see a young boy pointing his own gun at him. "Are you Billy?"

The boy smiled the same evil smile Sergeant Hustelange had seen on the other boys' faces, and then—

What the hell?

—he pulled the trigger.

A HOODED FIGURE stepped from the shadows. "Excellent job, Billy. All of you boys did. Once the others get here, we'll all go to the clubhouse. You'll get to see the inside for the first time."

Billy handed over the gun. "O-o-okay … Dr.-Dr. Von Faust. You're sure we're not gonna git-git in any trouble for this, right?"

"Billy, Billy, Billy, I've told you and the others numerous times, you're never going to be forgotten, hurt, or taken advantage of again—ever again. You're one of us now."

The other boys marched in from the field, cutting a wide path around the lifeless body of Sergeant Hustelange. Staring at the blood and brain matter scattered among the rotting leaves as they did.

The hooded figure could feel the soul energy emanating from the boys.

Fear.

Guilt.

Pleasure.

The young's energy is so, so chaste.

These were the last children he'd have to recruit, before attempting to open the gates that would allow Sheut 'Ba passage to this plane. He had exceptionally strong teams in place at *all* of the potential gate sites. But New York was the most likely entry point. The boys and their pure ki would stay right here.

When Sheut 'Ba materialized, he would be the only god the inhabitants of this world would need to worship.

And at the right hand of Earth's new master, Von Faust.

ABOUT THE AUTHOR

Tim A. Majka teaches high school social studies, along the shores of Lake Erie, in his hometown of Dunkirk, NY. He resides there with his best friend and bride, Bridget, their two college-age sons, Jacob and Alex, and two rescue cats: Stanley and Corky. He is hard at work molding the minds of America's youth, as well as writing book two of the *Blood of the Ancients* series.

You can follow him on Facebook, Twitter, and on Wordpress at timmajka.com.

Also By DevilDog Press

www.devildogpress.com

Zombie Fallout by Mark Tufo

Burkheart Witch Saga Set By Christine Sutton

The Hollowing By Travis Tufo

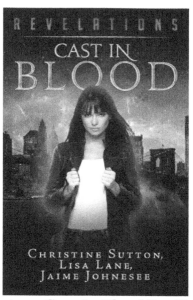

Revelations Cast In Blood By Christine Sutton, Jaime Johnesee & Lisa Lane

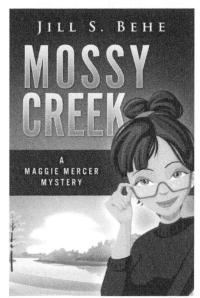

Mossy Creek By Jill S. Behe

Thank you for reading *Prey*. Gaining exposure as an independent author relies mostly on word-of-mouth, please consider leaving a review wherever you purchased this story.

Made in the USA
Monee, IL
08 July 2022